THE CITIZEN

THOMAS GODBER

Copyright © 2024 by Thomas Godber

Cover: Shaun Stevens

ISBN 9798322270317

The right of Thomas Godber to be identified as the author of this work has been asserted by him in accordance with the Copyright, Designs and Patents Act 1988.

All rights reserved. No part of this publication may be reproduced, stored in retrieval system or transmitted, in any form, or by any means (whether electronic or mechanical, now known or hereinafter invented) without the prior written permission of the author, except for the use of brief quotations in a book review.

This novel is a work of fiction. Names, characters, places and incidents are either the work of the author's imagination or used fictitiously. No identification with actual persons (living or dead), places or products is intended or should be inferred.

This book is sold subject to the condition that it shall not, by way of trade or otherwise, be lent, resold, hired out, or otherwise circulated without the author's prior consent in any form of binding or cover other than that in which it is published and without a similar condition including this condition being imposed on the subsequent purchaser.

For all lovers of stories

1

The figure in front had to be a Beast. No citizen would sit on an empty pavement like that. My stomach tightened: '35 seconds', my contact lenses said, and I would have to walk past this 'UNKNOWN OBJECT'.

Most citizens would switch to another route. Most citizens took the zip, and you never saw a Beast on public transport. Desperate to escape my routine, I was braving a rare walk to work, so I ignored the adrenaline urging me to turn back.

It was male and dressed in a dusty green coat made of an old fabric I had no name for. Wrinkles criss-crossed its face, and it would probably qualify as senior if it were a citizen. This one was harmless.

'Good morning,' I said. It was the first time I'd spoken to one of the avoided. I held my breath.

'Good morning to you too. It's not often I see a citizen on foot around here.'

I stopped. 'Fine day, isn't it?' What else could you say to a Beast?

Its face melted into a smile. 'I know, it's beautiful.'

It was hard to look away. The purity of that smile—how could it co-exist with such degraded skin?

The uniform leaves of safe trees rustled overhead. I tilted my head back, and through the leaves a large display at the level of the zip and the air taxis displayed—as if on cue—an elderly woman with perfected skin, talking about the benefits of stem cell therapy.

My grandfather came to mind as I glanced down at the hunched figure of the Beast, and the sadness flickered in my chest—time to get away before it surfaced. I waved and rushed on. It was only as I focused my eyes on the directions my lenses put up that the explanation of that smile tugged at my attention: I'd just been met by a lens-free gaze.

What once was London was now merely part of Megacity. As I walked on, the towering white blocks built by China Jia gave way to a short stretch of three-storied buildings Megacity hadn't transformed. An alert on my lenses warned me I was about to pass a hazardous site—a reminder that public transport delivered a much safer commute. Sure enough, between two of the buildings an opening came into view, sealed off by barricades and sheets of corrugated iron. A sign hanging across the sheets flashed red with the word 'TOXIC'. I wasn't going to wait for the onslaught against my skin and took three big steps towards the curb, upping my speed.

On Bishopsgate, the phosphorescent store logo of Dwellings competed with the sun. I ran the last stretch and bounded into an elevator that smelled of fake roses.

My colleague stood at the entrance of Wise Words, waiting to be relieved.

'You're late, Ben,' she said.

It was 9:01, and I was about to apologise, but she shot into the elevator, unaware of how much I would give for a short chat.

The story shop was starving for customers as usual. I

walked through the merchandise section, overflowing with unwanted gifts and toys inspired by the week's bestselling adventures and games, past the immersive film and gaming booths, till I reached my workstation.

As there was never more than a trickle of customers, each shift only required one member of staff. Dwellings insisted on providing human contact in its fleet of stores for the few customers who still expected it. A display above my station boasted, 'The greatest shopping experience anywhere or your money back!' It would be amazing to claim some pride from what I did, or rather didn't do—I was more or less useless there.

As always, the yawning began a couple of minutes into my shift. Battling lethargy, I drifted over to the books section, if a mere four shelves could be called a section. It was Year 118 of Megacity, and Dwellings still hadn't got rid of books. It made you wonder. Perhaps to some people the printed page still carried a touch of class, or maybe we all needed it to embody a romantic dream of the past no one could quite remember.

The bottom two shelves bulged with humour books and the four latest thrillers spewed out by the most popular artHuman authors. On the upper two shelves a selection of custom-made volumes showed themselves off, some of them luxury versions of the books underneath, that a few wealthy citizens had ordered as gifts or merely for decoration, maybe to place in a guest room. The artistry on these shelves made this by far my favourite place in the shop. Some of us clung on to the fact that no two such books ever looked identical. They were bound by human hands.

I skirted two senior citizens and their artHuman droid carers and scanned the plush spines on the upper customised shelf, until one of them caught my attention. A pattern of diamonds embroidered its cover of pink fabric that carried the title in gold lettering: *Paradise — Growth of Megacity*.

I pulled it out, knowing by the title it would have nothing to offer beyond the knowledge every citizen had been fed from the early years, knowledge that was—again—enjoying an upgrade in new packaging. Leafing through it, I saw the familiar progression of maps, describing the common history of human societies across the planet. At first swathes of germ-infested rural land dominated the maps in black. But over time they shrank, overwhelmed by the colourful shapes of towns and cities expanding with the Great Urbanisation until their outermost suburbs joined forces.

And as I turned the next page, there it lay: Megacity completed, sparkling like vast jewelled mosaics that stretched across each continent from shore to shore. Perfect, except for the occasional blotches of black, indicating toxic swamps that were still too dangerous to treat. The names of different countries also appeared, but they only referred to geographical locations with no political influence. Regional elections for presidents and prime ministers were merely another form of entertainment. Megacity was, of course, one single state.

I told myself for the millionth time not to feel guilt for having to suppress my disgust of Megacity and the idea that it was a gift to us. Guilt for wishing I'd been born into the vanished world of nature we were taught was so primitive. Guilt for the box still sitting in my wardrobe at home that nobody knew about.

My lenses dragged me to the end of my shift by convincing me to play a torrent of infuriating games. I descended two floors to the zip station on Level 28. Looking back at Dwellings as the train arced into the night, I read the pink letters of the evening update on the building's gargantuan eastern face:

**POLITICS FACE-OFF
BEGINS SATURDAY
LIVE AT YOUR LIVERPOOL STREET DWELLINGS**
Sponsored by your Supervisors

My response was automated as usual: I thanked the Supervisors for everything they'd given us citizens. After all, life had never been better. Still, it perplexed me that I could feel gratitude towards people I'd not seen an image of in all my twenty-seven years.

The view of Dwellings was eclipsed by ads on the zip windows for wafer-thin earpieces. When the images subsided, I turned to watch Building 303 speed into view, waiting to receive the train onto its 32nd floor, fifteen stories below my apartment.

I thought of the Beast and wished I could see my grandfather once more.

The sadness stirred.

None of the other passengers looked unhappy. Should I augment the colours of my surroundings or accept the uplifting track I was being offered? That's what you normally did. Strange how we took for granted that our tech could get us through every hour of every day, always keeping the sadness at bay.

I left my visuals and audio as they were. What was the worst that could happen?

Two minutes later, I was asking my apartment what was for dinner.

'Do you like the sound of hot and sour dumpling soup? You haven't had it for seventeen days, so I figured—'

'You're *right*.' I slammed the wall, irritated that my apartment knew me better than I did myself. 'That's exactly what I want.' My lenses informed me 4.5 citydollars had been deducted from my wallet.

I devoured dinner and opened funfriends 3D on the coffee table to see who was looking locally. A thirty-one-year-old woman called Ella just a block away spotted me. She was tall—maybe she thought I'd make a good fit. Obviously we were both testing negative for disease. We managed a chat, and she invited me over.

I showered and was about to pop a Bliss pill, but flung the pack onto the kitchen table. The sadness hadn't got me yet and I wanted it to. Why not? It was welcome to interrupt the endless loop of my days.

When I got to Ella's place, she was watching the news. I joined her on the sofa.

'Mmm, they look good,' she said about a report on a series of consciousness coffees with gentle sensory effects about to flood the market.

'Yeah,' I said, noting the stale smell of the apartment. Clearly, Ella was used to incarcerating herself all day.

Another Beast had been removed from the streets in another purge, this time in Rome. I longed to share my morning encounter with Ella. Was it really so important to hate Beasts?

In the United States the recent world champion figure skater in the ladies' singles had been elected President.

'But she's only twenty-one,' I said.

'We all know that's the main reason she got in.' Ella turned to face me for the first time. 'There aren't that many of us young ones around, are there?'

We got through the awkwardness of glancing each other over. It was unlikely Ella was as young as thirty-one, but she'd fool anyone. The unnatural blue glow of her skin told me she spent a lot more on anti-aging than most of my funfriends hook-ups.

The stilted foreplay of conversation plus news watching continued. Mundane, yes, but at least I had someone to talk to.

Just to be in the company of a fellow human—was that the real reason I was drawn back to funfriends every time?

It dawned on me that what I craved most tonight was for Ella to look me in the eye for a few minutes, but she kept avoiding my gaze, as though she expected me not to like what I saw and leave.

It was a clear irony that sex was supposed to inhibit the sadness. Obviously I experienced pleasure, but even as I was about to come, I saw my old friend loneliness, staring at me from the other side.

Ella wasn't used to dates staying over, and not having taken a Bliss, I raced home.

I'd not felt so clear-headed in months: there had to be more to it—to Ben Lee's existence.

Back home on my sofa, I told my apartment to call Max.

'Yes?' Max appeared on the wall of my livingspace.

'You sound happy to see me. Let's go for a drink one night this week. It'd be nice to catch up in person.'

'This is in person.'

'Shut up, Mr Tech.'

'You OK?' Max asked.

'Remember our talks at uni?'

'What about them?'

'Well, you know there are some things that are best discussed—'

'Yes, yes, I get it. I can do lunch on Friday.'

I could tell my secrecy horrified him, both our identities being unmasked. 'OK! See you then.'

Rolling into bed, I resisted the temptations of sleep soundscapes and supplements for a change and removed my earpieces. It had been a day of experiments, and I wasn't about to stop. I had to see if the melancholic state that was normal for me anyway would intensify. The only other time I'd tried this my anxiety had quickly ratcheted up, and I'd reached for my supplements long before I could tumble into the arms of the sadness.

It was weird having zero sensorial input from the earpieces, those transporters of the citizen's consciousness.

Half an hour passed.

The ache of loneliness was the main thing, but that was always there. Sure, my anxiety was up, but not like last time. The whole sadness thing, though, was beginning to look dubious as hell.

Anyway, I was too preoccupied by then to dwell on the absence of sadness: disturbing pre-thoughts that lacked the definition needed for complete understanding were bouncing around in my head. I'd always known they were there, but I decided that from tonight I would stop suppressing them.

Having also committed to passing the night without sounds or pills, I made one further decision. I would walk to work again tomorrow in the hope of seeing the Beast.

Not Beast. Man.

2

The mealer opened, and the smell of baked dough blasted the kitchen. Hoping the old man knew what croissants were and would enjoy them, I slid the four of them out and into a bag. Jittering after an almost sleepless night, I dashed out to the elevators, heart thumping, neck tensing.

Why the hurry, when I'd allowed an extra quarter of an hour to get to work?

The green figure sat slumped on the same spot of pavement. I relaxed. He'd seen me too and was smiling like yesterday.

'Breakfast is ready,' I said.

'Thank you, very generous indeed. You didn't deny yourself the convenience of the zip just to bring me this, did you?'

'I wouldn't have walked if I wasn't hoping to see you. Do you mind if I sit?'

'Well, that's a first. Sure, make yourself at home.' The man beamed again, lighting my insides.

If any citizens being driven past at that moment weren't lost in their lenses, they would be appalled at the scene: a citizen lowering himself socially and physically to the dirt of the ground, to speak with and eat with a Beast.

Then I got more radical. I stripped my eyes of their lenses and removed my earpieces. This was legal but socially unacceptable. It fed people's paranoia to see you going naked—it suggested recklessness, insanity or criminal intent.

Looking into the man's eyes, there was nowhere to hide. It was unprecedented: two lens-free individuals under the all-revealing sun. The awkwardness of it was like a first sexual encounter. Without the clutter and filters of my lenses, each of us shared a reality as concrete as the pavement beneath us.

'I must ask,' the man said, 'what can you possibly hope to gain from spending time with a Beast?'

'Even *you* call yourself that. Maybe you can start by telling me why you sound refined instead of bestial?' I laughed.

'You flatter me,' he chuckled. 'I suppose it's because I grew up reading a lot of old novels, the sort you can't find nowadays. When I was a young man, an agent discovered my collection and confiscated it. He arrived at the scene a little late. I was already self-educated. But I must thank you for your compliment. I imagine most citizens assume we speak a coarse or unintelligible version of English. We are, it is true, entirely incapable of conducting conversations on anything that relies on technology, which seems to be most things if you're a citizen.'

He savoured the first bite of a croissant. My proximity to him revealed that the belief non-citizens created a noxious stench wherever they went was utterly unfounded. Neither of us spoke for a while, though I struggled with the silence. How could he be so happy to eat without chatting? It wasn't as if he could read or watch or listen to anything. Just sitting and eating.

'Forgive me,' he said at last, 'but if I may be so bold—as a citizen you have everything, yet it also looks to me as if there is an emptiness inside you.'

How in Megacity did the old man know?

'Do you ever have the sadness?' I asked.

'What do you mean?'

'Never mind.'

The agitations of my mind were jostling for clarity. How to give words to them? And was it safe to? 'Have you seen London change a lot over the years?' I asked, choosing superficiality to shield us from questions I still lacked the courage to verbalise.

'Of course. Many of those white apartment blocks—you probably live in one—are quite new. The zip has only been around for thirty years. But you know all that, surely. You're going to see many more changes in your lifetime than I have. We don't live nearly as long as you—bit of a relief, come to think of it.'

I went deeper. 'Do you think the Great Urbanisation was really necessary?'

He was quiet for a moment. Then he mouthed something I couldn't hear.

I moved closer.

'Eviction,' he whispered. 'Not Urbanisation.'

I could have guessed he'd say something like that, but it didn't stop a sour taste filling my mouth.

It was difficult to judge time and distance without my lenses. Not wanting to be late for work, I hoisted myself up and prepared to leave.

The old man held out a hand. 'It's been a pleasure. My name's Lanh.' He must have seen my surprise or remembered the socially distanced ways of citizens as he quickly withdrew his hand. 'My father had Vietnamese ancestry, hence the name. You look like you've a little Eastern heritage yourself.'

'My grandfather was Taiwanese. I'm Ben Lee.' I stood up, thanked Lanh for the chat and left.

After a few steps, he called my name.

I turned round.

He was squinting at me through the bright morning. 'It's been a real pleasure talking,' he said, 'but it was probably for the best you weren't wearing those things in your eyes and ears. Indeed, I would advise you to limit such exchanges. You may find yourself sitting here like me one day.' He cackled.

I could imagine worse things. Saying bye, I put my lenses in and crossed the road in time to get some distance from the 'TOXIC' sign I'd seen the day before.

As I approached my workstation, still digesting my conversation with Lanh, two messages appeared on the display. The first was from Entertainment.

Happy Thursday Everyone!

A reminder that we are hosting the politics face-off in-store this weekend. Getting the show here is a massive achievement and our sales figures are about to go crazy. We aim to become the most popular Dwellings in the whole of London, which we think is achievable given our proximity to the tech and fintech industries.

Ensure your uniform is clean and be extra friendly to customers.

Hope you too enjoy the competition!
Entertainment.

Ensure your uniform is clean? I dragged my fingers across

my chest. Hadn't the artHumans of Entertainment been trained? The nanotextile of our uniforms dissolved any dirt in seconds on its own.

The other message was a response from Visual Merchandising.

*The whole store will be closed for rebuilding between 22:00 on Friday and 6:00 on Saturday ahead of the politics show which will kick off at 10:00. All staff must vacate the building by **22:00 on Friday**. Take personal belongings home after work as items always go missing during rebuild.*

A 3D map will open when you've finished reading this for you to see your store's new location.
VM

An upright ovular structure sprang up on the desk, a dim light pulsating near the top of the southeastern section on Level 55. This was where Wise Words would be situated. Ten years after the arrival of Dwellings branches across Megacity, the total transformations of these cities within cities still astonished citizens. On Friday evening, the VM team would rearrange the numerous blocks of the store between different levels and building faces, and by next morning a new monolithic structure would invade the sky, far taller than the current oblong sprawl.

From the map it was obvious this rebuild would be dramatic. The bioparks would be stuffed indoors for a few weeks; the zip track would be directed to Level 0; Wise Words would be sandwiched between a social networking bar and a relax zone; the Blended Lenses store now on Level 10 would be just around the corner from me. Restaurants and anti-aging clinics would be further down, while nightclubs would stay in the basement levels, to be joined by top-end fashion boutiques boasting new fabrics our home devices couldn't compile yet.

'Where's your politics section?'

I jumped.

A teenage girl was staring past me. She could have been an adult who'd started anti-aging early, but her easy posture screamed natural youth. Either way, it had been weeks since anyone young had been in. Like Ella said, young people were a fading demographic. If you went partying at night, citizens aged sixteen to fifty ruled the world; not in the streets and stores that were lit by day, though.

The politics and celebrity section was an exhibition of glossy publications, mainly magazines with interactive page displays. I led the girl halfway in, past the propaganda of the Transhumanist Party, whose members had been the poster girls and boys for much of Megacity's history, helping to get public buy-in for the tech and medical revolutions that made us who we were. Now the classical parties were enjoying a spell of popularity. On the right, everything revolved around Noah Black of the Born Again Conservatives. Some covers were close-ups of Black, celebrating his stubble, cheekbones and radiant teeth, while others sported his optimised lean body mass.

The girl was focusing on the left, where blonde Prime Minister Linda Bennings flaunted her curves in tight outfits for Labour of Love.

'Have you got your money on her?' I asked.

The girl flinched, startled by actual conversation. Seconds went by. 'Yes, you?' she got out.

'I'd need to ask the artHumans who wrote the script.' I quickly regretted saying that.

The girl stepped away to shut me out of her life forever and refocused on Linda. I left her to shop; a few minutes later she was striding out with a pile of magazines and a bag stuffed with Bennings merchandise.

'Bye,' I said aloud to myself.

In the last ten minutes of my shift I was desperate for something to do, so I guiltily removed my lenses again, then my earpieces. Nothing happened as far as the sadness was concerned. Even my loneliness had diminished. I scanned the shelves for rubbish, anything. The artHuman cleaners hadn't missed a thing.

I was about to reinsert my lenses, when I saw something. Rising up out of nowhere, Lanh's face hung in the space in front of me. His eyes held me: real, human eyes unhidden by lenses. In them, terror and urgency coexisted with strength and a peacefulness. There was sadness, but also happiness; the distance of horizons and the up-front confrontation of intimacy.

How could I feel such a connection with someone I'd only just met?

Yes, I may have been adding meanings to things, to Lanh and to our meetings, but I couldn't ignore the beauty and power of the picture in my mind. It was like Lanh's gaze had broken through the great social divide between Beast and citizen and called to me.

As I stood there, time disappeared.

My breath was the only sound, except for an occasional bleep somewhere in the store.

When I got home, I went to the wall opposite my bed. I wanted to be near one of the few fragments of family life I owned—a scroll of Chinese calligraphy my grandfather wrote for my mother when she was a child.

道 天 地 人
法 法 法 法
自 道 天 地
然

Humanity follows the earth,
The earth follows the sky,
The sky follows the Way,
The Way follows nature.

It was a quote from Laozi, an ancient philosopher. That's all I knew. Everything about him had been deleted, along with most pre-Megacity texts and movies. But it didn't matter to me that these lines were an enigma. The comfort lay in reminiscing about the afternoons when my grandfather opened his box of brushes to teach me calligraphy. His tranquil face as he prepared the utensils, the grind of the ink stick on stone and the nutty smell it made. The calm that filled the room when one of us swept the first black stroke onto a crisp clean sheet of the whitest paper.

Maybe it wasn't surprising that I was thinking about my grandfather more than usual since meeting Lanh. Both had a connection to Asia, and both stood for everything Megacity wasn't. There was Lanh's age as well, though I didn't have enough experience of non-citizens to estimate it.

All these thoughts and the anticipation of the next day left me restless: was I ready to entrust Lanh with my most radical thought of all tomorrow? And would our chat indicate some new direction I could go with my life?

Unable to sleep, I walked over to the wardrobe and pulled out the box containing the source of so much guilt, asking yet again what the real reason was my grandfather had left me it. A miracle that the ancient VR headset still played the one game installed on it. I say game; it was really just a virtual walk.

Soon I was on the path, climbing the hill I knew every pixel of. Sun, shifting clouds, crashing of a waterfall on my left. My breathing slowing. Another two minutes and there it was, just over the brow of the hill, waiting to swallow me up.

The forest.

That mysterious realm where light danced on leaves, where shadows and endless shades of green allowed me to pretend the 'Great Eviction' had not happened yet.

This was my bliss.

3

Lanh wasn't there the next morning. I swallowed hard and laid a coffee and a bag of croissants on the ground.

I paced around the shop floor until it was time to meet Max for lunch, then I left my lenses at my workstation and went down to Level 3, where I wandered out into one of the four bioparks.

Sliding a plate of spicy tofu off the Dawang snack bar, I used my Mandarin to thank one of the few human vendors still around. Auto-interpret made speaking another language unnecessary, and I knew the Chinese-named vendor spoke more English than Mandarin, but I needed to believe my Chinese degree had not been for nothing.

A voice in my earpiece said, 'We have detected irregular use of your lenses in recent days. To keep enjoying your citizen benefits, we recommend you wear your lenses at all times when you are not sleeping.'

Was that just a threat? What would actually happen if I never wore them again?

About a third of the fifty or so pods dotted around the small biopark were occupied. Max wasn't there yet. In the middle stood an artistic recreation of a Pre- Megacity outdoor bench. Realising I hadn't ever inspected it closely, I walked over. It was made of fake wood the colour of diarrhoea brown. A note next to it listed the harmful bacteria that polluted the countryside before the Great Urbanisation, and at the bottom you were welcomed to 'Try it out!'

I lowered myself onto the bench. It squeaked as the sharp edges of plastic planks dug into my thighs. I glanced over at a pod that featured a massage chair, 3D immersion and a free-of-charge mealer. The contrast worked, and gratitude to the Supervisors went off in me. I tried to override the automatic response by considering how much a designer had been paid to create a bench as uncomfortable and displeasing to the eye as possible.

'Are you OK?' Max's scrawny figure sidled into view from behind me. He was wearing black shades. 'What the hell are you doing on that thing?'

I stood up, towering over Max, and gave him a hug.

Max shrank. 'Hey, people are watching. It's weird enough you sitting here.'

'Like I care,' I said. 'Take your shades off. Your lenses will survive, and it would be nice to see your eyes. Join me on here, it's comfortable.'

We sat down, and Max winced. He removed his shades, glanced at me, then looked again.

'Yep, I'm going naked,' I said. 'I know you're not supposed to, but I've decided I don't need them.'

'Still got the attitude, then? Speak to me. What's up?'

Although I was glad to see him, sharing my question was going to be a lot harder than if I was talking to Lanh. Max was a citizen, after all, albeit a highly intelligent one.

'I can't stop my independent thoughts at the moment,' I said, going as gentle as I could in my opening move.

'You'll have to snap out of it, won't you?' Sarcastic tone—to be expected.

'At uni, we were the only ones who didn't care how people judged our views. I wouldn't have survived those boring parties without our chats. We weren't afraid to challenge everything, despite the risk of being overheard. What happened to that?'

'I see, you want to reminisce?' Max bristled. 'I've only got a few minutes today—can we go for a vitabeer next week?'

'I'll try and be quick. I can't stop thinking there must be more to human existence than consumption and tech, pleasure, Bliss. I mean, where does the sadness come from, and why are we virtually forced to avoid it?'

I was sure some of the surrounding pod occupants were training their lens cameras on us. It was easier not to care without my own lenses in.

Max sighed and turned away. 'It's not the first time you've talked about this. I thought we concluded that citizens are defined by a need to consume and—'

'What about redefining? There must be alternatives. We're no different from artHumans.'

'*You* a robot?' Max chuckled. 'You've got a way to go yet. Anyway, what's the point of asking these questions? Life's comfortable now, you've got a job. Imagine being one of the billions of work-free wasters living off Global Citizen Income, putting on weight, constantly looking for the next game to keep the sadness away. You and I don't need alternatives.'

I put my hand on Max's shoulder; the chat was still far from where I wanted it.

'Where's your curiosity?' I asked. 'Who are the Supervisors? Do you even remember us asking that? We see their messages and live in their city, but never a picture of them. You used to dream about finding out who they are.'

Max's features hardened. He blinked slowly to remind me he was wearing eye and ear devices. 'Look,' he said, 'our student days were fun while they lasted—hey, you're still my best and only friend—but this is the real world. I'll tell you this much and no more: there's a reason we don't know the truth about everything. If we've been fed a few lies, those lies must be good for us.'

'You amaze me,' I said.

Frustration gnawed at me. I wondered whether to go on, but needed to express it—the question my life had been growing towards, though I'd only begun to realise it in the last few days. The spotless gravel surface of the biopark and the small number of safe trees and designer flowers only increased the pressure to open up to Max.

I breathed deeply and let the words come out.

'I have a hunch that the countryside still exists. I'm talking about streams, trees, woods.'

I waited.

Max forced a smile. 'Why am I not surprised you'd come out with something like that? Has anything in particular led you to this fantasy?' He was trying.

'I guess I'm still influenced by my grandfather.'

'Of course you are.' Max's tone had softened. 'You're lucky you got to spend so much time with a human when you were little. Shame he only lived to a hundred and thirty.'

'Seeing my mother and father more than once a month would have been nice too. I'm still angry human parenting went out of fashion with our parents' generation. How could they become so self-absorbed that looking after their own children was just another inconvenience?'

'Well, the artHumans became too good at parenting, didn't they?'

'I wouldn't use the word "good". Anyway, you're right—

I'm grateful my grandfather made the effort to visit me every day. He had so many happy childhood memories of the countryside before he left it. Yet Megacity's done everything to control or suppress nature. And not just out there, but with human nature too—the ways we behave and relate to each another.'

'Yeah, yeah. You've often said this.'

'Do you have to be so condescending?'

'Whoops, sorry—I just don't have much time. Is there anything else?'

I tried to regain calm. 'Yes. I've been experimenting with letting the sadness in. It's actually not as painful as you'd think.'

Max straightened. 'Be careful. You know that playing around with the sadness is a downward spiral.'

'The strange thing is, I feel more alive. Like the sadness has been part of who I am all along, not something to avoid. We're twenty-seven—I can't believe it's taken me this long.'

'As long as you don't get depression.'

'There's something else I need to tell you,' I said. 'I've made friends with a guy who lives on the street.'

'You what?' Max slid along the bench away from me.

'He has to get by without any of our devices, but he looks happier than you and me combined.'

I knew I'd gone too far.

'OK, be open-minded towards Beasts then, but leave tech out of it for once. It's not responsible for your miseries.'

I never understood why Max had to defend everything tech-related like it was something personal, even if he did work for the biggest lens firm in Megacity.

'I'm not saying the tech itself is bad,' I went on, 'I just wonder why we let it tie us to the grid all day. Surely this is just one way humans can live—the way we've been prescribed because "life has never been better."'

'What do you suggest then?'

'That you hear me out before you go. Throughout school and uni, we weren't once given the chance to question anything. All I'm saying is that if the sadness doesn't kill you and the people we call Beasts can be happy, maybe other things aren't as they seem. Maybe the countryside hasn't been completely destroyed.'

Max pointed at a clump of flowers that was safely fenced off.

'Bioparks don't count,' I said.

'You've seen the maps.' Max was fidgeting, my time was almost up. 'The only countryside you're going to find is in your mind.'

I couldn't challenge him here, not given the power of lens maps to flawlessly direct every citizen on the planet, every day.

'So you've got a good job, but are you happy?' I asked. 'I mean really fulfilled? This life is boring as hell as far as I'm concerned. I have to at least attempt to find out if anything else exists. Just the tiniest trace of something that was once widespread.'

Then the worst thing that could have happened did: Max laughed. 'You actually want to go looking for countryside? Look around you—the city is everywhere. If you want to visit a mountain or two, be my guest. Last time I checked, the valleys and foothills of every mountain range were piled high with the waste of pre-Megacity. Oceans are poisoned. Dead. Where are you going to look?'

'You've never really understood me, have you?'

'More than you understand yourself sometimes, I'd argue.'

I'd had enough. 'Yeah? So what is it that you understand so well about me? That I'm insane, right? At least show some respect and pretend to be interested in my ideas for once.'

Max glanced around, putting a finger to his lips. 'Hey, let's go for those vitabeers soon. We need to spend more time together again.'

He could have said anything for all I cared. I stood up and got the hell away from him.

4

I yawned and opened my eyes, as day one of the politics face-off lurched into view.

How to survive another day in Megacity? Max was the only citizen I could talk freely to, and his judgment—however justifiable—had left a bitter aftertaste.

Popping my devices in out of habit, I obliterated the sadness with an uplifting morning playlist as I read the day's headlines on my livingspace wall, the first of which conjured a hint of a smile on my lips, even in my anguished state: 'Liverpool Street Dwellings—the only place to be today!' It was too late for a chewable meal, so I swallowed an all-in-one breakfast capsule and went down to the zip.

The train was brimming with overweight fans. After a minute, it abandoned the heights and darted underground. I half hoped the train had been hacked, then remembered the rebuild. Sure enough, we soon emerged from the city's intestines to traverse the new Level 0 in Dwellings, before drawing to a halt next to a rail of Wagingo chameleon jackets.

A voice in my ear said, 'Alight for Politics Face-Off. So you too can enjoy it, you're entitled to four hours off work today and one free Bliss pill. This event is proudly sponsored by your Supervisors.'

Gratitude began to rise up in me. I swore at in my head, and it faded.

I exited the zip with almost every other passenger.

As I blinked away an inane talk show I hadn't realised was playing and looked up, my heartbeat accelerated. The open-plan ovular structure rose around me, sixty stories in height and around three hundred metres in diameter at its widest levels. Daylight flooded through six giant hexagons at the top. Continuous balconies formed rings on every level, so customers could wander out of shops sporting new accessories or sipping enhanced coffees to take in the spectacle on the central stage. Most of the balconies were already packed. For a few moments longer I could tell myself the ritual about to unfold had never been born.

Clumps of fans were piling into the forty-or-so elevators that would take them to the upper balconies. I pressed my way into the nearest one, and it shot up. Through the elevator's transparent walls, my eyes followed a tower that reared up in the middle of the expanse, draped in red, velvety curtains. The tower stopped as we passed Level 13 and plummeted below to reveal a vast, red-carpeted stage.

I watched the balconies fall beneath. Half of London had squeezed itself onto the different levels. Those of us who were not walking were being fed 3D images of Noah and Linda through our lenses, expressions of heightened anticipation radiating across their faces.

Above the low hum of the masses, the chanting of hardcore fans thundered through Dwellings. Supporters of both parties were waving flags; teenagers were gearing up to scream, fall down and be carried off; and a number of young men and women clutched bouquets they dreamed of pressing into Noah's or Linda's hands.

As usual, there were also a few citizens adding variety in fancy dress, impersonating Beasts. Despite their provocative outfits, most people tolerated them as they too had dressed up like that two years ago when bestial rags had been in fashion. Toddlers sat on their artHumans' shoulders, a few senior citizens stood propped up by their carers, and the air buzzed with swarms of tiny invisiDrones, dancing in the immensity of space, communicating with each other as they optimised the filming of the event.

The elevator glided horizontally around Level 54, letting people out at intervals. I shuddered at the thought of what lay stirring in everyone's minds. Just as we rose again towards Level 55, a short female presenter ascended the steps from a hole near the edge of the stage, appearing gigantic on the displays that hung from the ceiling.

Why did Dwellings go to the trouble of setting up extra displays when consumers got close-ups on their lenses whenever they pleased?

The presenter walked into the centre, tilted her head back and raised her arms as though to include the human specs on the uppermost balconies. I fixed my eyes on the blue shine of her dress, dreading having to witness the citizens when I turned round to exit the elevator.

We were moving sideways towards Wise Words.

Better to get it out of the way now than to wait for my stop.

The chanting had died down as the fans prepared to submit themselves. I removed my lenses and turned round to the masses behind the glass of the elevator, squashed against the railing a couple of metres away.

My stomach lurched as the faces streamed by under hypnosis. All the action was happening in their brains as the Bliss took effect, their earpieces released playlists from the main feed and their lenses displayed colour journeys, or—provided the users had reached seventeen—streamed scenes of foreplay with one of the two candidates.

The doors opened, and I stepped into the crowd.

Despite the lack of visible commotion, the mass desire hit me like a storm. I sensed the electrical currents taking over minds as if it were happening to me. I couldn't block out the smells of cold sweats being unleashed, as the pleasure hormones in the politicians' legions of virtual lovers were collectively released.

I hated myself for the flickering of arousal I felt in response to theirs.

Without my lenses, I could see more clearly than ever before how the bulk of citizens were replicas of each other. Those who had not made the trip to Dwellings and followed the show from their apartments, clothing removed by now, would be touching themselves in the belief they were in love with their politician of choice. When the show was over, everybody would go back to their isolation, not questioning whether they had spent their time well, focusing only on keeping the sadness at bay for another night, another day.

I pushed my way through bodies towards Wise Words, just as the covers were being drawn over the hexagons above. The drama continued to unfold on the displays of the empty story shop. The presenter had left the darkened stage and a spotlight was trained on the steps Noah Black was ascending. I flinched as Black, dressed in a tight-fitting black costume with glitter across his chest and shoulders, jumped onto the stage and began to dance to electro backings and then mouth the lyrics of the first verse of his song, 'You and Me', over the artificial voice that had been selected to be sexier than his own and, no doubt, more in tune.

But who cared about Black's musical abilities? The great fantasy was everything. Who was concerned that this superstar

—physically perfected through bioenhancements—might not be a politician at all, that he would never influence Megacity? At least this impotent candidate for the premiership had our best interests at heart. At least he could connect with us, his people.

At least—and this was enough to dissolve all doubt—he *loved* us.

I sighed. What had driven citizens to throw away power over so many areas of their lives? How much had they chosen this, and how much had been forced on them through the course of history? Slowly. Subtly.

And what about me? I had begun my separation. As Lanh indicated, my questions had set a process in motion.

Each situation throws up new possibilities: like all employees, I'd been given four hours off work to 'enjoy' the event. A gift.

I had to get back on the zip.

Having checked the shop was running itself, I set off to brave the swooning masses a second time. Creating an opening to get to the elevator looked impossible. I hurled myself through a group of young women, apologised, jostled past an expansive couple kissing and stood at the elevator door, panting.

The train drew into my block.

I didn't get off.

My mood soared as the northwest-bound zip traversed sections of city I barely knew. It wasn't long before I was passing through the endless suburbia that adjoined the outskirts of the Coventry and Birmingham districts. Behind the colours of displays by the tracks, the edges of Greater London formed a single desert of conurbation made up of buildings my lenses—now hugging my eyeballs again—labelled as fruit and veg labs, meat factories, research parks, data centres and football stadiums. There were hospitals paired with anti-aging clinics; shopping malls without shoppers; artHuman-run restaurants largely devoid of customers; swathes of medium-sized apartment blocks; and seas of housing developments complete with gardens of artificial grass, where no doubt fields or woodlands once lay.

On the surface, there was nothing strange about this assortment of places. It was the lack of human beings that made the cityscape so unreal, frightening. Like a ghost town in a horror game.

The obvious question hit me hard. I say obvious, but I genuinely doubted many citizens would think it worth asking: if humans were barely using all this space, why had the Great Urbanisation been so necessary? How could the toxicity of the countryside be the only reason?

At the final stop, I and the only other remaining passenger, an elderly man looking a little lost behind his lenses, slipped out onto the grey expanses and parted ways.

I had no idea where to go or what exactly to look for. The maps did little to inspire, showing only the bright, continuous stretch of Megacity in yellow, interspersed with the occasional disease-free biopark in brown and a few toxic waste swamps of varying sizes in black. I wandered past an air taxi charging port and into a car park that extended for two and a quarter square kilometres, my lenses said.

Stretching my arms out, I turned on the spot, heart racing: across most of London space above ground was too valuable to allow for single-level usage, yet here was an old-fashioned open-air car park!

Aside from the occasional empty car coasting past to collect a commuter from the zip stop, I was alone.

I kept walking, and the further I went into the car park, the fewer cars there were.

Again: so much space unused.

After walking for twenty minutes, I caught sight of something 'natural', blowing in the breeze in a space devoid of vehicles.

I held my breath and ran towards it.

A small bunch of weeds clung on to its existence through a minute fissure in the asphalt.

I hesitated, unsure if it was safe to touch them, then stroked one of the stalks. Caked in dust, it left a black mark on my fingertips.

Any hope these shreds of life produced was polluted with despair, as my gaze travelled ahead to where the vast flat roof of a warehouse spread out into the grey continuum below the car park's slight elevation.

Despite my complicated feelings towards Max following our talk, I shared an image of the three sprigs with him.

Seconds later, a reply arrived:

Better than nothing.

I crouched. My hands grabbed on to the weeds and clung till my knuckles whitened.

Wasn't this something? Pitiful, but something.

Somewhere there would be more. More life not grown by humans, waiting to be uncovered. If somebody told me this was all I would find, I'd have given up immediately and decided to live out my days as a good citizen, taking more drugs than anyone else, fucking my life away with robots and one-night stands, subduing every real thought I had with the games I was force-fed.

If there is more, I thought as I stared at the weeds and the empty parking spaces surrounding me—if there is anything outside this shithole of an existence, guide me. Show me the way. Take me there!

Startled by the power of my emotion, I wiped at my eyes, stood up and returned to the zip stop.

5

The following evening after work, I bought myself the only model of handheld camera I could find that didn't need to be connected to the grid to function. I took the zip towards the west, again until the final stop, where I carried out the same hopeless recce as the day before, this time capturing a few images of a sprawling tech research and development park.

Over the next two weeks, evening research trips took me in numerous directions. Each location I ended up in was a variation on the same urban desert. One day I ended up in a theme park teeming with children and their parents or artHuman carers, one or two safe trees the only sign of plant matter. At the end of another I was wandering through a sports village. One final stop was a new Dwellings store, and when the floral fragrances concocted to attract customers streamed through the opened door of the zip, I gagged and couldn't bring myself to get off.

Any idea of using my annual leave to fly overseas died before it could breathe. Dwellings had sent me to train new staff at branches in Germany, the USA, India, China and Russia on a number of occasions, and they were all much the same as the UK: the same revolutionary technologies and aging populations and artHuman carers. Die-hard coteries of youth partying hard. Often, when abroad, I'd taken public transport between what had once been different cities. You could think you were coming to the end of a cityscape, only to find it enmeshed in the outlying tentacles of a neighbouring one. The only major variations between global regions were climate and topography, and even these could be recreated in London through immersion games.

I walked to work whenever I had the energy. Thinking about Lanh motivated me to keep looking, keep thinking. Each morning I suffered the same little burst of anguish as I saw only the empty pavement where the old man and I had shared a few words on those two mornings.

Finally, I stopped walking.

On a weekend outing to East London, my third trip in this direction, I alighted at one stop before the end of the line where the zip had just met ground level, and walked back for forty minutes in the heat of midday sun towards a long stretch of road I'd spotted. Not only was it entirely free from buildings—a rarity in Megacity—but a long slanting wall that ran along it parallel to the zip and rose up about fifteen metres struck me as interesting.

Even before I arrived at that section of road, I was hit by an inexplicable stench I'd not been able to smell from the train. Signs reading 'Health Hazard—Do Not Ascend!' had been drilled to the wall at regular intervals.

Is that all you've got, I thought. Think that's enough to stop me?

At first sight the wall looked as if it had been designed to be too steep to climb without anything to hold onto, but the soles of my trainers gripped the slanting concrete, and I managed to scale it with ease.

Halfway up, a whirring found me: the invisiDrone homed

in on my face and arced over my head. Before I could react it was gone, my confusion immortalised in its footage, my appearance instantly matched with 638ad3+71Q*8d978e&F593, my citizen ID. If I had my lenses on instead of in my pocket, messages would no doubt be popping up.

Since I'd already been seen, what difference would it make if I kept going? It was only a few more metres to the top anyway.

Peering over the rim, I saw the source of the stench: a sea of scrambled colours, shapes and materials.

Although I'd never seen a collection of waste before, there was no doubt this was like one of the landfills I'd learned about in history.

Hang on, that was impossible: all waste not dumped in the ocean or mountain ranges was recycled nowadays.

But the scene the sun lit suggested a different story, as the household items, clothing, shoes, gadgets, cans, furniture and endless plastic shapes continued to pose while my camera drank in the evidence.

Had nobody else ended up here and shared images of the landfill? Unlikely. No citizen in their right mind would bother to go by foot from a zip stop to a nondescript stretch of road that failed to offer a single fun activity. Who knew? Maybe I wasn't unique, but with Max no longer questioning anything, it was hard to imagine another citizen being this intent on pushing at the seams of the city and scrutinising it with my obsessiveness.

What would anyone care if they did, by a strange turn of events, find themselves at this urban wasteland? I smiled. Even that wouldn't happen: it wouldn't occur to a 'mentally well' citizen to disobey the public warnings on the wall.

Back at the zip stop, I put my lenses in. So clever how all the workings of a city are automated: I'd been fined four months' salary by Megacity Law Enforcement and warned not to break the law again. A hefty fine for going past a sign and looking at a pile of waste. My top-notch apartment gobbled well over half my income. But I'd be OK. As an employee I was luckier than most: I had savings.

I sat and stared as trains came and went. It was too early to leap back into Central London; possibilities had long since escaped from there. The landfill represented an unmasked scar of the city and had shifted something in me. It wasn't just that a piece of truth had emerged, though that was important. There was something else, and it frightened me because I hadn't known it before. My breath quickened, until my nose was puffing the air in and out.

Whatever this shift was, it felt good.

I lowered my gaze, clenching my hands into fists till the veins on my arms stood up. I counted my achievements: I'd made friends with a Beast; the sadness either had no power over me or didn't exist; I'd discovered a hidden landfill and, in the process, broken the law without a second's thought.

Liberation—that was the shift.

6

When I finally did get myself onto the zip half an hour later, my elation was peaking. I'd become a warrior. Like one from those games everyone played, only I was self-trained, and my opponent wasn't a monster or another character, but the city itself. The real city. Not the one everyone took for granted as the truth.

But how could I continue the fight on my own? The burden of revolutionary thought was too much for one person to shoulder. To get any further in my subversive explorations, I was going to need at least one accomplice.

Who, though? Who would be willing to risk as much as I was?

A message from the Supervisors reminded me it was urgent to vote and that it only took one wink at a candidate's face on my lenses. I chuckled, pretending I didn't care, but already the taller buildings of Central London were rising to vacuum up the zip—and with it me and my newfound warrior strength.

A return to numbness.

I pressed my hands on my face, the sadness close to the surface again, the throb of loneliness welcoming me back.

What if I could persuade a woman on a date to question her lifestyle? It could only happen during the euphoria after an orgasm. Those few minutes capable of creating emotional connection between two people that was so rare in our lives. Perhaps then I might find my accomplice.

I opened funfriends, scrolled the list of women looking for an immediate date and selected *Iambeautiful 25361885*. Apparently twenty-six, she was sporty looking with radiant skin. You had to love the convenience of funfriends: she lived just around the corner from the next zip stop.

She selected me back.

I exited the zip, telling myself that although she managed to look twenty-six, she was likely to be older.

A message:

Welcome to my place, Ben. I'm in the shower but come in! Grace

Whenever I went to a date's home, I hoped to come into contact with something new: a part of town with some outdated architecture I'd never seen; an interior décor with a story of a vanished era. This fantasy proved harder to realise than my sexual ones. The white building today's date awaited me in was similar to my building. It was an older, less hi-tech version without a zip stop, but the security, elevators and amenities were probably regularly updated and no different.

As I approached the apartment, conscious that my clothes carried smells from the landfill, the door opened, and a tall, impeccably dressed man beamed at me—Lawrence 12vq, my lenses informed me.

'Come in, you must be Ben.'

Only an artHuman could smile at a stranger with such openness.

'I'm Lawrence, Grace's assistant,' he said superfluously. 'She's expecting you.'

'Make yourself at home,' Grace shouted from the bathroom.

'Thanks,' I called back. 'Could I use your shower when you're done?'

'I'd ask you to shower either way. You know how this goes, I'm guessing? I'm getting out now.'

Lawrence gestured down a corridor towards the bathroom. I walked towards it. The apartment smelled of floor polish—Lawrence's work.

Grace opened the door, wrapped in a towel and looking a lot rounder than on her profile. She attempted a smile and failed. Holding her nose, she walked straight past me and down the corridor till she was a good five metres away. She turned to face me, speechless.

'I'm really sorry about the smell. I forgot to message you about it. I got a bit close to a landfill.' I couldn't resist saying the word.

'Hilarious,' Grace said. 'Supervisors! This is just ... weird.'

Lawrence detected concern in his boss's voice and looked about, waiting for a command to usher me out.

'Actually, I was at my mother's,' I said. 'She calls me out of the blue when her waste builds up. Look, I promise I'll only smell of soap in five minutes.'

'Doesn't your mother have a carer for housework?'

'Of course, but she likes it when I go round. Lets the rubbish build up, then pretends she needs me. Human contact, you know?' I wished my mother did want to see me. Sure, I wondered what my parents were like now, but I was so resentful of their absence as a child I couldn't bring myself to contact them.

'You're strange, but kind of interesting,' Grace said. 'And I saw you've got a job—you're lucky.' She leaned against the wall. 'I'm probably only in the mood for talking today. In bed's fine. If that's OK with you, go and take a shower.' She walked towards the bedroom. 'Mind leaving the door open while you wash? Lawrence and I like to know what's going on.'

'Sure.'

'I wish I knew my mother,' she called as I went into the bathroom, where I spotted a difference immediately: in my apartment, a clean towel came out of a hole in the wall when you needed one. Here you had to fetch one yourself from a pile in the corner that Grace or Lawrence must have washed and placed there.

Wrapped in a dressing gown for male guests and presumably Lawrence, I shuffled through the apartment engulfed in the sadness. The bedroom door was open and Grace was sitting up in bed watching the wall display.

'Do you always watch stuff during dates?' I asked, climbing into bed.

No response at first, then a grunt, and finally a vacant look at me. 'What?'

'What are you watching?'

'*Serious*?' Her eyes widened. 'It's face-off results night. What planet do you live on? Freak.'

'Oh, Supervisors! Of course.' I smiled to myself, proud I'd managed to dissociate myself from the election with such ease. Compared to the political pageantry sweeping London, my explorations had been time well spent.

'Ah, this is unbearable,' Grace moaned. 'Still one and a half hours to go before the result. Come on, Noah!' She lowered the volume. 'I suppose we should talk a bit.' I thought of leaving if giant Linda and Noah had to accompany us, even if they were now barely audible.

'Doesn't it ever annoy you?' I tried.

'What?'

'That politics is just about celebrity. That it's all an act.'

'No. Should it?'

'I mean, is it really worth pouring so much energy into

supporting a candidate when politics is nothing more than a staged reality show? I've not once seen politics make any changes to Megacity.'

'Why does it have to make changes? I thought it was just meant to be fun.'

'Do you sometimes wonder whether we could live differently?'

'Differently as in …?'

'How about freedom from the grip of tech?'

'Supervise me!' she swore. 'Do you actually mean what you're saying? You do, don't you? OK, lemme tell you this—you got your words the wrong way round just then. Tech frees you from the grip of your own sadness. You wouldn't have met me if it wasn't for funfriends, would you?'

I wasn't yet convinced meeting Grace was something to celebrate. 'Sure, but here we are lying in bed and we don't even know each other,' I replied. 'You don't want to have sex. I'm fine with that. It wouldn't make me much happier if we did—either way, we'll have forgotten each other's names in a couple of weeks. Soon I'll leave this building and never see you again; we both continue to exist in Megacity pretending we're happy until we die, perhaps in our hundred-and-sixties. What are we doing apart from trying to make the time pass, just waiting to be released from boredom and loneliness? What if … how shall I put this? Say I realise I like you so much I want to see you again. What then?'

'Well, maybe you will if you can stop asking silly questions and prove you're not some psychopath.'

'I don't mean just seeing you again once. I'm talking regularly. What if I got to a point where I wanted to spend the rest of my life with you? What if then, after a few years, one of us wanted to have children?'

'Freak!' Grace attempted a laugh. 'You would never like me that much if you got to know me well. And I probably wouldn't like you in that way either. Anyway, that's exactly the way it *was* before, right? The mess of childbirth, screaming babies and sleeplessness, destructive marriages ending in hatred and divorce. You know that shit. Sure, a few people still do it, but physical families are so pre-Megacity. C'mon—I can't believe I'm actually having to say all this.'

I had to go deeper. 'OK—just one more question, then I'm done. What if all that stuff made life more interesting? More meaningful? What if it made us love more?'

'Infatuation's good enough for me.' Grace paused. 'You think too much,' she said with earnestness.

Her eyes had become watery. She blinked, gave her eyes a short rub and pulled my face towards her lips.

'Supervise me! That was *good*,' Grace sang on a high note when her orgasm had subsided and we lay there, covered in a light sweat. 'Poor Lawrence still hasn't quite got it. Nothing like the real thing, right?'

'Robots never did it for me,' I said.

'Now, now, don't discriminate. Lawrence is an artHuman, not a robot.'

'Anyway, that was great. Thank you.'

'Don't thank me, thank the tech for hooking us up.' Grace chuckled. 'Big night, tonight. You going out?' She put on a track from her good-breakup playlist and stared at a close-up of Noah on the wall display.

I shook my head. 'Can you look at me for a moment?' Grace dragged her face away from the election coverage. 'Before you kissed me, I mentioned love and you looked—'

'I think it's time for you to go.' Grace's tears of connection were resurfacing, but my chances of coaxing her into an inquiring state had crumbled. Lawrence would already be on high alert.

THE CITIZEN

. . .

I'd never felt so alone as I walked to the zip.

What had I expected? You can't undo an education's conditioning with a few words and an hour of passion. But one hour was all I'd been given.

Just two hours ago, the evidence of the landfill had given me some much-needed faith in my subversive views. But that faith was gone, along with any dignity I'd disposed of with my ejaculation inside yet another person I felt nothing for.

So I'd discovered an endless landfill—great! That only confirmed how our ancestors had, on a much larger scale, squandered the mountains and oceans. It was time to be honest with myself: there was no logical connection between my discovery that afternoon and my far-fetched idea about pristine landscapes existing somewhere on the peripheries of the city. What was my grandfather's countryside anyway beyond an outdated concept referring to a buried place I might never have felt at home in? Maybe there wasn't anything wrong with history, and the urbanisation of all 'untarnished' land—to use my grandfather's word—was a necessary step in human evolution.

I was the problem, not Megacity, not the Supervisors. I and my stubbornness stood in the way of enjoying life as a contented citizen.

As lights of evening flourished into action, I accepted a twilight that would bring the final darkness, in which I would turn off the part of my mind I'd celebrated—the independent thinker, the rebel, the asker of dangerous questions. I was like night and day, needing to be entirely for or against. I couldn't tolerate uncertainty for long. The time had come to end my mad hunt for a gap in the city and my challenges of the life other citizens accepted without fuss. I would give my mind back to Megacity. I would take Bliss and do my best to rejoice in the bright lights; I would surrender my identity and try on all the roles in the games cyberspace offered, craving nothing, satisfying desires even as they arose. No thought would be entertained if it had the power to separate me again.

Stick to the grid, I told myself. Follow your lenses and be a good citizen for once.

A message from Max read:

Sorry wasn't more supportive. Been thinking a lot, and truth is I admire you for standing by your convictions even if I don't share them. Vitabeer and catch-up tomorrow evening?

Too late. Admiration meant nothing to me now, though I was grateful I had Max and agreed to the meeting.

The displays onboard the zip were celebrating Noah Black's victory, and people were already out for the Bliss-fuelled inauguration parties, dressed up in varieties of Linda and Noah costumes. A message from the Supervisors appeared on every wall and window:

We congratulate Noah Black on his election. We know he is going to make an excellent Prime Minister. Thank you for supporting the election and making the effort to vote. Now you can all get on with your beautiful evenings. Life has never been better.

'I didn't vote,' I said aloud.

Nobody noticed.

A low chant began to spread through the carriages: 'No-ah! No-ah! No-ah! No-ah!' It grew steadily into a roar, and I had to max out noise cancelling.

7

I made a final trip northwards the following evening to a vast motorway bridge a few stops north of Central. Having seen it a few times from the zip, I'd decided last night to visit it and mark the end of my search.

It was still light. As I got closer, the twelve-lane bridge towered up much higher than it'd looked from my passenger seat. There must have been around a hundred metres separating it from where I walked below, on a disused stretch of tarmac punctuated by a few ancient warehouses Megacity had ignored.

The bridge had been built of concrete in the pre-zip-and-air era to carry traffic between a sculpted hill I was approaching and the northernmost reaches of Greater London. It would have seen more traffic back in the days of mass commuting, but it still served a steady stream of ground vehicles. Amazing to think that once, every one of the thousands of cars that crossed the bridge each day had been driven by a human.

I scrambled up the embankment until there were only about five metres between my head and the bridge. I sat panting at the edge of the cavernous, dusty space and gazed over north London. A murky red splodge of sun was setting to the left opposite my perch.

My lenses had lost the grid, and a warning I'd strayed into dangerous territory appeared. I removed them, taking care not to get dust on them.

What a gift: over the past two weeks of exploration, I was drawn to forsaken spaces like this. They allowed me to shut out the overstimulating fairground of Megacity. Despite the cars grumbling on the road above, nobody and nothing waited to serve me here; no augmented realities had provided for these forgotten vantage points, and I was free to think for myself. Although this was my first time under the bridge, I sensed, as I had yesterday at the landfill, that I was probably the only citizen to have ventured into this corner for who knows how long, and this made the location special, secret, my own.

I pictured the maps in the book, *Paradise—Growth of Megacity*, and as the sun set I gathered my notions of countryside once more and smiled at them, accepting at last that I was a dreamer driven by a hopeless imagination. The loneliness of being the only one chased by obsessive doubts about reality had hung around too long already.

I had this strange need to address my grandfather, or at least the part of my personality he represented. It's not your fault, I said to him in my head. I can see how you would want to cling to the things you knew. But I was born in a different era. This concrete jungle isn't comparable to the places you loved so much, and although I'm sad I never got to see them, I have to find a way to make living here worth it.

As the sun slipped behind the buildings, I whispered, 'Goodbye, dreams. Megacity, I'm back.'

I watched as iridescent pink, peach and orange turned to blue between buildings, roads and zip routes. Heaving a sigh, I took out a bag of Bliss, popped one on my tongue and half stepped, half skidded down to the concrete flat.

With euphoria reaching into me and stroking parts of me I'd almost forgotten existed having not blissed for so long, I reconnected with my feeds and got on the zip to the West End to meet Max.

I alighted on Oxford Street and entered a Dwellings that was a lot smaller than the Liverpool Street branch. I ran up two escalators to Wise Words for a browse. A new title called *Ultimate Guide to Extreme Sports* caught my eye. I picked it up and preview text appeared on the cover:

Thanks to new limb enhancements in development, base jumping, once considered the highest-risk extreme sport, may one day be as safe as football.

'Extreme sports next, eh?' a voice behind me said.

'I doubt it. Come here!' Max let me hug him properly this time.

We avoided the elevators and made for the stairs down to the bar. Taking the stairs had been a tradition at university whenever we went out together. It was good for talking when we didn't want to be overheard, stairwells being another place most citizens never frequented. Cameras were rarer there too. Sometimes we lingered for hours. In those rebellious days, we weren't afraid of arousing suspicion, and thanks to Max's hacking prowess, we often doubled our privacy and blocked all the feeds to our lenses for a good hour or two.

'How did the search go?' Max asked.

'Oh, that. Big disappointment. I've had to accept that I've been dreaming.'

'I wasn't joking when I said I admire you,' Max said as we took seats and ordered vitabeers. 'You were right. I seem to have completely forgotten my capacity for independent thought.'

'Well, you're better off for it. Mine has been stopping me from getting on with my life.'

'I disagree,' Max said with a sincerity I didn't expect. 'Never lose it, Ben. One of us has to keep thinking, even if the logic gets a bit lost.'

'It's your turn then. I've had enough. Look, can we just change the subject?'

'Whatever. Sorry.'

Wondering if I'd be able to enjoy the evening, I let the Bliss wash over me and asked, 'How's your love life?'

'Still just distance dating for me.'

'I can't believe you haven't tried funfriends.'

'Not my style. You know I couldn't do physical. It's so unhygienic.'

'That's why you never have a good time. Knowing you're making immediate physical contact with an original human body that's a hundred percent alive is the ultimate excitement. I still don't get why most citizens prefer virtual, with so much distance from the other person. Or how sex with artHumans can really be any good.'

'Maybe because most of us were brought up by artHumans.' Max downed the rest of his drink. 'Plus, it's easier to hide what you feel. And not everyone has your good looks. Anyway, stop trying to convert me. How did it go?'

'She was empty like the others. I don't know why we bothered.' My turn to finish my drink. 'It doesn't matter, though, right? Take Bliss, party, have sex, repeat. What else is there?'

'Well, I'm pretty empty-headed myself nowadays, and you still hang out with me.'

'Maybe she was right. She said I think too much. If I never had the desire to question everything—'

'Shut up,' Max interrupted. 'It's OK, thinking is part of

who you are. Sometimes you just get a bit carried away. Anyway ...' He hesitated.

'Yeah?'

'I've thought about our last meeting. I'm sorry it went the way it did. Also ... how shall I put this ... it dawned on me that the only person I've really felt any love for is you.'

'Where did that come from? You don't do emotion.' I said. 'One day you think I'm a lunatic, the next you tell me you love me. The only reason you feel anything is that—unlike your dates—we've actually sat in the same room.'

'I never got to see any relatives,' Max continued, 'not that there's anything unusual about that. But you're the only thing resembling a family I have. It's hard to admit, but I'm realising I don't have much of a life. I spend all my time looking at displays, women don't seem to like me much, and it just hit me last night that you've always been there. You're the one loyal person I've known.'

'Max, you're lonely. Loneliness is what we all share if we're honest about it.'

'I know, but sometimes I've even wondered if I could find you attractive,' Max said, blushing. 'I can't believe I'm admitting it.'

I blinked. 'You've only ever talked about women.'

'Yeah, but my friendship with you feels deeper than anything I've had with a woman. I even caught myself thinking we could be happy together if we were attracted to each other.'

'Max, I love you too, but I'm not interested in a romantic relationship.'

'I'm sorry. I don't really get my feelings. I guess I just wanted you to know I've got struggles of my own. I've never really acknowledged that I might be unhappy. But when you stormed off the other day, I felt like shit. I think what you said about the sadness made me look at myself.'

'It's fine. I understand,' I said, trying not to show too much of the surprise still resounding in me.

'So tell me about your adventures of the last few weeks,' Max said, looking and sounding relieved to be changing the subject.

'It was all quite predictable. I should have listened to you.'

'No surprises? Nothing?'

'You almost sound like you wanted me to find something.'

'Well, after you told me you were going to try, a bit of me did want you to get somewhere, even though the odds were against you.'

'Actually,' I said, 'I did get *somewhere*. Just not where I wanted to.'

'Tell me more.'

'I found a massive landfill.'

'Yeah right.'

'I did.'

'Stuff waiting to be recycled?'

'There was too much of it.' I took out my camera, ignoring Max's horror at its basicness, and brought up the first photo on the screen. 'It covers a few square kilometres. Could be the last one in Megacity, for all I know.'

Max fell silent as he absorbed the images.

'Shame I didn't find something a bit more inspiring, right?'

'And you didn't use Artware or anything to create these pics? I forget, you don't have a clue what Artware is, do you?'

I smiled, pretending to enjoy his banter. The emotional turmoil of the last two days had carved me hollow. The bar was filling up, debates and flirtations bouncing off the walls. Everyone was smiling. A blonde woman opposite was looking at me over the shoulder of a man, or was it another artHuman who couldn't fulfil her needs? Perhaps it was time to top up on Bliss and go clubbing to celebrate my return to Megacity.

My lenses activated. Max was including me in a map search. 'What are you doing?' I asked.

'Where exactly is the landfill?'

I located the stretch of road by the diagonal wall and highlighted the area behind it. Why hadn't it occurred to me to run this check myself?

'That's odd,' Max said.

There was no landfill.

Of course there wasn't.

I would have predicted it, but I still felt an element of surprise. Instead of the landfill, a huge solar farm filled the space behind the wall I'd scaled.

Max gawked. 'You're definite that's the exact location?'

I nodded. The long slanting wall was unmistakeable.

'And this camera hadn't been used before you bought—'

'Stop questioning me, Max. I took the pictures with a camera that is so cheap and so basic it cannot lie.'

His mouth fell open.

I waited for him to speak.

'The implications of this could be huge,' he said in a low voice.

Then I too had an insight: if the maps lied about the landfill, why trust them on anything else?

'I've been such an idiot,' I said.

'What do you mean? Clearly you haven't.'

I shook my head and got up. 'I need to leave. Here, have the rest of my pack.' I dropped my bag of Bliss on the table.

Max stared. 'Where are you going?'

'I haven't given up. I've changed my mind.' I removed my lenses and earpieces for whatever was about to come out of my mouth.

'Meaning?' Poor Max. I'd clearly rattled him.

'I've just decided. Fuck this city! Fuck being a good citizen!'

I knew that was risky language, but Max would erase any records for me.

Max clenched his hands on the table as though enclosed by fear. I leaned down and kissed his cheek. 'Swallow a pill, and you'll be alright. Take care, Max.' And already I was walking out, putting my lenses back in as I made for the taxiport on the roof instead of the zip platform: sometimes speed was more important than price.

There was one place left to explore.

8

Fresh hatred clamped my heart.

The taxi's windows flashed a barrage of ads at my lens-free face. As I flew towards my block, my heart rate shot up, and not because of the Bliss or vitabeer.

I got out and broke into a run across the taxiport, sucking the cold night air into the furnace of my chest. Pausing at one of the windows around the rooftop, I drank in the panorama. Elegant, majestic and glittering with confidence wherever I looked, Megacity was ravishing from this perch as it wrapped itself around my tenement block like a giddy smile.

I rushed into my apartment; confirmed there were willing subs if I took some of my leave allowance; downed a glass of water in three painful gulps; placed my devices on the kitchen table; scribbled a note the old-fashioned way with a pen in case something happened to me; grabbed the camera and ran back out of the apartment, my brain on fire.

I took the emergency staircase—couldn't face the company of a single other citizen. Descending two steps at a time was easy at first, but the stairs were endless, and halfway down my untrained legs weakened from the pull of gravity. Pausing to regain control, I pushed open a window. It squeaked with under-use as a confusion of warm air wafted in and mingled with the stagnant cool.

All sweat, I ran a hand through my hair. Such aliveness. Rebellion may be the only liberation I would find, but I would settle for it. I would deal with the loneliness freedom brought. For now, all my cells were fizzing with the desire to attain some new type of existence.

I spat through the crack in the window and continued my run down, tripping twice, hardly noticing my body smacking the floor, scrambling up and flying on down through the zigzag artery of Building 303.

Outside at last, I charged through the lit-up night, propelled by a raw power my radicalism had awakened. If my renewed search failed to reveal anything tonight, I could always choose another approach tomorrow. I would get a posting to a country I knew nothing about or quit my job and risk my health sailing the polluted seas.

I was on track. Up ahead? Yes.

Nearing the spot where I first saw Lanh. The pavement looked yellow at night. It didn't matter that the old man wasn't there; I hadn't expected him to be. Why would Lanh want to expose himself to the naked garishness of Megacity at night? I had no intention of staying here myself.

I should have tried this on day one of the search.

Past one more building, till there, coming into full view, just a few metres separating me …

The sign told me I'd arrived at my destination.

Destination TOXIC!

9

My skin began to crawl.

I cared little for the whirring invisiDrones working at predicting my next action. Out of a sense of decency, though, I waited for a lull in the road traffic to minimise my chances of being seen by fellow citizens.

The toxic waste I was about to get closer to could be fatal, but risk was the one companion I desired. I swung myself over one of the metal barricades and examined the layered sheets of corrugated iron. Pulling one of them and pushing another that went behind it, I managed to create a gap and squeeze through. The sheets clattered into place behind me.

Desperation surged: where was Lanh, the one person who thought differently? Was this where he slept when he left the streets?

In the darkness, my sole orientation was the knowledge that I was standing between the two disused buildings about three metres apart that were visible from the street. Slowly my eyes adjusted, and I took a step forward. The air was damp, and I wondered if I should have brought some kind of mask.

Pushing on, my foot hit something and I almost fell. I bent down, moved a finger along the ground. It was uneven.

'Lanh!' I jumped at the volume of my own voice. 'It's Ben Lee.'

No reply.

I edged left, groping for the wall.

Cool bricks.

A few steps on, the bricks ended, giving way to upright sheets of hard plastic. I followed this makeshift wall, stroking my hand up it till it ended about twenty centimetres above my head. Somewhere the zip purred; I turned and watched it shoot past, high over the street I'd left behind.

I jumped as high as I could to peek over the edge of the sheeting. Black space on the other side, beyond which the lights of Megacity glinted in the distance before gravity pulled me down. I saw better now, and as I pushed on I realised I was on a track that started between the two buildings behind, leading away from the street I'd come from. It bent right, and I continued along a straight section for almost a minute.

Then gently downhill, curving slightly left. I'd rushed out without a coat, and now that my sweat was drying, coldness pushed its way through my skin. It would be wiser to run back to the comfort of home and bed. And that was surely the smell of something burning.

I coughed and spat.

The track kept veering vaguely left, and I guessed I was descending in a wide, gradual spiral. About forty minutes passed. I had to be fifty or sixty metres below street level.

Foreign smells circled. Enough exploring? Any moment, and I might reach the bottom that could still be thick with hazardous waste.

The growing unevenness of the ground made it difficult to walk, and at one point I fell, only to leap back up in panic: the damp ground had been so destroyed that bits of it were disintegrating and had attached to my hands.

Or perhaps it wasn't destroyed. I allowed in the thought that should have followed my fall. I knew what it was of course, the stuff on my hands, but I hadn't been near such a large concentration of earth before, let alone walked on one. I knelt down and scooped some up, half expecting my hand to fall apart with the alien-smelling substance.

Soil—that was its name.

Courage from surviving so far pulsated through me. I stood up and continued down the steepening track, my steps becoming strides.

After ten minutes or so, I stopped: my rhythmic steps were not the only sounds. Not far from where I stood, sprinklings of words alternated with laughter. Where the hell was I? Did Lanh live down here after all? I continued down, halving my speed, painfully aware of every movement and sound I made.

A few metres on the track ended. I stood at the lip of an open space, where the cause of the smells was revealed: small fires, near and distant, created islands of light for clumps of people huddling round them on an undulating expanse of earth about eight football pitches in size.

I hadn't seen fires in the open like this. Looking up, I realised I'd gone deep into the bowels of Megacity. Although I made out a thin zip train and the dots of a few air taxis, virtually no buildings were visible along the vast conical rim of the forgotten pit that was, I could at last assume, devoid of heavy toxicity.

The nearest fire, about ten metres away, crackled and released a flurry of sparks above a semicircle of six men and two women. I slipped the camera under my shirt, nudged it behind my back and took a few paces towards the group.

'Watch out!' a female voice called. Before I could identify its owner, they were climbing to their feet.

I swivelled, ready to sprint back up the track.

'Stay!' called a deeper voice.

I froze, heart thwacking, and looked back. The whole group stood raised by a mound of earth behind the fire, two of them holding swords like the ones you saw in games set in the dark ages. The eight faces stared, decorated by shifting tattoos the flames painted. Rags hung from their limbs and swayed, grey with dust from the floor of the pit.

I assumed the second voice had come from a man with a ponytail who stood at the highest point on the mound, right hand gripping an upright pole. His black eyes locked into mine.

I blinked a few times just in case I was dreaming.

The ponytailed man flexed his neck and repositioned his gaze. I entered a terror I hadn't known existed, as the urgency to run battled with the risk of disobeying the command to stay. I took a deep breath and exhaled as slowly as I could. Even with the mounting tension in the smoke-filled air, some of my terror thawed.

Seconds slowed. I could barely hear the zip or the traffic so far above. For a moment there were only the flames elongating and vanishing, the breeze caressing my face and playing with the rags of clothes opposite.

'Seize him,' the man with the ponytail shouted.

10

Despite total shock, I could just about process what was going on.

A tall, wiry man with blond hair straddled me, pointing a long knife at my throat. Hands wriggled in my pockets, while somebody wrenched my shoes off. Somebody else wrestled the camera out of my shirt. The whole time, the ponytailed man stood over me yelling, piercing my mind with his dark eyes.

'*Nobody* comes here. Nobody but us. How did you find the dividing line? Speak!'

I was so shaken no words would arrive.

The torrent continued: 'You think you can come down here and film us, then go back up unscathed and report us, because we are powerless—'

'The camera isn't connected to the grid,' I cried. 'That's why I chose it—nobody can access the pictures.'

'No weapons on his person,' said a woman who had been going through my pockets. The blond man loosened his grip.

My thoughts sprinted. I shouldn't have brought the camera. What would they do with me? How much longer would I be alive?

The ponytailed man shrugged, turned away and flopped to the ground. He sounded like he was crying.

Bizarre, was all I could think. Clearly I had a lot to learn about these people.

'You barely have any clothes on,' said an older man, flinging what looked like a rare animal fleece onto my chest. 'Have this—the subterra gets cool at night. I am Elijah, by the way.'

I sat up cautiously and wrapped the fleece around me.

The man with the ponytail wiped his eyes, twitched his head in my direction, looked away again and spoke into the expanse. 'Come, citizen, join us by the fire. Do not take my behaviour personally. Times are hard, and I have suffered. My name is Duc, these are my friends. Your name?'

'Ben Lee,' I replied, wondering whether times were always hard if you lived here, or if something particular had happened.

I stood up and took a step towards the fire, unsure why I was trusting him and whether he really trusted me. It amazed me to see another person openly expressing the sadness.

At the same time, every narrative that had been engraved in my childhood and adolescent brain was urging me to use this lull to charge the hell back to the track. There was a sliver of chance I could make it all the way up to the streetlights.

Although my apartment wasn't far geographically, I felt like I'd just woken up in a separate universe or had entered the most immersive game ever invented.

I moved closer and sat down. 'Thank you for not killing me,' I said, cringing at my words.

Duc chuckled. 'So, tell us, what drove a young whippersnapper off the smooth streets, all the way down to this wretched patch of earth? Are you escaping from somebody, or have you committed some terrible atrocity up there? Don't worry, we are not here to judge you.'

'You could say I'm escaping from everything up there.'

'Do we not all spend our lives escaping?' said the blond man who'd held a knife to my throat. 'I'm Hendrik, by the way.'

'Nice to meet you,' I said. 'Actually, I'm looking for somebody.'

Duc flinched. 'How would you know anyone down here?'

Hendrik put his hand on Duc's arm.

'I don't really know him, I just met him a couple of times. I thought maybe he lives down here.'

'You'll need to be clearer,' Duc said.

'His name is Lanh. You know the pavement at the top of the track I came down? Two and a half weeks ago I passed an old man near the entrance, and we had a chat. I saw him again the next morning, but I haven't seen him there since.'

Duc and the others looked at each other. Nods were exchanged.

I felt uneasy but continued, 'Interesting man. Although neither of us said much, I thought I could learn a lot from him.'

Having sat down again, Duc was looking straight at me. 'That was my father,' he said. 'He was a good watcher.'

'He was a good watcher,' the others echoed.

'Was?' I asked, still digesting the knowledge I'd just met Lanh's son. 'Has something happened to him?'

'He was taken from us in a recent street purge,' Hendrik replied. 'Arrests are sudden. He would have seen it coming, but it would have been too late for him. He is dead now. I am sorry you won't get to see him again. Lanh was much loved by all of us.'

Duc's emotional state made sense now. Fury rose from my belly. 'I'm so sorry to hear this,' I said.

'It's what happens,' Duc said.

'Are you sure he was taken?'

'It's all over the news up there,' Duc replied. 'One of our

watchers saw it on TV in a Vietnamese takeaway. The new Prime Minister, Black, had the nerve to refer to us as terrorists again. My father was the most peace-loving man I have known. If my brothers and sisters here hadn't restrained me, I would have gone up there to hunt down the prime minister and skin the fucker alive.'

'The press release from the Supervisors wasn't much better,' Hendrik said. '"It is these dangerous elements,"' he continued in a mock-official tone, '"that highlight why we need to maintain absolute privacy, so we can continue to serve our citizens. There are still forces in Megacity who would come for us if they could, whose sole aim is to destroy everything in our lives we hold dear."'

'"Well, "' a woman with hair that looked bizarrely silver said, continuing the impression, '"let us tell you, they will not succeed." You must have heard press releases like that.'

'Of course, all the time. Sorry, what is a watcher?' I asked.

'All so-called Beasts you see up there are watchers,' she continued. 'We in this pit are watchers. Although we find ways of accessing the news, we need to know more for our safety. By spending time on the streets, we keep abreast of the real trends that might affect us in the long run. And we can pick up food at the same time. Most watchers, unless they're retired, are fast runners. We need to be able to escape agents and get ourselves down the nearest hole at any moment. Lanh insisted on continuing despite his old age. He knew the risks, but he always said watching gave him a sense of purpose. So the community allowed it, as long as he sat somewhere near the track. You looked for him in the right place.'

A quietness descended and settled around and between us, as smoke gently stroked us. I stared at the glowing embers in the fire and listened to the sparks popping as I mourned Lanh. I thought of the many news reports of street purges I'd watched over the years, framed as victories or cleansings. It was different when you knew the victim. The taking of this warm, harmless old man was evidence of a maliciousness in the power structure I'd somehow been blind to previously.

One by one, everyone in the group made eye contact, some tearful, some smiling.

'Our spirits are victorious to the end,' Hendrik said.

'Our spirits are victorious to the end,' the others repeated.

After a pause, Duc said, 'Ben, I should tell you, I know about your kindness towards my father.'

'What?' I sucked in smoke.

'Yes. When you said his name a moment ago, I knew it was you. He spoke highly of you.'

'I only gave him a coffee and a few croissants.'

'It was more than that. Do you not realise the significance of what you did? For as long as any of us can remember, no citizen has spoken to us in a way that remotely granted us our humanity. We are not as simple-minded as you might think. We know about the conditioning against us that goes on up there. We get to feel it, Ben, as soon as we set foot on a pavement. Citizens speed up and veer to one side when they have to pass us. Children run to their carers when they see us. Think about how your kindness would have made him feel. You greeted him—you actually smiled. This was big news in the community.' Duc paused. 'Were you yourself not programmed to avoid us?'

'I was.'

'Then either you are an accomplished actor attempting to infiltrate our ranks, or you are blessed with an ability to think for yourself.'

'I'm not here to spy on you.' I raised a hand.

'It may seem bold of me to make assumptions,' said Duc, 'but I suspect you did not come here this evening merely in search of my father. I also doubt you would have been open to the type of exchange you shared with him if you did not have other things on your mind. Is there not some truth in what I say?'

Was it safe to unpack my most personal questions again?

'Oh, come on!' said Duc, 'something must have emboldened you to desert the streets of slumbering, mechanised citizens and push past the warning sign?'

'I've been looking for the countryside we lost. I know it sounds crazy.' I closed my eyes, my cheeks flushing with shame.

'Wait,' Hendrik said. 'If you've been having such unusual thoughts, I imagine it has been unsettling for you.'

The fire blurred; my eyes swelled with tears. Duc wrapped an arm around me and said, 'Shh, don't you worry. You must let your feelings out. I promised you we wouldn't judge you.'

I swallowed hard. How come I had to trek all the way down here just to be understood by another human?

Courage pushed me to ask my next question. 'Even if the countryside doesn't exist, why was the Great Urbanisation—Eviction—even necessary? The world's population is nowhere nearly big enough to fill up the city. It can't have been as toxic as we were taught. I mean, look—I'm still alive down here, and you live down here.'

'Questions are good,' the woman with silver hair said. 'Philosophers once explored all the big questions. Schools even encouraged students to doubt.'

I stared at the fire. I'd had to challenge my entire reality and risk everything just to find this dusty corner of the world where people could be open and honest.

'But isn't it pointless to be possessed by dreams that only lead to disappointment?' I said. 'I convinced myself the countryside might still exist, but to what end?'

Elijah, who'd given me the animal fleece, cleared his throat. 'Having dreams is what keeps us going. Citizens dream as well, even if only about upgrading the technology that runs their lives, or about some hot politician or celebrity, thanks to all those shenanigans and games I hear you play up there. Dreams of sex and romance have kept humanity going for as long as we have been on this planet. But you—your dreams are different.

'Hopefully, you realise we are harmless,' Elijah continued. 'If we were not, the agents would unleash a few swarms of drones, and that would be the end of us. It is pretty obvious the Supervisors need us. By taking one of our kind now and then, they remind citizens of the dire consequences of ignoring societal norms. The truth is, we pose no threat to Megacity; it is simply that we are feared up there like a pest. People cannot comprehend how life is possible outside the comfort of the grid, so fear is their natural response.'

The fire's warmth drained away some of the tension in my shoulders.

Hendrik winked at me over the flames and said, 'You have come to the right place.'

So this was what support felt like.

11

I woke up to the disbelief that I'd slept outdoors. These people did it every night.

Initially I didn't want to open my eyes in case none of this was real. I listened to mumbles about breakfast, cutlery tapping on plastic, the crackle of fire. A whiff of fried cumin greeted me. I stretched on the cracked, hard earth and lifted my eyelids. Grey tufts of weeds vibrated in the breeze.

I was so far below ground level that I wondered if day had even arrived, but looking up I saw the tops of three white apartment blocks painted golden in early sun. The sides of the buildings facing us were devoid of windows that could provide views of the pit. I tilted my head back. Into the upside-down view a zip train emerged, passing the rim of the pit.

'What I don't understand,' I said to Duc and Hendrik as we ate a refried bean stew, 'is why we never see this pit from the zip or air taxis.'

'Window ads,' Hendrik said. 'I've not seen them for a long time, but I gather they are still used.'

Had Hendrik been a citizen once? I stored the question for later as the realisation dawned: hundreds of times I'd wondered why ads seemed to come on at the same points on every zip journey.

'You will have work to get to, no doubt,' Duc said.

'I don't. I sorted that out before I came down.'

'He's clever, isn't he?' Duc winked at Hendrik.

'Where are the others?' I asked.

'Some of them have gone up to watch already,' Hendrik replied. 'Others have begun the search for good scraps of food. Ensuring meal supplies is our main focus every day.'

'This is tasty,' I forced myself to say.

Duc smiled. 'You don't have to lie. But you've got to get something inside you. So, do you intend to go back up after breakfast?'

'I'm in no rush.'

'But you'll have to go back at some point, right?' Duc said.

'I own an apartment up there, so it's hard to imagine not going back. I could stay down here until I die, but that wouldn't be long—I don't have your survival skills. The problem is, I've seen through some of the brainwashing citizens go through, so I don't know if I can take life in the grid anymore either.'

Duc scanned me up and down and said, 'I'd not normally say this so soon after meeting somebody, but I believe you have the necessary integrity to hear it. I would like to encourage you to continue your journey.'

'Where is there left for me to go?'

'Trust me, you have not seen some of the places we pit dwellers have,' Duc responded. 'For example, have you explored beneath the city? No, right?'

My heart fluttered. 'Sounds interesting.'

'Hendrik would be your guide, wouldn't you?'

Hendrik smiled.

'For now, all you would need is the initiative to begin. Hendrik, do you want to add anything?'

'See it as a sort of self-discovery,' Hendrik said. 'About fifteen years ago, I was where you are now. I was not born among watchers. I found my way here by mere chance. The guided journey changed me completely, and I am grateful every day that I took the step. But the decision must come from you.'

My heart beat faster. 'Is it dangerous?'

Duc smiled. 'Physically, you should remain safe—if you stick with Hendrik and do not start trying to control situations you will no doubt encounter. Mentally and emotionally? That depends on your resilience. But I think you are ready, would you not say so, Hendrik?'

'Absolutely, but your willingness to keep going would be key.'

'How long does the journey last?' I asked.

'Six months,' Hendrik replied.

'What? I can't go,' I said, my enthusiasm shrinking to nothing. 'I took annual leave to come down here. I'll never be allowed back into society if I'm away that long.'

'There is that,' Duc nodded. 'But the offer is there. You may like some time to think about it.'

'Yes, I'd definitely be grateful for that,' I said in a sarcastic tone. 'Is there nothing else you can tell me about it? Surely you can understand this is a pretty big decision for me.'

'Sorry, Ben,' Duc said, ' but anything we add to your knowledge could detract from your experience. Accept or decline our offer. We will leave you in peace to think. I suppose I could say this—as you weigh everything up, you may want to reflect upon how mainstream society has been serving you.'

Great. Helpful.

· · ·

Even as they left me, my instinct was to say yes.

I watched as Hendrik and Duc began a slow walk around the perimeter of the pit. Tall and fierce close up, they looked smaller and more powerless the further away they went. With every step they took, my resolve thickened. I couldn't help smiling. I'd taken a huge risk last night and followed through on what had seemed like a deranged plan, yet here I was, still breathing. Accepting this offer posed a far greater long-term risk than pushing past the TOXIC sign, but my appetite for adventure had broken out.

How could I decline? The danger, the freedom, the journey, a new life—it was made for me.

Still, was I being too easily persuaded? I felt sad at the thought of not saying goodbye to Max. It was disturbing to think I might never be a citizen again. Despite my revolutionary thoughts and actions, the offer and its suddenness had caught me off guard. It wasn't only that being away for six months would erase all hope of returning to a life of comfort and the security of the grid. It would, no doubt, also shorten my life expectancy substantially.

Yet this was what I'd been waiting for. I was starving for anything that might show me a different reality. Last night I had crossed the dividing line—maybe there was no going back.

'You look like you've come to a decision,' Duc said when the two men returned after a full circuit of the pit.

'Yes, I'm going.'

'Back up to your old life?' Duc asked.

'No, on the journey.'

'Wise choice,' Duc said. Hendrik nodded.

'Can you at least confirm that I won't be forced to have sex with anyone?' I asked.

Duc glanced at Hendrik and broke into laughter. 'Do not

worry, it is not that sort of rite of passage, although now that you mention it, why don't we add something in, Hendrik?'

'Come with us. Your journey begins,' said Duc.

'Right now?' My brain was exploding.

'You've made your decision, haven't you?'

'Don't I need to pack? I hardly brought any clothes down here.'

'We have backpacks equipped for trips such as these,' Duc said.

'Are you giving me back my camera?'

'We destroyed it last night. You don't really think we could have trusted you with your camera down here having only just met you, do you?'

And already the two men were walking away towards a distant edge of the pit.

Irritation electrified my nerves, and a stubborn child in me resolved not to move from my spot.

I bit my lower lip. How did they know I was going to follow them? Was my desperation that obvious?

Beyond Duc and Hendrik I spotted three small black holes at the foot of the pit. I got up and went after them through the morning air that had warmed up, watching as little billows of dust were lit up by the sun in the wake of their steps.

12

The black holes turned out to be entrances to three small caves. Duc beckoned, and I followed him and Hendrik towards the middle one. A few metres inside the entrance, water trickled out of a hole from somewhere high up, before spreading over a dark rock face and flowing to the ground.

I stepped into the cool space of the cave that was lit by burning torches on the walls. Next to the water stood a figure holding a staff—Elijah, his black eyes reflecting back miniature pictures of the torch flames.

'Kneel,' Elijah said.

Hating the commanding tone and wondering what in Megacity was going on, I dropped to my knees.

Elijah put a hand on the rock face so the water washed over it. He closed his eyes, took a deep breath and touched my forehead with the backs of his wet fingers. 'Hold your beliefs and your doubts in your mind. Now let them be washed away— clear and ready for a new beginning. Cup your hands and drink. You are one of us now.'

My concepts of hygiene were being challenged down here, but I thought I might as well hydrate while I could. The water tasted OK, but not being used to the hand cup method, I spilled half of it down my chest.

'It is time,' Elijah whispered, pointing to my left.

Duc had gone. Hendrik was waiting for me on the other side of an opening to the adjacent cave, holding an electric torch. I walked through the opening and followed him deeper into the cave.

I said goodbye in silence to the pit somewhere to my left—that place where I had experienced being understood so completely just yesterday evening. Bringing Max to mind and Dwellings, my apartment, the zip, a few one-night stands, I said goodbye to Megacity as I'd always known it. When I next walked the streets, perhaps it would be as a watcher. I grinned: had Lanh foreseen this when he advised me to limit our chats?

Hendrik beamed his torch along a narrow passage that led steeply uphill. Two old backpacks lay at our feet. Had someone put them there before I'd even been told about the journey?

'That one's yours,' Hendrik said. 'You will find two water bottles in the side pockets. Use them wisely. They need to last a while. Here's your torch.'

How did watchers get hold of torches? Landfills?

'Where's Duc?' I asked.

'He stays behind. Keep following.'

'How did you manage to get water flowing in the cave?' I asked, a few minutes into our ascent.

'That's the beauty—we didn't need to do a thing. It's been flowing for years now. Some of us think it was pure chance, that some pipe burst somewhere above and never got fixed. Others, like Elijah, believe it's a miraculous gift from some spiritual world that keeps flowing because it's our destiny to survive. Whatever your take, it's become a symbol of life for us in the pit.'

We climbed in silence for about half an hour before the path flattened. A wall to our left shimmered under the torchlight: tiles. 'Where are we?' I asked.

'Guess.'

'Well if most of Megacity is layered on top of old London, are we in some basement of a Victorian building?'

'Nope.'

'An old tube station. We're on a platform.'

'That's right.'

As a boy I went on a rare school history trip to a museum in a preserved tube station dedicated to the ancient progenitor of subway systems around the world, the London Underground. It hadn't occurred to me that remnants of the network might still exist intact away from public view. Everyone knew the zip sometimes dived into stretches of tunnel once used by the underground, but those sections had been completely gutted and re-built with high-spec materials.

At the end of the platform, I climbed down after Hendrik onto a three-railed track.

'Careful not to trip,' he said. 'You'll be fine if you stay between the central rail and one of the outer ones.'

Moisture from somewhere. About forty-five minutes later, it was clogging my lungs.

'How much further underground?'

'A few hours, that's if we maintain pace. Asking questions like that won't make your journey easier. We're heading south. Now, let's walk.'

I swore in my head.

As hours dragged by in the dank and motionless air, I had to cough. Here and there we made turns into other tunnels.

'How do you remember the turnings?'

No answer.

I tried to distract myself from the alternating anxiety and boredom by picturing the Underground in its heyday. Billions of forgotten lives, each so important to the person living it.

Out-of-town families before the days of Megacity, visiting the capital for dinner and a show perhaps. Drunk partygoers before the arrival of healthier drugs, hassling passengers on a Friday night without fear of lenses recording them. Planeloads of tourists from around the world ferried between Westminster, Oxford Street, Madame Tussauds, the South Bank, Brick Lane, Camden Town. Some of these places had vanished even in my own lifetime, devoured by history to be replaced by smarter streets and neighbourhoods and Dwellings stores, which would one day also go. Strange how the version of Megacity I knew felt like it would dominate forever. How architectures and technologies are constantly presented as pinnacles of achievement, while obsolescence waits to delete them, one by one.

'We need to keep the pace up.' Hendrik strode ahead. 'Otherwise we won't cover the necessary distance today. I am not going to carry you if you pass out.'

'Charming,' I muttered.

Then, a few hundred metres on: dull grey. Hendrik silhouetted against filtered daylight. The tunnel had ended in mid-air, as though the rest of it had been sawn off.

I joined Hendrik on a small ledge in the middle of a jagged cliff face far below the mainstream city at ground level, but equally far above a chasm.

'The guts of Megacity. Quite a sight,' Hendrik said.

I looked over the edge, and my heart quickened. Inverted towers hung down around us, as if the city had been turned upside down and painted black. The towers were the underground data storages, malls, hotels, gyms and nightclubs that continued all the way up to the man-made urban crust that redefined the height of street level with no regard to where the original surface of the earth had been. From where we stood, the word 'underground' no longer made sense: humans had re-sculpted the city's bowels and constructed their own levels wherever they wanted them.

Citizens only ever saw smoothness, shine, colour. Views of this haunted lower region were shrouded by displays and windowless walls inside the structures. I shivered: the dark monolithic shapes that hovered around us had a weird splendour. High up at what was street level and beyond, tiny lights twinkled like layers of sugary decoration arranged on giant chunks of dark cake below.

'Have you looked enough? We will eat now—sit. It's just leftovers from a Chinese takeaway.'

'Thank you.'

I gagged and swallowed my saliva, grateful that Hendrik missed my expression. 'It will get me in touch with my family background.'

My foot hesitated mid-air and fumbled at the first tiny slice of foothold as I departed from the ledge and navigated round a protrusion of cliff face. I glanced at the chasm beneath, and a surge of panic threatened to end my journey.

'I thought it was safe,' I shouted at Hendrik, who had already climbed around the corner out of sight.

'You will be fine. There are more handholds above if you keep looking.'

I scraped my way around the protrusion.

Hugging the cliff, we continued on narrow planks someone had somehow affixed to it, sacrificing their own safety for people like us on bizarre journeys. Whenever we came to a slight overhang, rope handles dangled from metal rings that had also been fixed to the cliff. I say cliff, but it was really a mix of brickwork, cement, concrete and metal beams—architectural hangovers from vanished days.

Around an hour later, we reached the end of the planked cliff path and joined the curve of a dusty lane that had presumably once been used by cars. Actual lanes were rare these days, most roads consisting of multiple lanes that wouldn't descend this far. No agent vehicles or cameras would bother us down here.

'Where does this road go?' I asked.

'Nowadays, nowhere.'

'Marvellous.'

'You sound annoyed.'

'I am annoyed. I don't know this area like you. I haven't got a clue what we're doing here or where I'm going.'

'You need to focus on the journey, Ben, not the goal. In the pit there's a saying—be patient, and your path will guide you.'

My self-control imploded: 'I am *not* a patient person. You might be used to feeling timeless and free, but I've just come from a world where I get answers—'

Hendrik gripped my arm. 'Ben, it is simple: I need to know, can I trust you, or can't I?'

'Chill out.'

I remembered the threatening look in Duc's eyes last night. Hendrik might not hesitate to get rid of me if I became too much trouble.

'You can trust me.'

'OK. We're going to see some brothers and sisters. I can't give you any more than that.'

Despite the vagueness, I didn't push for further details. My legs were weakening, and maintaining forward momentum had to be my focus now.

To my surprise, even with the exhaustion and my lens-free state, the sadness hadn't been bothering me. That's not to say I didn't crave the stimulation my eyes, ears and mind knew so well, but I was bound to suffer some sort of withdrawal symptoms.

'Sing me a citizen song,' Hendrik said as we set off up the winding lane in the direction of light.

'I don't have the energy. Anyway, the tunes I know are so over-produced and distorted you can hardly sing them with a human voice. Citizens don't sing much generally, except as stars in concert games that make anyone look and sound amazing.'

'I had forgotten,' said Hendrik. 'That is sad. We watchers could not get by without singing. When someone is sick, we sing to them. When someone is dying, we sing to them. When we are cold and exhausted and feel like we're not going to make it through the year, we get together and sing. One of the things we always agree on is the power of song to heal and give strength and hope.'

'Let's hear one of your songs then.'

Hendrik hummed a short melody, then sang it again with lyrics.

> *I wander on down the hillside,*
> *Valleys before me open wide,*
> *Scent of dew under trees,*
> *Winter by spring is appeased.*
>
> *I wander on down the hillside —*

'Wait,' I interrupted.

'You don't like it?'

'Did I hear the word "trees"?'

'Yes.'

'Who taught you this song?'

'We all know it. It's been around for ages. It's not that special.'

'I don't think I've heard a song with trees in it.'

'Well, we sing—and talk for that matter—about many

things citizens don't. Our stories still reside in an age long forgotten by much of humanity. It goes both ways, obviously—we don't understand much of what is churned out by the media up there.'

'Can you sing it again?'

I listened closely.

'What's dew?' I asked when Hendrik had finished.

'A form of condensation.'

'Keep singing it. Please.'

It was twilight when we neared the top of the dusty lane. A low-slung overpass hummed ceaselessly twenty metres above our heads. The lane stopped a few metres in front of us, swamped by rubble and square boulders that continued below the overpass as far as I could make out in the gloom.

We stood there a few moments, me ready to sleep.

Hendrik pointed at the rubble.

'You're joking!'

He climbed onto the first boulder.

'Isn't there another way we can go?'

Still no words.

'Are we going to eat soon?'

'Must keep moving.'

I spat as I climbed onto a boulder, exasperation turning to desperation. I was already through one bottle of water. My body, unaccustomed to climbing and obstacle courses and long walks in darkness, wanted to shut down from the exhaustion.

If I looked up to the left or right past the underpass, shapes of turquoise evening sky were visible between the criss-cross patterns of building tops, roads and zip lanes. I tried to reframe my situation. Although I couldn't escape Megacity, at this moment I was entirely removed from the life I'd always associated with it, and whereas before I'd explored corners under bridges alone, now I had a companion, even if he was leading me on an endless and painful journey to nowhere.

It grew too dark to see, and we stopped.

'Here,' Hendrik said, handing me a small, dark lump.

'What is it?'

'A handmade protein ball. I would not ask what's in it if I were you. Have a sip of my water if you're low.'

We continued with our torches, hours trickling. Tiredness weighed on me like a ton of concrete, and twice I slipped and grazed my shins on the rocks. All I could do was focus everything on getting over the next boulder.

Then came the moment I'd stopped hoping for, as Hendrik sat down on the flat top of a rock and unpacked a pair of thick, decades-old sleeping bags that released a cocktail of smells I decided not to analyse.

After a breakfast of more protein balls the next morning, the scrambling under the overpass resumed. I accepted the boulders now as facts of life. Hendrik was in a good mood and sang sporadically. I tried singing along. My mind slowed as the constant view of concrete and rubble—framed by the dark grey foundations of tower blocks either side—narrowed the range of things I could think about. Had Hendrik chosen this monotonous route to tease out and wash away some of my entrenched thought patterns?

Another break, another protein snack.

'Supervisors! We'll be at Brighton District soon,' I said through the nutty flavour of a ball I swore would be my last.

'We're not quite halfway to Brighton. The terrain slows us down a lot.'

'No kidding.'

When I lay down that night, even though the noisy traffic on the overpass refused to respect my bedtime, I noticed a stillness inside, as if the clouds of my worries had drifted apart to reveal a clear sky. Soon I was coaxed away from the assault course of the day by a dream of long multicoloured veils, hanging from the edges of the overpass and wafting over me.

I awoke to the warmth of sun rays on my face. I sat up, stretched and stared down a long slope that wasn't visible when we arrived in the night. A sweep of dark buildings spread out below as far as I could see. Some were domed, others pointed. I rubbed my eyes. Through the morning haze, I could barely discern the colour of the buildings—dark grey seemed a safe bet. Here and there stood a pole, perhaps a streetlamp turned off now it was morning, except that most of these poles where bent into odd shapes.

I looked again. Perhaps the buildings were a dark green. But I knew I was out of my depth here—I had arrived at a place unlike anything I'd seen during my searches or on trips abroad. The cars were still audible above me, but the cacophony of horns and beeps that connected you to the pulse of the city—even in the most far-flung districts—was absent.

In fact, this wasn't a district at all. The domes and spikes moved back and forth, jarring with the narrative I'd come to know too well, until they finally shed their identities and I saw them for what they were, swaying in the breeze.

I swallowed in disbelief and let bliss gush through me, but not the kind from a pill.

In front of me lay a forest.

13

'Hendrik,' I yelled. 'I've seen it!'

My voice vanished into the ocean of green. I yelled some more, but the world consisted just of me for now.

Hendrik had left me an energy bar, but nothing else, not even a note. I decided I couldn't wait for him: I needed proof I was looking at a real forest and not a film set or simulation or some kind of illusion.

I got up, put my backpack on and took a few steps down the slope before stopping. Strange to be alone so suddenly. I craved the security of systems and directions to give me my location and send me to the nearest café or entertainment hub.

But I couldn't let anything hinder me and I began to run down the slope.

Childhood conditioning kicked in perfectly on cue, the warnings against germs, disease, pain and death saturating my thoughts, conjuring terror. I tried pushing them away, but they wouldn't budge. The fear was paralysing, and I had to stop several times. Part of me knew I was probably imagining the dangers, but my education had been too effective, even despite the level of independent thought I'd reached.

Squinting, my face turned to one side, I managed to use gravity and move my legs in an awkward downhill jog, forcing my way through the paranoia with each step. Somewhere deep inside me, a longing propelled me as well—a sort of pure desire to blend with the green mass rising up to meet me. Tears streamed, as a foreign air poured into me and introduced me to the smells of a morning forest—dew, wood, earth and leaves.

Birdsong that hadn't existed outside historical simulations greeted me with startling intensity.

I approached the nearest tree, half expecting lethal gases to envelop me. The bark was grey—wasn't it meant to be brown? Had it been poisoned?

Most of the trees were thick with leaves, which surely had to indicate life.

A little bird flew right past me. Its feathers were blue, green and yellow, and I wondered if someone had painted it as a joke.

I shouted Hendrik's name again. Nothing but questions: why hadn't he waited? How was I supposed to survive out here on my own?

A few minutes of just me standing. Computing. Almost disconcerted that I felt so well. I took a few steps past the first tree and began to explore the brown, wrinkly bark of a different species. I bent a twig from a branch towards me and pressed its leaves to my face and neck.

I sat between two roots, still learning to accept I was surrounded by naturally grown trees.

Yet somehow it was familiar. Had the many hours on my grandfather's VR forest game given me the imagination needed to challenge my conditioning?

My gaze drifted back up the slope and hovered at the overpass with its grey barrier, and more bricks in the wall of my programming were dislodged: the roads and zip lanes linking Greater London to districts like Brighton, Oxford and Birmingham were sandwiched between these grey barriers at various points—many of them lined with displays.

No traveller would glimpse this forest.

All those journeys I'd made to these places, blindly assuming the barriers were added to reduce noise pollution and enhance passenger entertainment.

But wasn't it too soon to believe this single collection of trees was anything significant? It could be a one-off. Countryside as a whole could still be nothing more than a dead concept related to a social history long gone. If I walked for five or ten minutes, I was bound to come out at the other side and arrive back in Megacity. I reminded myself I was homeless now.

My mind wandered back to the streets, to Dwellings, the political face-off and the fans. I wondered at how I'd managed to get from that to this with no other transport than my legs.

I plunged into the forest.

The air under the canopy was cooler. Twigs snapped under my trainers, and beneath the twigs the ground was spongy. Leaves from different tree species I wished I could name emitted subtle smells—some rich and nutty, others delicately aromatic. And everywhere on the forest floor was the dew Hendrik had sung about. I passed a row of cars, rusted, half sunk into the earth—relics of a non-self-driving era.

Here and there, strips of torn-up plastic bags lifted skyward by the growth of trees wafted like short streamers from branches, hangovers from the party of pre-Megacity. Beyond this evidence of plastic pollution, the forest seemed untouched.

And this space, this knowledge had been sealed away all this time. I brought Max to mind, colleagues, Grace, other women I'd slept with, Lanh. Then I went further back to the faces of classmates. Every one of us ignorant.

Starting small, a wave of fury spread through me: the scale of deception was hard to grasp.

. . .

For all I knew, this might be my last night if I didn't find Hendrik. But bathed in the green air I couldn't bear to go back to the rocks in search of some form of safety. As I went further, I sang Hendrik's song.

> *I wander on down the hillside,*
> *Valleys before me open wide,*
> *Scent of dew under trees,*
> *Winter by spring is appeased.*

The act of singing gave me courage. The air seemed so clean it could wash me, and I had the curious sensation of being born again.

For a moment I thought I could hear my heartbeat, steady and unusually clear. But that was just my mind messing about: the beat wasn't coming from inside me. It was a faint rhythm in the distance—drums of a dance track at a music festival somewhere in the city? I was probably nearing the end of a narrow strip of trees, and my adventure would be over in a few minutes. Perhaps that would be the best outcome: I might live to see tomorrow if I could find a way back to the streets, a way to slot back into the comforts of my apartment. I followed the beat, trying to increase my pace. The ground was far from flat. My grandpa's game hadn't been able to recreate the experience of walking on an uneven surface.

It wasn't an ordinary drumbeat. The tempo and drum rolls resembled those of the dance music I knew, but the regularity was lacking, so that a few of the beats arrived haphazardly. And the tone, light and mellow, had nothing of the crisp, mechanical punch we jolted our bodies to in clubs. I had difficulty imagining a beat that was not electronically produced.

Was this what live drumming sounded like?

About half an hour passed; no sign of concrete. I wondered if I was being lured into a trap. Having walked some distance already, I was amazed by the way the music travelled. You rarely heard sound from far away in Megacity, partly because people didn't play music outdoors and partly because you didn't have to set foot outside the interconnected buildings and transport systems in the first place. Nobody opened windows, and the magic of noise cancelling meant you could live adjacent to a nightclub and easily pretend it didn't exist.

The drumming grew louder and more frantic, now punctuated by occasional shouts. It seemed to come from the top of a slope I was stumbling my way up.

I reached the top, too tired and dazed to hide, but still tense and ready for flight if need be.

14

A few metres in front, a group of maybe thirty men and women, most of them naked, were leaping, gyrating and air-punching as if they'd taken three Bliss pills. Opposite me, in the middle of the whirl of bodies stood a wilder version of Hendrik, his legs akimbo around a large, goblet-shaped drum, hands pounding out the main beat. Two additional drummers stood either side of him. He grinned at me under a knitted brow.

Hendrik whooped in a high pitch. The dancers spun round to face me and slowed their movements. Still looking at me, one by one they raised their arms and fluttered their hands, whooping.

My shoulders relaxed, and I took a few steps forwards. The dancers formed a circle around me and the drummers, held hands and skipped round us anti-clockwise, then clockwise.

Hendrik winked at me as the dancers linked arms, tightening the circle and skipping closer to us. Although some were dripping with sweat, the stale smell citizens masked with antiperspirant was absent. Their scent was an intensification of the forest's smells, infused with a hint of garlic.

A sequence of smiling faces floated by. I tried to meet the gaze of each man and woman. Their eyes were so alive, but so peace-filled as well. It was like Lanh was looking at me through them.

The drumming continued, the beats quieter, and I slipped into a delicious trance. The blue eyes of one woman seemed to channel the clear sky that gushed into my brain. The brown eyes of a man grounded me on the forest floor. The varying shades of green in two other dancers' eyes linked me to the numberless leaves.

Euphoric gratitude rushed through me, and I couldn't rationalise a thing.

The dancers and drummers gradually disbanded and grabbed shawls or blankets. They formed a circle, including me, and we sat on the earth.

It was silent, except for real birdsong and a breeze shifting the trees.

'So,' Hendrik said finally, 'this is it. You were right, Ben—this has been waiting for you all these years.'

Applause from the group. A number of congratulatory shouts. As for me, I was a reservoir of emotions and struggled to speak.

'How come you didn't tell me your "brothers and sisters" lived in a place like this?' I asked Hendrik.

'I had to see if you could be trusted not to desert us midway,' Hendrik replied. 'It would have been easy for you to leave during the first night when I was asleep and inform on us or give away the destination of our trip. The Supervisors probably would not do anything based on one citizen being taken out of the city, but we can't risk a thing. Now I know I can trust you, let me say that it has been an honour to accompany you on your journey the last two days. Do not worry. All these people are your friends, and you won't get agents following you out here. It is not worth their while.'

A woman next to me on my right spoke: 'Every year or two, a citizen makes it down to a pit or out of Megacity alive. It's become clear to us that for the Supervisors, this is a tiny price to pay for the limitless power they enjoy. And so we're still here, surviving.'

'This is Fern,' said Hendrik. 'How long have you been with us again, Fern?'

'A year and a half.'

Fern had green eyes and cheekbones that looked too familiar.

'Have you seen me before?' she asked.

'How did you know?'

'Wouldn't surprise me, I was a news anchor.'

'Are you *the* El—'

'Elektra, yes. That's who I was.'

'You were everywhere. Didn't you—'

'Yeah, I died.'

'The Bliss overdose?'

'That's the one.'

I'd seen Elektra's face hundreds of times online and on the covers of fashion magazines at Wise Words. I'd once dreamed I was having sex with her and woke up masturbating furiously.

Blood rushed into my face. 'What made you leave Megacity?' I asked to distract myself.

'You can only willingly disseminate fake news for so long,' Fern said. 'My job got me thinking—a lot. It highlighted the indoctrination all too clearly. How can any human brain actually be interested in and believe the bullshit the media vomits out? So I started questioning the many beliefs I clung to that defined everything I did. Like you, I was lucky to find the pit.'

'I'm Jack, this is Andrea,' said a man who could have been in his sixties. Judging the age of a non-citizen was a challenge. And Jack was balding—you didn't see that in Megacity.

'We're natives,' Jack continued. 'The forest is all we've

known. Our parents were members of a small group of rebels who found their way out here. They worked with the founders of our community.'

'Jack and Andrea are our teachers,' Fern said. 'They're masters of survival and farming. Horticulture too.'

'Your story is also unique,' Hendrik said, looking at me. 'You have been driven here by an unshakeable belief in nature, despite the wealth of fake evidence. You show a level of intuitiveness rare amongst citizens.'

Nods all around. Cheers.

'Thank you,' I said. 'Thank you all for letting me come.'

'You will be hungry,' Hendrik said. 'We should head on.'

'Now you'll see where we live,' said Fern.

'I still can't believe I'm here,' I said to Fern, as we made our way over small hills. I looked up at the boughs of four tall trees and asked, 'Why do some trees have grey bark?'

'That's their natural colour. Those are beech.'

'And those?'

'They're my favourite—oaks.'

'How can you hide something as big as a forest?' I wondered. 'What about the views from skyscrapers or the zip or air taxis?'

'Think back to when you were a child. Did you never see bits of green or brown far away through cracks between buildings on one of your trips out of Greater London?'

'Not on my recent searches. But I think I might have asked a carer a few times about them.'

'And what did she say? Or was it a male model?'

'Female. You know the answer.'

'That it was an untreated site or that you were lucky to be far away from it.'

'That's about right.'

'And soon you stopped asking,' Fern said. 'That's the way it goes. The key is, we lost interest. We got seduced by immersive displays, social media and virtual experiences. When you're in that head space, your physical surroundings become the least interesting thing in the world.'

'An inconvenience, right?'

'Precisely,' Fern replied. 'An inconvenience that takes you away from the stuff you're taught really matters. That's what pisses me off most—the education games are so well engineered that any patches unaccounted for by the grid become completely invisible. Even if your average citizen were placed right in front of this forest, they wouldn't see it, or they'd immediately scamper back to "safety". Did you know that a number of uninhabited districts have also been added to Greater London purely to create the illusion that the city is endless?'

'Makes sense. Why do you think the Supervisors want to hide this from us if it's not even dangerous?'

'Social control.'

'I hate them,' I said. Being totally unmonitored out here, uttering that little sentence was pure satisfaction.

A series of large shapes came into view. I asked Fern if they were natural boulders.

'Those are our homes, silly.' She laughed. 'They might be mossy, but they're houses. The remains of an ancient village called Forest Row from before the Great Eviction.'

The same word that Lanh had used.

'Forest Row,' I said a few seconds later. My skin tingled: a place named after a forest. 'I imagine this is just a small woodland now, right? The black dots on the maps are tiny.'

'It's not as small as you'd think,' Fern said. 'You know not to trust the maps, don't you? Sure, Megacity is massive, but some areas of forest and farmland were clearly ignored and even allowed to spread in places. This forest is an expansion of an area that was once known as Ashdown Forest. There are bound to be other similar areas, but we don't hunt for them. We're bloody lucky we found this one.'

'Were buildings really made that small?' I wondered, as we drew closer to the houses covered in plant life and draped with creepers.

'They're a mixture of houses and shops from the 21st and 22nd centuries Pre- Megacity,' said Fern. 'A few go right back to the Victorian and Georgian eras. You're walking along an old road right now.' She pointed to an ancient sign half a metre above the ground that read, 'Priory Road.'

We entered the remains of a crumbling pub. Beneath what seemed like an impractically low ceiling, Fern motioned for me to sit down at a long wooden table laid with an assortment of cutlery and chipped crockery of many colours that must once have looked clean.

I detected onion in the air, and Jack appeared, piled high with dishes.

'What's it today?' somebody asked.

'Plain salad, roast vegetables and sourdough bread. For dessert we have apple and blackberry crumble.' Walking past my chair he added, 'All organic, of course, and not modified in any way, although I hear Megacity stopped labelling GM food long ago, so I doubt that means much to you.' He looked around and called out, 'Will you hurry up and take your seats, ladies and gentlemen.'

Children ran over and slithered onto the benches, as the adults and three teenagers left their conversations and made their way to the table. Hendrik sat to my left, Fern was on my right. Andrea took her seat at the head of the table, and the crowd fell silent. Everyone closed their eyes. The only sound was real birdsong, amplified by the absence of glass in some of the windowpanes.

Andrea spoke: 'Let us give thanks—for this food, for our

freedom, for this forest and each of us who has been lucky enough to thrive in it. Thanks also for the new member of our family.'

After a pause, everyone joined hands and said, 'We give thanks.'

I didn't have a clue who they were thanking. I was just relieved it couldn't be the Supervisors.

'Ben,' Jack called, 'I won't be offended if you don't touch it. We don't know how your body might react to healthy food.'

'Fern has offered to put you up,' Hendrik said.

My knee twitched. I tried to picture Max's reaction if I told him I was living with Elektra.

'That's amazing, thank you,' I said.

Turning to Hendrik I asked, 'Where the hell were you this morning?'

'I wanted to let you meet the forest on your own. I knew you might struggle at first, but it makes the culmination of the journey a lot more powerful. We had a couple of people looking out for you in case you didn't make it down the hill or didn't follow the sound of the drums. But you got here on your own.'

It was weird to taste the real flavour of vegetables without sauces or added flavourings. After a few mouthfuls I told Fern how much I wanted to let my friend know about this place and suggested we could come up with a way to spread the word among the citizens.

A clatter. Fern had dropped her cutlery onto her plate, and now she was putting her hand on my thigh. I jumped. She was staring at me.

'Are you alright?' I asked.

'You do know that you're not going back, don't you?' She searched my eyes.

'It isn't allowed,' a woman said opposite. 'Not for any of us. We've got children to think about. Just to be seen returning is a risk to the community. You've been unconditioned and will find it impossible not to try and convert others.'

I swallowed irritation with some root vegetables.

'I can see you're not enjoying hearing this, but it's better we get it out of the way.'

'What about the watchers?' I asked. 'They go up from the pit to the streets all the time.'

'The pit is not the forest,' the woman said. 'Watchers rarely attempt to convert a citizen. And what applies in the pit is not what applies here.'

'As long as we don't bother any citizens or alert them to our life here,' said a man to her right, 'we can go on living our harmless existence. You'll soon be glad you have to stay. I know we don't have access to hospitals, dentists or coffee, but I promise you'll forget about that in a matter of weeks.'

'We've evolved our own therapies and survival modes,' the woman said, 'although it's fair to say our life expectancy isn't nearly as long as the citizens'.'

'How come you go back and forth?' I asked Hendrik.

'Occasionally one of us makes the trip to carry news between the pits and the forest or to escort a rare newcomer like yourself. But these journeys must be strictly limited, and we never speak to citizens about life beyond the pit. It is the only way to safeguard the community and know we can trust one another.'

'*Now* you tell me I'm never going back. I thought this "journey", as you call it, was going to last six months,' I said.

'It is,' said Hendrik. It will take you some time to learn our principles. The main one is trust, which cannot be built overnight. When the six months are up—'

'You can stop there, Hendrik.' It was the woman opposite again. 'We have to be careful in the early days.'

'Ben's an intelligent man, Maria. He deserves the full picture.' He turned back to me. 'When the six months are up, you can decide if you would rather remain here or be posted to a pit. If you choose a pit, we cannot force you to not go back to your former life, but we will discourage you.' Hendrik smiled. 'You might find it reassuring to know that so far nobody has found it necessary to leave their new life behind once they get used to it.'

'What would happen to me in a pit?'

'You would become a watcher like the others. Like me. We in the pit have chosen to sacrifice the freedom and pleasures of the forest. We're nothing more than guards, really. Our priority is the safety of our children—it is they who will one day be the energy that carries our community into the future.'

Not wanting to ruin my first night in the forest, I nodded and said nothing.

We walked under the half-full moon to Fern's house. Her hand reached for mine, and I swallowed moist forest air.

Steps in unison, joined in darkness.

A decision to stop.

Me putting my arms around Elektra's neck.

A single warm kiss against the cool night. For a moment I thought I heard traffic or drones, but it was only the strange sound of wind passing through many trees.

'That was by far the best kiss I've ever had,' I said.

She hugged my tightly. 'Pretty good for a first kiss.'

We reached a small house Fern said was called a cottage and went inside. She spent a few minutes lighting candles with an ancient fire starter she said was made of magnesium.

We fell onto a dusty sofa, our mouths searching and finding each other.

'That's enough for tonight,' she said after we'd torn off a layer of clothing. 'There's no need to rush.'

'I agree.' And I meant it. It would be refreshing to see what waiting was like, even if I'd never been so ready to merge with another human being as now.

'This could be special, who knows?' she said. 'Better not to waste it.'

Lying in my arms, Fern drifted into semi-consciousness, and I gazed at her face spotlit by the moon shining through a window frame that had once encased glass. She looked so much older than the Elektra who'd been the face of Megacity.

I marvelled at how far away this moment was from anything I could have predicted. Trees swayed and creaked, their leaves whispering. Some kind of forest creature sent out the occasional hoot. Pristine air explored my lungs.

Fern heaved herself up and away from me. 'Have the spare room, or sleep on the sofa. Goodnight.' She went to her bedroom and closed the door.

I couldn't leave the sofa. I wanted to absorb the warmth of it into me, as if staying there could extend our embrace indefinitely.

What would it be like, my first night in a forest? Sure, I'd come to the right place, and this might become a life worth living. But armies of questions tarnished by that other universe that seemed so distant—yet was a mere walk away—prevented me from arriving fully. And although I glimpsed a blue land of sleep that promised ultimate oblivion, I would not enter it yet: tonight, thoughts of Megacity were on the march, and I lay awaiting the fretful dreams already circling.

15

A week went by, and except for midnight desperation for Fern, I slept more soundly in her spare room than I did with all the supplements and audio programs my apartment could produce for me.

I absorbed the basics of community life. You could thrive without caffeine. Carrots, kale, beetroots and pumpkins could be grown in the clearings and were so much better direct from the source. You could also eat certain mushrooms and leaves from beeches, birches, hawthorns, nettles, dandelions. Your sleep and mood improved when you awoke to daylight and lay down soon after nightfall.

I encountered a range of animals with names such as rabbit, squirrel, fox and deer, and I learned first-hand that numerous species of bird still existed, from robins, blue tits and pigeons, to jays, magpies and tawny owls.

Wherever I looked, whatever I did, there was that same feeling—connectedness. With my environment, the people around me and myself. With Fern I perfected the human kiss, and although my desire to sleep with her had become a war I had to fight in silence, I was mostly happy to take things at a prehistoric pace.

I saw my grandfather everywhere, playing in the streams and collecting leaves, sticks and fir cones.

The notion of the sadness as a state that endangered your sanity was revealed for what it was—one of the many ploys to keep citizens hooked up to tech, Bliss and entertainment. Instead, sadness was just one of many emotions flowing in and out of your day.

The only times I really felt sad were when I imagined what the Great Eviction must have been like for my grandfather and countless others. The concept of a Great *Urbanisation* as taught in school allowed for the possibility that many families might have actually chosen to relocate to Megacity in its early years, attracted by everything a smart city promised. Whilst I'm sure many were excited to move, now that I'd experienced the beauty of life here it was obvious that force had been used on a gigantic scale, and it hurt to imagine the brutality involved in forcibly evicting whole populations from their centuries-long homelands.

And all for what? This was what no-one was able to tell me.

On the afternoon of my eighth day in the community, I was digging in a clearing with Jack. He was talking about how to grow different types of vegetables. I was trying to convince myself I was interested, when really, I was waiting for the right moment to ask him something totally unrelated. He'd just finished on courgettes, and I jumped in with my question. 'Have they never come looking for you out here?'

Jack jerked himself upright. 'No.' He got back to digging.

'Not once in all the time you've—'

'Luckily not,' he interrupted.

'You can tell me, I can take it.'

He stopped digging for a second. 'Just the occasional visit.'
'From agents?'
He nodded, back turned to me now and busy with the spade again.
'How many times have they come?'
'Four, but the gaps seem shorter every time.'
'What happens when they do?'
'They … sorry …' Jack sounded like he was choking up. 'They take a member of the community. It's a reminder—a warning to us and the watchers in the pits that starting a rebellion is futile. The third time …' Jack fell silent for a moment. 'The third time was when they took Andrea's sister.'

This beauty, the green forest, the place I'd imagined might come to be my home … it wasn't beyond the tentacles of Megacity after all.

I stared through the trees, the utopia of the community shattered.

Flames fanned into life in my chest. I clenched the handle of my spade, unsure whether I could do any more work.

Then I slowly released my grip and let it fall to the ground.

I paced over to the hut Hendrik stayed in. He was out. Three hours stood between now and dinner. Three hours I would use to think.

It wouldn't be easy to say goodbye. I'd already begun to love this place and had imagined the forest dwellers becoming like family. The thought of leaving Fern was painful. If it wasn't for my relentless desire for truth and justice, I might have tried to make a go of things here.

That evening Jack—somehow—managed to serve the communal meal with his usual serenity. Hendrik sat opposite me. He'd been gathering wood in a different part of the forest and looked like he'd fall asleep if it wasn't for the need to eat. I forced myself to smile and make small talk until everyone had finished their meal.

Then I blurted, 'I have to ask you, has the community ever thought of doing something in response to the abductions?'

Fern stared at me. 'Ben, not here, not now.'

Hendrik was caught off guard. 'We have not come here to think about that tonight.' He leaned forward and looked down the table at Jack. 'I am not sure Ben was ready to hear about the visits.'

'It was me,' I said. 'I asked him.'

'How could I lie?' Jack said.

'Ben,' Hendrik said, 'this can wait.'

Nobody spoke. A throat clearing here and there.

I didn't like what I was about to do, but the pain of my new knowledge meant I could no longer just slot in here as if everything was fine.

'I was shocked to hear about what happens,' I said addressing the whole table. 'But haven't you at least thought of how to prevent another abduction?'

Fern elbowed me in the ribs.

Frowns everywhere, parents hurrying children out, a doubling of silence.

Hendrik took a slow breath. 'Ben, believe me, it is not a pretty sight when they come. Do you think we don't wish every day that it won't happen again? But we have to accept we're no match for the agents.'

'I understand,' I said, 'but isn't it also true that by doing nothing you're choosing for this continue?'

More people getting up.

I heard someone say, 'He's gone mad.'

Hendrik stabbed a potato and chewed it in silence as though he was the only one in the room. When he'd finished, he wiped his mouth, got up and left without even looking at me.

A handful of people who had remained at the far end of the table began making lamenting sounds. Jack broke into a slow melody in a minor key; the others joined in, some branching off into wails that produced gut-wrenching harmonies, so that I was unsure if they were singing or crying in song.

A barrage of wind flexed the boughs outside until I thought they'd snap. The song grew louder, before dismantling itself note by note, as its producers prepared to carry themselves home.

Well, that went well, I thought darkly.

At least I'd been honest—sooner or later they had to get to know the real me.

'I need to get back,' I said to Fern as her cottage came into view.

'Be my guest—run on ahead. I could do with some space, Ben.'

'No, I mean back to Megacity.'

'You know the deal.'

'Fuck the deal. People have a right to know.'

'What do you intend to do?'

'Well, I know this place exists now. That's a start, isn't it?'

'You've been here one week, and suddenly you can solve *our* dilemma that's been going on for decades? Do you know what an arrogant prick you are?'

'I hate inaction. You're intelligent. How can you live happily here and pretend everything's fine?'

Fern ripped the door of her cottage open. She lowered her pitch and almost whispered, 'You know nothing about the compromises we've had to make to be able to live like this.' She went into her bedroom and slammed the door behind her.

I stood in the living room for a minute, seething. I went

back out, slammed the front door and walked towards Hendrik's hut.

Hendrik said nothing when he opened the door but accepted me into the room with a diagonal nod. We sat on a pair of floor cushions.

'You are different,' Hendrik said. 'You seem incapable of just being grateful for what you have found. Newcomers usually put up with the small risk of being chosen by the agents one day. They are happy to savour the many fruits of forest life for however many years they are lucky to get here.'

'How can you expect me to enjoy the many fruits if I had to witness you, Fern or Jack being taken?' I shrugged. 'I'm sorry if I haven't expressed enough gratitude. I love everything about this place and the way you live. I didn't set out to complicate things. But how can I live in this reality now that I know the other half of the story?'

'You have a lot to process after what you heard today, I know, but you've got to stop being so forthright with your words. You are hurting people. Everyone here has worked hard to develop the community. If you keep challenging and questioning things, you will start putting your personal safety at risk.'

Great, so now I wasn't allowed to have my own thoughts and speak my mind, just like my life before. That made me want to leave even more, but where the hell was there left for me to go?

A knock on the door—Fern had guessed my whereabouts. She stepped inside and found a cushion.

'Fern, can you speak some sense into this man?' Hendrik said.

'He's got sense, he just doesn't want to use it. I heard the last bit through the door,' she said looking at me. 'You just need to choose your audiences more carefully. And don't shit on everyone right before dinner.'

'I can't believe Jack told Ben today,' Hendrik said to her. 'We normally wait at least three months.'

'Well, it's done now,' said Fern. 'Ben, is there anything we can do that will put your mind at ease and stop you threatening our entire way of life?'

I took a deep breath. 'We can discuss my return to the city. Not the pit. I want to go back into Megacity. And it's not to betray—'

'Other than that,' Fern interrupted. 'We'll consider almost anything other than that.'

'If the Supervisors are the only reason we and the citizens can't be free,' I said, heat rising, 'I don't understand why there's no dialogue—either here, or in the pit—about finding out who they are. That's all I'm trying to ask—who the hell are they? And why did they forcibly evict vast numbers of rural inhabitants from their rightful—totally healthy and uncontaminated—homelands? Why is nobody asking these questions?' I paused for impact. 'If something is ever going to change, we need to know who the enemy is. Before I found out about the abductions, I might have been able to swallow my hatred of the Supervisors and settle down here for longer, but knowing this is too much. The level of power they wield over us has become absurd. We're all just miserable little pawns in their game. Yes, even out here.'

It was Hendrik's turn. 'You don't think the Supervisors are prepared for people like you—renegade psychos happily risking your own and other people's lives to play at chasing them down? If they do not want to be found, they won't be. If they know you're after them, they will squash you.'

'Maybe I'm willing to take that risk. Sure, I might not find out anything about them, and even if I do, it might not help the world much. But if nobody tries, there's no hope for anyone either. And if I do learn something, just the tiniest thing, maybe somewhere someone will continue the search when I am gone.'

'Yes, and you'll be gone pretty quickly,' Hendrik replied.

'What do you propose, given that they've always been invisible?' Fern asked.

'I don't know, but sitting in this forest isn't getting me anywhere.'

'Maybe he has a point,' Fern said. 'I would definitely feel some satisfaction if I knew who they are, especially as they're probably not even artHuman, but mere mortals like ourselves —eating, fucking and shitting. Come to think of it, that was probably another reason I left the news channel—the moronic ignorance about who pulls the strings and comes up with the stories.'

At last a scrap of support from somebody.

Hendrik looked as if he'd eaten sour berries.

Fern was gazing at me with a deeper intensity than usual. I felt so close to her in that moment. It was uncanny how much she meant to me already.

'Thank you for saying that, Fern,' I said. 'I just can't understand why somebody can't make a start on this. Surely we have a right to know who's oppressing the entire world?'

Hendrik shifted about on his cushion. 'I appreciate your coming here and talking to me about this, Ben. Unfortunately, we cannot change the rules for one person. I'll be happy to continue this conversation in the coming weeks. We will support you as you process these and other feelings that will inevitably come up. Fern, are you happy for the three of us to meet once a week in this hut?'

'Sure.'

Fern and I stepped out of the hut into the blanket of night. The wind sent the fragrance from the forest flowers up from our path and we linked hands once more.

Was it love, this feeling of never wanting to let another person go, or was I just infatuated? Regardless, it was tinged with melancholy as I knew I'd stop at nothing to go back to

Megacity and delve into the murkiness of who and where the Supervisors might be.

'You're a bit of a drama queen, aren't you?' said Fern.

'Call me what you like. I can't sit back and accept this. Anyway, I wouldn't have got here if I wasn't the way I am.'

Back at the cottage we didn't light the candles. We dropped all thought of holding back, unpeeled the extra layers needed for life in an unheated house and fused under the eye of the waxing moon, our breaths and cries agreeing with the wind's insistence and the sighing of the leaves.

16

'It must be the same in other regions,' I said, when we finally sat down to breakfast the next morning.

'What must?' Fern asked.

'Undocumented forests like this one.'

'I imagine. None of us have done research abroad. How are we supposed to get there? We're non-citizens.'

'True.'

'Are you OK?' Fern narrowed her eyes. 'You look weird.'

She must have picked up on me thinking rebel thoughts again. 'If I did go back early, would you come with me? You could stay in the pit while Max and I run some searches. He's a master hacker. As soon as he picks up anything about the Supervisors' location, I'll travel there and see what I can find. Then I'll come back to see you.'

'You can't stop, can you? Hendrik's not gonna budge. Anyway, what makes you assume I'd be happy to tag along and wait around while you explore the planet?'

'Sorry, but I had to ask you.'

'Why do you want to drag me into it?'

'I'm being selfish. I've not met a woman with a free mind like yours. I can't bear the idea of letting you go.'

'You know nothing about me.'

'I want to learn more.'

She was quiet for a few seconds. 'I'm really fond of you, but even if we did let you go, I couldn't leave this place.'

Although it would be almost impossible to find my way back to the pit alone, it was obvious that nobody could compel me to stay here, unless they were prepared to lock me up or follow me armed all day, all night. I pictured myself setting off alone, and a shadow of sadness passed over my heart. Wasn't everything I could hope to attain in life here in this leafy paradise?

Not just life. Love. I followed the curve of Fern's lips and kissed her once more.

'You're very romantic—I'll give you that much.' She smiled. 'You're beautiful too.' She leaned forward and framed my face with her hands.

She wasn't making it easier.

Fern's smile faded. 'But think carefully about going. You might not be allowed back.'

She was right, of course. I felt hollow at the thought of never being in her presence again. But stubbornness was my defining characteristic.

'Can we go and see Hendrik again today?' I suggested.

'No, wait for our meeting with him. It's just seven days away.'

'Do I have to go alone, or are you coming with me?'

I knocked on Hendrik's door an hour after his usual breakfast time. Fern stood a few metres behind me, arms crossed.

'Yes?' Hendrik rubbed his eyes. 'I had a late one—too much

beech leaf liquor. Why are you here again? If it's about leaving, you can forget it.'

'Let me go, Hendrik. Let me go and find something on these Supervisors and who they are. Then maybe one day we can do something about our predicament.'

'That's not going to persuade him,' Fern warned.

'Why the fuck should we trust you?' Hendrik spewed, sharing the stench of his hangover. 'Why should the community treat you differently from those who came before you? Huh?'

'You said yourself that I'm different. And I'm ready to dedicate myself to the cause.'

'He's definitely a fighter,' Fern said.

'Enough talking in the open.' Hendrik took a step back from the door. 'Get your asses in here.'

'As soon as I get back, I can hand in my notice at Dwellings. I will speak to *one* contact. His name is Max. He has access to tech you cannot imagine. We will strip the grid clean in our searches for the Supervisors. With Max's encryptions we will be untraceable. If we haven't made any progress after half a year, I can either become a watcher, return here or wait for death to take me, along with the secrets of the community—take your pick. Choose my fate for me.'

'This Max is a big problem,' Hendrik said. 'He goes straight to the agents, you're arrested for trying to brainwash a citizen with fake knowledge and we're all seized. Who is Max anyway? Why him? We have never let anyone make the journey back with the sole intention of talking to a citizen. Undoing conditioning carries extreme risk. You cannot predict the reactions and side effects. The watchers know this as well. That is why we call them watchers and not warriors.'

'Think back to when you met Lanh,' Fern said. 'I doubt he was actively trying to convert you or lead you down to the pit.'

'I hear your concerns. I know Max from uni. He's the only

citizen I've met who thinks independently. He knew about my searches for nature and had over two weeks to set an agent on me. When I tell him about this, he'll believe me. Plus, I'm the only friend he has. He loves me way too much to betray me.'

Hendrik looked from me to Fern and back again. 'I'm still not convinced.'

I'd come expecting this. I nodded, gave Hendrik a few moments to feel heard, prepared to soften my tone and tried to assume a calm authority. 'I'm so grateful to have been brought here and welcomed into the community with such warmth.' I took Fern's hand. 'I'd be sacrificing too much if I betrayed anyone here.'

Fern squeezed my hand.

'Here's my proposition,' I said, 'as far as I know, nobody here or in the pit has been able to explore abroad. If we can't find any loopholes in the structures of knowledge through searching in London, there are other locations we can try from. It's a big world. My eye and ear devices are waiting for me at home, and I've got money saved up. In addition to working with Max, I can travel overseas. Technically I'm still a citizen on annual leave. Dwellings is expecting me back in six days. If you let me leave tomorrow, I'll just make it and there won't be any blips in the narrative.'

Hendrik sighed. 'This is determination.' By the tone in his voice, I knew his resistance had lowered. Finally, we were getting somewhere.

17

It was mid-morning on the following day when Fern and I trudged up the incline I'd careened down after my first sighting of the forest a week and a half ago. Just hours after the second talk in Hendrik's hut, he'd come to our cottage and given me permission to leave, with the condition that my departure was quick and silent to limit any further conflict.

Halfway through a briefing with Hendrik about the route, Fern had—to my excitement—done a turnaround and agreed to be my guide on the journey back to Megacity. There were also friends in the pit she wanted to see.

As we reached the rocks where I'd slept under the overpass, I wrapped an arm around Fern and thanked her for coming.

'I admire your courage,' she replied. 'I wouldn't have done this for anyone else.'

'I know. I'm lucky.'

'You are, you bastard.' She kissed my cheek.

The first day of clambering was as easy as breathing. A magical force that was sexier than Bliss drove my legs and fuelled my arms as we battled the boulders and helped each other up the steep faces.

We stopped now and then, but what were supposed to be rests rippled into waves of kisses. As evening approached, we couldn't hold back and our bodies found each other. I pressed her against the slant of a boulder and lifted her skirt. She tugged my belt open and pulled me into her. I scooped deeply as we owned our rhythm, her moans birthing harmonies with the groan of traffic above us. Faint smells of the city carried on the twilight air mingled with her natural scents that overpowered me, till I seemed to grasp the reason for my existence.

When we emerged from the cave into the smoky pit after two days I wished would never end, dusk was falling.

'Fern!' someone shouted.

People around various fires looked our way, and in seconds many of them were walking or running towards us. I stepped away and watched as Fern became a magnet attracting about thirty men and women jostling to embrace her; three or four children skipped around the edges of the huddle.

After allowing them to celebrate her return, Fern motioned for them to move away. 'Give us a moment.' She looked in my direction.

The crowd peeled away, and Fern walked over to where I stood. 'I'll be fine here,' she said. 'These are my friends. Go up and do what you've got to do. Now that I'm here, I'll probably stick around for a few weeks. Come back and see me. I won't go until you do.'

'I'll try to visit you in a couple of days. Tell Duc I look forward to seeing him again and that I'm forever grateful to him for sending me on the journey. In case something happens to me and I don't return within a week, here are Max's contact details.' I handed her a scrap of paper I'd written on before we left the forest. 'Are you sure the watchers won't turn on you when they realise why you helped me come back to the city?'

'Shh! Don't worry about me. Hendrik's highly respected—he'll smooth things out for me. Just don't fuck up. A lot of people depend on you to not make any mistakes.' She kissed me. 'Good luck, and don't let anything happen to you. From a selfish perspective, I'd like to see you again.'

I checked the others were no longer watching, kissed Fern once more and turned to leave.

Only as I walked to the mouth of the track did the full force of my decision confront me. I turned and saw Fern approaching a group in the middle. As if she could feel my eyes on her back, she turned and waved before merging with the group.

As soon as I was out of sight, I leaned against the fencing and slid down onto my haunches, breaking into violent sobs. Why? I didn't know. Sure, I was leaving Fern for a while, but I'd see her again.

This world of fully-felt feelings was still so new to me. My own tenderness and the power of my love for another human had split me open. They seemed to dwarf my absurd idea of pursuing the invisible forces controlling Megacity. Could I even survive back up there? Wouldn't I be giving myself away? Was it better to stay? I could just spend the night in the pit and return with Fern to the forest. We'd live out our days there as long as we could. We might even plot to be abducted together and die in each other's embrace.

Or perhaps I could persuade the watchers to let me remain in the pit for good. Fern could either stay with me, or I could make an occasional trip to the forest like Hendrik and visit her there. I liked the pit: my journey to the place I'd dreamed of had begun on the floor of this forsaken crater, here where the smell of bonfire smoke and the enlightenment of free thought existed dangerously close to sterile routines and the oblivion of mind control. To live in central Megacity, yet within a hidden pocket that maintained a link to the land protected by trees—was it possible to be more in touch with truth, if there was such a thing?

I stood up and wiped my eyes. Fern and I would find a way to make this work. I was no longer the person I was, but some things remained unchanged: if I failed to at least attempt the task I'd set myself, the regret would never leave.

My jaw hardened as I focused on the track. I pushed myself uphill and began my journey back to the lights and the loneliness awaiting.

18

Edging up the gradual spiral, part of me looked forward to the hygiene and convenience of Megacity. I also knew, though, that attaining peace of mind up there would now be an impossibility.

I waited till there were no vehicles before slipping through the corrugated iron onto the street, smiling for any invisi-Drones that may be on duty. The evening streetlights blinded me after the darkness of tunnels and the night-time forest; it was as though someone expecting my return had turned them on to expose me.

My front door opened at my approach and the apartment clicked into life. Wall displays dazzled me with their abundance of blue light and richness of colour. Lighting, air purifiers and the temp controller watched, listened and communicated with each other. The mealer hummed itself awake, while adjustable furniture twitched as it tried to anticipate my moves.

To think I once found it peaceful here. Homely.

I stared at my possessions, estranged: I didn't need a single one of them.

In went my lenses. The dread of wading through thousands of missed messages was dispelled by a notification from Megacity Law Enforcement that I was banned from all social media for one year. I'd risked my life by knowingly entering an Untreated Toxic Site. The ban was for my own safety, and I was strongly advised to seek therapy, which Dwellings would be happy to pay for.

Banned from all social media—the average citizen would choose suicide. I couldn't care, but it was a pain not being able to call Max. I wanted to go straight to his apartment but was starving, so I ordered a strawberry-flavoured liquid meal and downed it. Still hungry, I washed my mouth out and ordered a selection of dim sum.

By now it was too late to disturb Max. I'd visit him in the morning.

I had no idea how my story would affect him. He'd believe me but would need time to digest how conditioned he'd been. He might even try to kick me out. Either way, he'd be swamped with fear at the idea of running any searches to help me. He'd have to refuse.

At first.

I knew Max well. It'd be easier for me to persuade him than Hendrik. I hoped I wouldn't have to resort to manipulation, but I also couldn't allow my one contact to let me down.

I needed sleep, but the experience I'd lived through and was waiting to share with Max stood in the way. At 3 a.m. I got dressed and left my apartment. I wasn't yet banned from the zip, so I took a trip to Max's block.

Max was either ignoring me or sleeping through my rings. Of course he might also have hacked and disabled his doorbell.

I walked to a 24-hour pod service halfway down the next

block, paid for a relax pod and set an alarm for 6 a.m. It was Saturday, but Max was always up early.

The sounds, lighting, fragrance and back-and-foot massage in the relax pod enraged me, and I asked for complete stillness. The pod said that wasn't on the menu. I exited the service and sat on the ground outside, smiling as I remembered Lanh's warning I might find myself in his position one day. I relished it when the occasional citizen walked past, avoiding my gaze.

At 6:30 Max finally let me into the building.

'What the fuck!' he said. 'I thought you were dead. I thought you'd taken a euthanasia pill or something. You looked crazy when you left me that night.'

When old friends meet again, there are no words for the warmth inside. 'I'm so happy to see you again,' I said.

'Where have you been? I called you a hundred times until I heard a message you were disconnected.'

'It may take a while to explain.'

'Tell me over breakfast. Coffee and eggs Florentine for you?'

'Am I that predictable?'

'Of course.'

I interlocked my fingers, then pulled my hands apart, looking around Max's apartment.

He understood immediately that I was asking him to disconnect every device that might be listening.

'Ben, if this is true, it changes everything,' Max said.

'What do you mean, *if* it's true? What would I gain from lying to you?'

'This is a lot to take on board first thing on a Saturday morning, asshole.' Max pushed his chair back. 'I don't actually want to believe you, but I recognise I might have to.'

I leapt up and shook him by the shoulders. 'I've been

looking forward to this moment so much, the moment when we both know the truth.'

'Relax, will you? I need time to process this. There's a voice in me yelling that you're spouting bullshit, but I suppose this is where you leave me no choice but to say, well done.' He patted my back. 'Your hunch about the countryside was clearly more than fantasy.'

'Thank you,' I said, sitting down. 'You know what happens next, right?'

Max's eyes widened; he shook his head slowly. He knew alright.

'We've got work to do.'

'*We*? No, I definitely don't understand.' Fear in his voice.

'I need your help. The community needs your help.'

'My help is not on offer.'

'I won't get you into trouble. All I ask is that we run some searches over the next few weeks. You can do them in the evenings after work.'

'What kind of searches exactly?'

'Well, it's likely to involve hacking into networks to try and find out who the Supervisors are. That's the first step before any sort of dialogue can occur.'

'Dialogue?' Max's tone had hardened. 'You mean before I end up executed? This is the most pointless idea. How do you think knowing anything would change a thing about the way we live?'

I gave him an almost identical spiel to the one I'd thrown at Hendrik.

'What makes you think I'd be able to find a safe way through the impenetrable fortress that protects them?'

'You've got multiple degrees in security systems and you only happen to work in the security department of CityLens, one of the most powerful firms on the planet. You know how to protect some of the very systems the Supervisors are probably hiding behind.'

'Even if I did find something, this is way too dangerous. Why should I risk so much?'

The atmosphere between us thickened.

'Come on, we both know you have all the tools to trawl untraced,' I said. 'There's barely any likelihood you'd get caught. It just feels wrong because it's illegal and you've never done anything like this before.'

'I can't do it.' Max looked away.

He wasn't buying it. That left me little other choice. I hated resorting to my trump card of pure manipulation, but I hadn't come back to the city for nothing. 'I thought you said you loved me. Man, we're like family!' The words came out genuinely, reducing my guilt.

Max stopped frowning. Had I touched a chord?

'Bloody hell!' he said. 'You think you can get whatever you want, don't you?'

'Yes, I do. I'm sorry. Seriously, though: now we know the truth, neither of us is going to be happy pretending there's nothing behind the facades surrounding us all day. Once the initial shock wears off and you've thought about this, you know you'll never be content again. Am I wrong?'

'You could at least have let "the initial shock wear off" before asking for help. That would've been nice. I've only just got out of bed, you wanker!'

The desperation in Max's voice signalled it was game over for him.

'Am I wrong?' I repeated, as if I hadn't heard. Fern was right; I could be an arrogant prick, but I had to let my determination run its course. I'd make it up to him later somehow.

'I hate you. You're this little child who believes in magic and fairy tales. What's in it for me?'

'Honestly, I don't know yet,' I replied. 'Definitely a good

conscience. You'll be doing me and a lot of other people an unquantifiable service.'

'I work from home, and you're asking me to stay at my desk and do more work after work? You know how tired my eyes get and how badly I sleep.'

'Can you call in sick for a few days and work during the—'

'No way,' he said, his voice rising over mine. 'I'll give you this weekend and no more.'

The adrenaline hit me: it was Saturday. That meant he could start today!

'I'm genuinely grateful, Max.'

'Don't mention it, shithead.'

19

The arrogant prick thing bothered me. Was it purely my ego driving me to imagine I could tackle the mysteries of the time we lived in? It was good to have principles and my strong desire for justice as they showed I had integrity, to use Duc's word. But I was one tiny pawn in the vast and impenetrable game the Supervisors designed a long time ago and had always been the masters of.

But I'd got Max interested now.

'This is massive,' he said as we walked over to his desk in the livingspace.

'You're seeing it, right? Once it sinks in and the whole picture takes shape, it messes with your mind.'

'Hell, yeah. Like why bother move that number of people into an urban environment for a start? So what do you want me to do?'

'I was kind of hoping you might know. Maybe hack into as many of CityLens's high-level communications as you can— see if you spot anything about plans or policies for Megacity? We both know the Supervisors must be connected in some way to such a massive organisation. Anyway, that could be a good start, couldn't it?' I had no idea what I was saying.

'That's hardly a strategy, Ben. It feels like you're trying to find a germ in Megacity.'

'Maybe start with the most heavily encrypted messages then. You're the techie—can you think of a better way?'

'Give me a couple of hours to gather my thoughts. Watch something in the kitchen.' Max powered up his apartment again now we'd stopped talking.

I went into the kitchen and asked for the most popular news channel.

'Welcome back to Megacity London with Zeb, your channel for all the—'

'Even just the *name* Megacity makes me want to puke!' I yelled through the open door, reaching out for some solidarity from Max.

He ignored me.

Zeb was a stocky, middle-aged man known for his gravelly voice. Despite the relentless demand for young-looking, slim presenters with doctored facial features, he had enjoyed the most subscribers among the thousands of news channels for a whole year, partly due to the very fact he looked so at odds with all the competition. Maybe his visible age also gave him a sense of authority people trusted.

'In bed with the enemy?' Zeb said. 'Prime Minister Noah Black has been photographed coming out of a hotel in North London by Birmingham, accompanied by Labour of Love leader Linda Bennings.

'Real or fake news? You decide. But following so soon after the two party leaders were spotted just a week ago sitting next to each other at a football match, this story is almost certainly going to add fuel to the widespread suspicion that the much loved politicians are having an affair. If they are, how could such a liaison affect the reputations and careers of these two—shall we call them—passionate politicians?

'Already comments are arriving from viewers. It warms my heart to see people around the world taking an interest in London's politics. Let's see … Stefan in Austria. Go ahead, Stefan.'

'I think a romance between Noah and Linda is exactly what we need. London's politics has become a bit dull recently, so I'm pleased with this development. Although some people will say there is a conflict of interest because they are from opposing parties, I think the benefits to both politicians could be substantial as many people are going to take a greater interest in the next general election, which I think may be called soon. It makes sense—you will get a much bigger voter turnout if they are having an affair, and both parties will sell a lot of merch and experiences.'

'Interesting, thanks for that. Let's go to Shanaya in Bangalore. Shanaya?'

'I think Stefan is right. There's going to be another election in the next few months. I've already told my relatives in London to vote Conservative many times. Let me just say, I love Noah. His images are plastered on all my walls and I listen to his music every day. Like lots of ladies out there, I'm very jealous of Linda at the moment. I think I will love Noah till the day I die.'

Shanaya's eyes had grown moist. 'A friend of mine believes Linda is just trying to get publicity, but that deep down she wants to be with a woman. This friend is crazy—she only dates British women who don't mind dressing up like Linda.' Shanaya giggled.

'This is hurting my mind.' I groaned. The volume of the news show decreased to allow conversation.

'What?' Max asked.

'Nothing.'

'This is an impossible task you've given me.'

Our short conversation was over. I knew Max would be whispering expletives in my direction, but I couldn't hear him as the volume had come back up.

'Well viewers, the possible blossoming of this romance is certainly exciting our viewers.' Zeb winked sleazily as he said 'exciting'. 'It will be interesting to see if this does mean yet another election is on the cards as Stefan predicted a moment—'

'Give me the top story.' I yawned.

'Citizens of London and the rest of Megacity'—Zeb looked charged with excitement—'today we bring you a special report on the optical breakthrough announced on the island of Taiwan just last night. Long ago the internet was born. Later the hefty devices cutely named "smartphones" gathered together social media, payments, music, cameras, maps and of course the phone itself into one handheld item. Then the lenses we all wear today did away with the need to raise your hand, or ruin your posture by looking down for hours. Now, fellow citizens, the entire way we live may be set to change again, as my scientist friend Oscar, who has followed the events in Taiwan, reports. Oscar.'

'Well, a brief recap of what we know so far, Zeb. Last night scientists in the Hsinchu region of Taipei published a hotly anticipated press release, claiming to have successfully grown the most advanced bionic eyes to date inside a human host. The host, a man who was born blind, can now see. Yes, you heard me correctly. And they're calling these new organs Fresh Eyes. The whole procedure has been funded by the Supervisors, so it's definitely legit.'

'But there's talk this invention could affect all of us one day, right?' Zeb said.

'Precisely. A spokesperson for the project has said the treatment could one day also be recommended to citizens with normal vision. As you can imagine, gossip about how to get added to a waiting list is already bubbling over in the streets of Taipei. It's likely to be a good few years, though, before we see this tech go mainstream.'

'Max, check Zeb's top story!'

'Hang on.'

'So what would an average day look like for someone with Fresh Eyes, Oscar?' Zeb asked.

'I can't comment on the user experience yet, but I can give you a bit of the science behind this extraordinary invention. At last night's press conference the scientists said it all begins with the removal of the biological eyes. Small, powerful devices wrapped in lab-grown tissues and nanofabrics are then inserted into the eye sockets, and the tissues are given time to fulfil their coding by growing and forming robust designer eyes.'

'What is this?' I called.

Max grunted.

'This is where it gets interesting,' Oscar continued. 'Apparently, what the large team of neurosurgeons, ophthalmologists, synthetic biologists and nanotechnologists has managed to do is hook up the eyes with the brain via fibres in the optic nerve. The material that meshes with these fibres is programmed to create offshoots that set up new neural networks in the cortex, enhancing the work of the various lobes by connecting them with the colossal stores of data held centrally in Megacity.'

'Sounds wonderful,' Zeb said. 'And no more need for lenses?'

'Absolutely not,' Oscar replied. 'This would redefine convenience. You would have immediate access to information related to whatever you are thinking, looking at, hearing etc. And we've been told that the material used in this procedure prompts the growth of entirely new centres in the brain that could, for example, speed up decision-making—'

'A cognitive upgrade then,' Zeb pushed in. 'Can we call it that?'

'It's precisely that. And because the eyes collaborate with the brain, you can get all the visuals, smells, sounds, tastes and sensations of basically any experience you want.'

I ran out of the kitchen and into Max's livingspace. 'Did you know about this?'

'Of course I did.' He slapped his forehead and said, 'Oh yeah, you missed it. There's been this huge build-up in the media for the past week. The Taiwan Experiment—it's all we've been hearing about. The results were only published last night. I've always known it was a matter of time till something like this was announced.'

'It's disgusting.'

'I think it's pretty cool. If you don't mind getting rid of your eyes, I mean.'

I stared at him. 'You're as sick as they are. It's one thing to give sight to a blind man—but citizens with normal vision? Why in Megacity get new eyes when your own are in perfect working order?'

'Why not? And what can you do? Our species can't stop innovating. This is just the next level.'

Although Max was inseparable from his devices, I knew swapping his eyes for artificial ones would be a step too far for him too.

'Time to catch up on some sleep?' Max asked.

'I don't know how to sleep at the moment. But I'm so exhausted, if I do sleep, I'll never wake up.'

'Why are you sitting straight as a skyscraper with your eyes closed, Ben? Are you meditating?'

'You could say that. I find my thoughts interesting.'

'Care to elaborate?' Max turned his apartment off again, rightly sensing I was going somewhere dangerous.

I took a slow breath. 'First we're given lenses at school, and a little later these bionic eyes are miraculously developed. All for citizens' benefit, of course.'

'Your point is?'

'Come on, you know it's not just about our species wanting to innovate. The reporter himself said the Supervisors funded this. They want to control everything.'

'Yeah. And?'

I went over to him and looked him straight in the eye. 'They want to control our bodies, Max. Isn't it obvious?'

He stared back at me in silence. 'If you say so,' he eventually had to say in classic Max, automated response. It did a poor job of masking his agreement.

'Can you run searches on Fresh Eyes? Examine any interesting communications or data you can find on it.'

'Sure,' he said simply, but with the blank face of someone seeing beyond the lies veiling their entire existence for the first time.

Max wasn't the only one with a lot to process; needing space to sift my own thoughts, I went outside and walked up and down the block.

I missed Fern. It was hard to grasp how waiting to see the person you love could cause such intense longing. It'd only been one day, but all this was still foreign to me. And what if Max's search led me somewhere that meant I'd never see her …?

I wondered how he'd react if I went back to the pit for a night.

A zip train whooshed over me. Back in Megacity I was lost. It was beyond doubt the Supervisors had the planet's most futuristic tech at their disposal, while I had nothing. I had Max, who was brilliant, but thinking we might somehow make a quantum leap from his livingspace into territory where we'd know and even bargain with the Supervisors was so laughable it was almost objectionable—Max had more or less said so. I wanted to go up and release my friend from the pointless work I'd pressured him into.

Another zip train sighed in the distance.

The small chance that the Supervisors' game wasn't as impenetrable as we all believed had evaporated.

Fern's absence was the real problem, and I had to solve it. My only hope lay with her.

20

I strolled out of the florist, and the balmy evening air brushed against my face. The bunch of slinky stems wriggled into new positions every few seconds, the colours of the bouquet's petals changing and swirling below my gaze. I doubted Fern would appreciate engineered flowers. At least they were programmed to last for months, not days.

Max was concerned about me going back to the pit; I was not. The music of traffic and the purr of the zip retreated as I descended; the smell of urine at one point on the track was a fragrance welcoming me back to simpler ways. A relief that I would soon be surrounded by enlightened individuals alternated with quivers of excitement in my stomach whenever Fern occupied my mind. I was so lucky to have this opportunity to experience love without swallowing any Bliss. Even the sky, which looked grey an hour ago, seemed to glow as it witnessed the burning truth in my heart.

The pit stretched out grey and uneven, peopled here and there by the watchers, many of whom were in motion, creating a layer of dust hovering a metre above the ground in the day's final hour. Despite Megacity's throb just a short distance above us, my return to this other dimension was total and instantaneous.

I approached an old, wrinkled woman and asked if she knew where Fern was.

She shook her head.

I asked a group of watchers in the centre of the pit.

They turned away.

I assumed I wasn't welcome back. They'd given me trust, and I'd betrayed it. After everything they'd done for me, I was the enemy again. An entitled citizen walking through their midst, parading a bunch of engineered flowers.

I began a circle around the edge. As I neared the caves, I saw Elijah talking to someone. I ran towards him and hugged him.

'Ben, it's good to see you.'

'Do you hate me for going back to the city?'

'That wouldn't help anything, would it now?

'Everyone seems to be avoiding me.'

'Is that so? Hey, you never gave me a chance to congratulate you on your journey.'

I thanked him.

'Have you seen Fern?'

Elijah gave a slight nod and turned his head towards the nearest cave.

I walked to the entrance that had been the start of my transformational journey.

In the final glimmers of daylight, I could just discern the body of Fern as though moulded from the warm shadows.

Fern arching and falling into Duc's embrace.

I stepped closer, caught the song of their kisses. Slow cries of ecstasy echoed in the hideaway of the cave's chambers.

I steadied myself, my knees suddenly weak.

The next moment Fern had seen me. She pushed Duc away and rushed out of the cave wearing only a skirt.

'Ben!'

My thoughts were still glued to the sex scene in the cave.

Duc sidled out of the shadows, quiet, expressionless.

My stomach tightened as licks of jealousy scorched my solar plexus and flared into my throat.

I tried to stand tall. I had to say something to her, but all words and thoughts seemed incoherent. 'I don't understand. Why?'

'I'm sorry, I wanted to tell you, Ben.'

'What exactly?'

'About my past.'

'Yes, and your present, clearly.' I looked away, then met her gaze again.

She came closer.

'I thought we had something special,' I said.

'We did.' Fern tilted her head, her brow furrowed in a look of anguish. 'We still do.' She tried to take my hands. 'It's more complicated than it looks. I've known Duc for a long time. We were together before I made the trip to the forest. If it wasn't for him, I would never have discovered it, just like you. And you and I wouldn't have met. I am sorry if you feel I misled you.'

'This is why you wanted to come back to the pit with me.'

'I didn't know this would happen.' Her voice went neutral. 'If I'm honest, I didn't think I'd ever see you again. No one down here has ever gone back as a citizen. It was hard to imagine any kind of future together. And we hadn't been close for long—'

'I left yesterday. You didn't give me much of a chance.'

'This is hard, brother, I know,' Duc spoke at last.

I was silent. I wanted to charge at him and punch his face repeatedly, never mind that I was certain to lose a fight.

As for Fern, part of me knew it was over.

Part of me wanted to kiss her.

I heard the bouquet fall from my hand into the dust.

I took one more look at Fern and Duc and walked away to the track, crushed beyond repair.

21

'What time is it?' I stretched on the sofa.

'Two in the afternoon,' Max said. 'I ate without you. Are you alright?'

'My head's killing me. Overdosed on Bliss last night.'

'Well, it's great to have your help with this search you asked me to take part in.' Max threw a worry ball at my head.

'Sorry.'

I told him the story of my pit visit and filled him in on the punishment I'd received for it when I got back last night and put my lenses in. How I'd then gone clubbing.

'Suspended from work indefinitely?' Max looked horrified.

'How's it been going up here?' I asked.

'You really want me to answer that?'

'Include Hsinchu in your searches,' I suggested. 'It's Taiwan's Silicon Valley.'

'Yeah, I know that. OK, I'll try.'

I went back to sleep. Three hours later, still lying on the sofa, my head felt better, but my emotions raged on. A broken heart was way worse than any sadness my fellow citizens could imagine.

I walked into the kitchen and opened Max's fridge. 'Let's have a vitabeer.'

Max followed me. 'You seriously want me to stop? It's Sunday, and I'm not touching this again from tomorrow.'

'I've been working you too hard.' I handed him a bottle, guzzled half of mine and asked him what he'd found.

'I've activated sweeps of all the encrypted data my tools could decrypt from servers at Noah Black's office, CityLens, artHumans Inc., Meatconstruct Inc., Global City Finances, Forever cityFit, China Jia, Eternally Citizen and your beloved Dwellings, and I've managed to mobilise about a hundred strangers to trawl comms content at other megacorps. So far every communication, including those about Fresh Eyes, comes from identifiable citizens who are definitely not Supervisors.'

'Unless the Supervisors are masquerading as normal citizens.'

Max goggled at me as if I was the biggest idiot in Megacity. 'How would we know who to focus on then? It could literally be anyone. I don't think—'

'Stop there,' I interrupted.

'I'm sorry?'

'We don't have to discuss this anymore.'

'Missing Fern, are we?'

'I'm more than missing her, but that's not the reason.'

'You're not giving up already are you?'

I was impressed by Max's genuine tone, given that he didn't share my fanaticism.

'You've forgotten: I don't give up. What I'm saying is, your trawling is over for now.'

'And your plan is?'

'Maybe to keep drinking. I'm not a happy man right now.'

'Hey, buy your own vitabeer. It's great you're visiting, but if Dwellings decides to fire you, you're paying your own way.'

'They can fire me. If they don't, I'm handing in my notice.'

I banged my empty bottle on the table and popped a second one open. 'Fuck Dwellings. Fuck Fern. Fresh Eyes is massive. Forget London, I'm going to Taiwan.'

'Always so impulsive.' Max walked out.

'Wanna come?' I called after him.

22

Max breezed through security.

After a week of relentless paranoia, the moment had arrived. I'd received punishments for discovering the landfill and leaving the grid on the two occasions I'd been to the pit. Would I also be denied international travel?

Or worse: would I suddenly have my citizen status revoked and be labelled as a Beast on the run?

I looked into the camera, trying not to swallow.

The see-through screen glided to the right.

My jaw unclenched, and I stepped onto the plane.

Persuading Max this would be a worthwhile jaunt hadn't been easy. I had no plan for how to proceed once we were in Taiwan; I only knew I'd struggle to achieve anything if I went alone. So I came up with the idea that Max should apply for a sabbatical, and to our surprise, CityLens granted him a six-month break. It was unpaid, but Max had ample savings. In the end, he'd even thanked me for the idea, and over the last few days he'd worked himself into a frenzy of excitement and nervousness about physical travelling, having only ever made remote immersion trips from the comfort of London.

THE CITIZEN

As we walked to our pods through floral-scented air, the inflight entertainment kicked in, welcoming us onboard and bathing us in a light display and Eastern Sky's chill-out track. Options based on my previous flights appeared on my lenses —games, Bliss, news, sleep programs, consciousness coffees, supplements, nanotreatments, rice noodles. I closed everything and sat down in a pod a couple of metres away from Max, only to see the same options pop up merrily on my pod's display. I closed them a second time. *Flight time 3 hours, 31 minutes* was the only data still hovering. Not a bad flight time.

As the aircraft began to move, I scanned the cabin's walls and smiled. The real reason planes were manufactured without windows was not to save fuel and flight time by improving aerodynamics and reducing the weight of the plane as I'd been taught. The windowless body was another piece in the perfect puzzle—the colossal operation to maintain watertight ignorance of the planet's corners that couldn't be hidden by the Megacity narrative alone.

Shortly after take-off, a new message advised me to select at least one service option or else head over to the bar or shops to avoid 'the harmful effects of the sadness.' My smile exploded into laughter.

My previous flights had been trips through the full repertoire of sensory pleasures. Abstaining from all the excitement brought a surprising sense of peace. All I heard was the engine humming; all I saw were other pods scattered across the cabin and the artHuman flight attendants seeing to passengers' needs. I asked one of them for water.

Sliding to the edge of my seat, I extended a leg and prodded Max's foot.

He jumped and shouted, 'What in Megacity!'

'Sorry. Try without any extras for a change, I'm doing it now. It's really chilled.'

'Leave me alone, I'm busy in here. Freak.'

I sank into my pod. Pangs of desire for Fern came and went, but now that I was flying far away from her, I could at last reflect with some objectivity on my first love. In spite of my knack for analysing the world and getting it right, the lover's heart still gets things wrong. At least in the midst of this unforgiving universe, romantic love—old-fashioned romantic love—was still possible. Even when it hurt.

Sipping at my water, I considered how I'd finally made it out of London—legitimately this time. Fabricated sunlight beamed through the cabin. I couldn't help but wonder what my grandfather would think if he could see me now on this flight to the Beautiful Isle, as he'd said the Portuguese once called Taiwan. It was my first trip there, and my excitement to see where some of my ancestors had lived had probably helped sway me that evening when I announced my decision to Max, though I didn't tell him that. If I wasn't so hell-bent on the task I'd set myself, I would have used this opportunity to trace my lineage.

I closed my eyes and brought to mind my favourite soundtrack that still played, somewhere south of where we'd departed from, hidden beyond the cut-off points of the grid: the symphony of leaves playing on the trees of my first forest.

23

Sweat dripped from my cheeks onto my clothes as we joined the tail of an endless queue outside Taipei's newest bubble milk teashop. No amount of climate engineering could defeat Taiwan's sweltering humidity.

After checking in at our hotel, we agreed to relax and recharge today and tomorrow before getting down to business. We still weren't sure what 'business' entailed but we agreed on a visit to Hsinchu Science and Technology Park as a first step.

Having discovered the forest in the UK, I was keen to find some version of countryside in Taiwan. I thought of introducing myself to any watchers we passed, but so far the streets seemed to be devoid of any non-citizens. It was probably for the best. Retreating to some wooded region would detract from the purpose of our visit. Anyway, Max would have a fit if I announced I was going off-grid.

Despite our intention to enjoy ourselves, the reason we were there kept ambushing my thoughts thanks to the ubiquitous news coverage of 新視野計劃—Project Fresh Eyes—on roadside displays keeping customers entertained as they waited.

I let my earpieces relay sound from the broadcast. It was stimulating to hear Mandarin again and understand everything. Max remembered a good deal of Chinese from his school days as well, though he admitted to relying on English translations from his devices.

The patient, whose name was James Lin, had left hospital. In his first press interview he was recounting how he was born blind and grew up without a future in a poor district in the centre of the island. He said how grateful he was to the experts and businesses whose research had helped make his dream a reality; to the surgeons, nurses and artHumans who had carried out such a smooth and complex operation. He thanked his parents. He thanked all the people of Taiwan for their support.

My self-drying clothes failed to keep up with my outpourings of sweat, and I was about to suggest we abandon the queue and buy water instead, when my skin tingled: at the end of James's emotional outpourings, he thanked one more group for giving him sight—the Supervisors.

Sucking at fat straws of overly sweet bubble milk tea, we wandered towards Xinyi District. Around every corner another huge display of James appeared on a building face or store window. Every other young person had selected a viral clip to display on their clothes of him smiling, then tilting his head back as he laughed, new brown eyes gleaming. We even spotted a toddler wearing it.

James Lin was already a national hero.

'His gaze is weird,' I said.

'Be happy for him,' Max responded. 'Imagine what it's like suddenly being able to see and do so much after living in darkness all his life. And he owns the best tech there is. Supervisors! Imagine what it's like to see other people's faces for the first time.'

'Is he really able to see them, though?' I wondered. 'How do we know his experience of perception is the same as ours? How do you define seeing? Can an artificial thing truly see or is it mimicking sight?'

'Does it matter?' Predictable irritation in my friend. 'Your life would be so much easier if you stopped mistrusting tech. You and I are both machines, just natural ones. The only difference between our technology and James's is we haven't modified ours to the same degree.'

'You're such a citizen.'

'Fucking Beast!'

Evening sneaked up on us: lights had come on wherever you looked. Taipei was ready to party.

'It's Friday night,' I said. 'We should grab a drink before we go back to the hotel.'

'I'm exhausted.'

We bickered a while. I searched with my lenses and suggested Bar 75. It was described as 'a humble, local bar oozing old-world charm.'

'Hey,' I exclaimed. 'It's got human service.'

'One drink,' Max said.

In a similar style to the zip, the Taipei metro made arcs both over and under the city—a gigantic rollercoaster with the addition of smoothness. I looked down as we shot over Central Taipei, the train's path interweaving with those of air taxis.

I thought back to my Asian history module at university. How fickle history could be: once a disagreement over Taiwan's national sovereignty had given the island an identity distinct from China's; now all that had been forgotten and there was just Megacity.

We zoomed down towards Heping East Road Station. Although outwardly Taipei hardly looked different to other regions in Megacity, I throbbed with excitement. It was more than just the feeling of being here for the first time: it was because—at this moment in history—I was on the very island the whole of Megacity was fixated on.

The entrance to Bar 75 was squashed between two derelict buildings and forced you up a narrow staircase in single file. As we arrived, a tangle of three or four people was scuffling down the stairs. Two of them were dressed in white and turned out to be paramedics. They struggled down the remaining stairs and onto the pavement, carrying an unconscious man.

A tall, athletic-looking woman wearing an agent's badge followed the paramedics. She bounced out of the doorway, blowing and popping a pink bubble gum. She winked at us and said, 'Don't worry, it's all safe now, go on up.' She grinned, gave us a manic stare, resumed chewing her gum and walked off into the crowds, as the paramedics put the unconscious man into an ambulance.

'Did you see the way she looked at us?' I said.

'She's high,' Max replied.

'I'm serious. She looked right through us.'

On reaching the top of the stairs, we agreed that the bar oozed more darkness than charm, but the air con was a relief. Bodies jammed the small space, many of them emanating bleeding-edge fragrances formulated to seduce. The décor and facilities certainly were humble. Light was minimal, and there wasn't a single large display. The luminous colours and swirls the ever-young partygoers had selected on the exteriors of their lenses pierced the gloom like tiny planets roving the night sky, as their wearers gesticulated and twitched, switched on by Bliss and chatter.

A few retro clientele were buying drinks with physical cash, which neither of us had seen before. We took lens clips of the glinting coins and creased notes changing hands and congratulated each other for glimpsing a moment of antiquity.

I pushed my way to the bar, which sold a selection of old-fashioned beers, wines and cocktails containing alcohol and no fabrications. I ordered two bottles of Taiwan Beer. I leaned against the bar, and a warm smile spread through me: it was made of solid wood. Real wood—from trees.

We really had landed in an aging establishment. I wondered how many other customers had noticed the wood during the life of Megacity.

I found Max and suggested we talk to strangers to refresh our Chinese.

'I'll stay with you. I hate talking to strangers,' Max said in Mandarin with sound grammar not quite matched by his pronunciation.

'You need to get out so much more.'

We chatted to citizens from a range of countries and met a clique of bubbly Taiwanese locals, who kept buying us drinks. I brought up James Lin in a few conversations, and invariably people's faces lit up as they raved about what an amazing achievement the bionic eyes were.

I was soon sick of small talk and couldn't resist asking one woman who was coming up on Bliss where she thought the Supervisors lived.

She looked at me as if I was insane and exclaimed, 'That's a bit deep for a Friday night.'

I was going to suggest to Max that we go back to the hotel, but he'd left my side. That wasn't like him. I looked round and saw he was standing right behind me, chatting in Mandarin to a woman who must have approached him.

'Where are you from?' she called over the ancient rock music playing, just within my earshot.

'London. My colleague and I arrived this morning.'

I stared down at my beer, not wanting to distract either of them.

'You must be tired?' the woman asked.

'I was, but this drink is refreshing me. Talking to you is also waking me up, which is nice.'

I could hardly believe Max was flirting, and face-to-face too. It had to be the travel factor.

'I don't travel often,' Max continued as if on cue. 'It's cool being in a new place.'

'What have you found most interesting about Taiwan so far?'

'I've just seen cash for the first time in my life. It's also fun speaking Chinese again. I'm definitely going to use it more when I go back to London. There's no excuse nowadays when everything gets translated by our devices anyway, right?'

The woman laughed. 'Your Chinese is excellent.'

'You're joking, right?'

She chuckled. 'Yes, I am. Hey, I can teach you a different language if you like.'

'Aha? What language is that?'

'A mountain language. I am a *shandiren*, a mountain person. You haven't heard of us before, right?'

'I haven't.'

'I'm one of Taiwan's indigenous people. There used to be a good number of ethnic groups, but we mostly mixed with the Han Chinese and, in recent times, with other races of course.'

'Interesting,' Max said.

I agreed; I wanted to turn around, ask if she knew anything about any remnants of countryside, but I didn't want to step on Max's toes. I focused on my drink.

'My people are called the Atayal. Unlike most minorities, small clusters of us still live together.'

'So you can actually speak the language of the Atayal?' Max asked. 'I thought only the big five languages were left.'

'I reckon there are hundreds—we just don't get to hear them as so few people use them. Anyway, my Atayal isn't as good as some of my relatives'.'

'How come?'

'I received an education. My brothers did not.'

'Why?'

'They stayed in the community.'

'I see.'

'My lessons were all taught in Chinese or English, hence why my Atayal isn't so good. Most people here have no idea we still exist, and they probably wouldn't care if you told them.'

This was too much; I sipped at my beer, desperately restraining myself from barging in on my friend's first face-to-face chat-up experience.

She asked him why he was in Taiwan.

'Business,' Max said. 'I have some meetings with tech firms in Hsinchu. Do you work?'

'No.'

'What are your interests?' Max asked.

My jaw tensed. He still wasn't asking the right questions. Great—he was having fun at last, but we also needed to get information from this woman.

'That's a hard one to answer,' she said. 'I actually quite like just to think. Does that sound strange?'

'Yes, but not unheard of.'

'I also like reading,' she added, '—mainly science and tech. Oh, and I listen to nuClassical. I'm a big fan of the Japanese band Beat Heaven. Can you believe it, most people don't even know their tracks are remakes of works by Beethoven?'

'Well, I'm one of them. Who's he, or she?'

She laughed. 'An ancient classical composer pre-Megacity. By the end of his life he was completely deaf, but he still composed—amazing, right? I've got a lot of time to research this kind of thing. Beat Heaven are actually performing in Taipei on Saturday a week from now? Not physically, obviously, but it'll be real enough. I'm going. I can get you a ticket if you want to come?'

'I'd love to,' Max said immediately.

I couldn't bear it any longer. 'Hi, I'm Ben, Max's business partner,' I said, joining them.

Displeasure bubbled into Max's facial muscles.

'My name's Yayuung.'

'Pleased to meet you. I couldn't help overhearing your conversation. You said that some of the Atayal still live together.'

'That's right.'

'May I ask where they are based?'

Fear shot into Yayuung's eyes. 'Why do you want to know?'

'I'm sorry if that was too personal—we've only just met. I'm genuinely interested.'

'People don't show interest in us normally.' She smiled, and her white teeth pierced the darkness like two strings of stars. 'Isn't there another reason?'

We couldn't hide forever. 'OK, there is,' I said hesitantly. 'I want to know if there is any countryside in Taiwan.' It felt good to let it out. 'I imagine the flat parts of the island are all urbanised as the maps indicate, but what about the mountains? They're marked as polluted.'

Yayuung's large eyes lit up. 'Your colleague has interesting thoughts, Max. I have never met anyone this inquisitive.'

'He's a nosy boy, ignore him,' Max said with a ring of jealousy.

'Well, the answer is yes,' said Yayuung, 'there's a lot of natural scenery left, if that's what you mean. There is a lot of pollution in some places, but the idea that whole mountain ranges were used as waste dumps is simply not true. It may be different in other countries. I can only speak for Taiwan.'

I could feel Yayuung's words rattling the foundations of Max's education like my revelation of the forest's existence had. Could it be that nature was easier to find than I'd realised? Perhaps if you scratched hard enough at the veneer of the city wherever you were, the green forces of primitive life sprouted up.

'And you are clever to ask about the mountains,' she went on. 'That's where my people live.' She stared at my face. 'And you're desperate to know exactly where, right?'

'No,' Max blurted before I could answer.

Yayuung laughed. 'I don't think your colleague agrees, Max.'

'Quite right. I'd love to know,' I said.

'Come on, I've only just met you guys. Let's keep it a mystery for now, shall we?'

She turned to Max and said, 'Look me in the eyes, and I'll transfer my contact details. You can see me again if you like.'

24

I was up at 11:00 on Saturday morning; Max wasn't budging. I left him a message and went to meet up with a woman I'd dated for a night when she worked at Dwellings. She now ran a local software company and could be a useful lead.

Wei Ling and I had lunch, and before we'd covered much ground were on our way to her apartment to 'talk more over tea,' which we both knew meant taking one sip of jasmine tea before climbing into bed to explore every sexual position our bodies inspired us into.

Even as we launched into the act again, I was under zero illusion that taking clothes off with Wei Ling hadn't been my wish all along, that I had wanted to discuss anything remotely software-related, and that I wasn't hopelessly attempting to drain the ocean of pain that flooded my heart when I caught Fern and Duc together.

As I worked up to expelling every last bit of energy, I saw myself sliding on an asphalt slope of loneliness, failing to claw back any of the dignity and self-confidence I'd left in the pit.

'Do you want to stay over, tonight?' Wei Ling asked. 'I have to go to work in the morning, but you can make yourself at home. Stay as long as you like.'

It struck me that before Fern, I would have thought being together with a citizen for more than a day and a night was quite a long relationship.

'I need to get back to the hotel,' I replied. 'I'm off to Hsinchu in the morning.'

I'd been an idiot to prioritise sex and my wounded ego over keeping Max company and discussing the next day. I'd battled to win his trust for this escapade of madness and couldn't take his help for granted.

He rang as I left the building and was understandably irate. 'Where the hell have you been. I've been trying you all day. Do you *want* me to get on the next plane back to London?'

'I'm sorry. I've been longer than I planned. I'll tell you about it later.'

'Damn right you will. I'm starving. If you're not back in half an hour, I'm getting fast food. Alone.'

'Please don't do that. Can we go to a Taiwanese night market? They're legendary. They have to be good if they've survived this long. Everything's on me.'

'Pick one for us then, but hurry. And thanks for the shit day.'

'Hang on.' My lenses were already suggesting night markets. 'Details for Tonghua Night Market coming your way. I'll wait for you at the entrance on Jilong Road.'

It was almost dark when we pushed into the buzzing night market. A plethora of food stalls lined the impossibly narrow street.

I ordered two portions of stinky tofu with chilli sauce, intrigued by the novelty.

'You don't really expect me to eat that,' Max said.

'Remember you're having an adventure. You can tell Yayuung you tried it.'

Max snatched the tofu and grimaced as he chewed the first cube.

We walked down the one-lane market, devouring a local speciality of ice cream wrap with peanut candy shavings and coriander. Amazingly, all the vendors were human. People of all ages were out, everyone chatting and laughing.

'What's up?' Max asked. 'You look like you're about to cry.'

He was right. I was moved that this sort of place still existed. 'Look how happy and lively they all are. I thought citizens had lost the ability to have innocent fun. When would you see people chatting away like this on a street in London?' It even reminded me of the forest community.

A group of demonstrating students marched by, shouting, 'Elect James Lin! James Lin for President!' Thanks to the insanity of Megacity, this new hero stood a real chance of becoming a candidate and winning a regional election.

We continued to browse as the end of the market came into sight. With my appetites for food and sex satiated, I was giddy with relaxation. The cool texture of freshly pressed papaya milk I sucked through a straw contrasted with the warm air and the barrage of glaring lights, now that night had taken over. Crackles and smells of fried foods, explosions of banter from vendors and the latest C-pop tunes blaring out of shopfront speakers completed the multisensorial concert. It had been worth the journey just for this moment.

I glanced at Max who seemed unperturbed and cheerful enough.

'Aren't you pleased I got you to travel?' I asked.

'Yeah, I'm enjoying it, thanks. Sorry I was pissed at you earlier. This may sound sad, but these last two nights have easily been the best nights out I've had.'

'I wonder where Yayuung's relatives live,' I said.

'Tell me about it. I've been trying to research the indigenous Atayal all day. I began by sifting through deleted folders located in ... '

My mind drifted as it usually did when Max described a process. The crowds thinned and stalls became sporadic. Tired-faced senior citizens padded around in the shadows at this end of the market, as though they'd finally accepted their age and had chosen this corner of Taipei for their final decade, in comfortable earshot of the liveliness.

Max was browsing nanobots in the final stall when I noticed a tall, muscly man in a black tank top and black trousers, standing with his back to us in the middle of the street about forty metres ahead. He was straight, motionless, arms slightly away from torso, as though he were ready to fight if somebody swerved into the market street.

I was hypnotised. This giant of a man had nothing to do with the people and activities of the market.

I simply had to walk past him to get a glance from the front. Max had finished, and we resumed our leisurely stroll, still with about thirty metres separating us from the tall figure.

The man rotated his upper body towards us and swivelled his head round. His eyes drilled into mine.

Max noticed him now and said, 'Look at that guy—straight out of an action movie. Is he even human?'

We stopped.

The man turned the rest of his body to face us. Took a step towards us. Another one.

His stare held me, and a shiver travelled from the back of my head to my shins: I'd seen those eyes before. We'd seen them all over Taipei from the moment we arrived. They were the eyes of James Lin. Only this wasn't James.

The man broke into a trot.

The soundscape of the night market morphed into a distant

jangling. Something was really wrong here, but we couldn't wait to find out what. 'We're out of here,' I said, grabbing Max's arm.

We charged back through the market, me ripping my lenses and earpieces out, yelling at Max to do the same. I glanced over my shoulder.

The man was now running.

'Faster!' I shouted.

Max knocked over a woman. Next he was on the ground himself.

I pulled him up and along behind me, dragging him through the many clumps of people. We darted past modified puppies, over piles of clothing, through stinky-tofu air and flung ourselves into a road taxi at the mouth of the market.

'Go straight,' I told the vehicle.

I looked through the back window as we pulled away from the curb. Our pursuer reached the edge of the market for a second, then disappeared back into the crowd.

'What the fuck just happened?' Max said between gasps.

As if I knew. Well, I suppose I did: the authorities were on to us.

I was the most arrogant person on the planet—thinking I could outwit the grid, the agents, the Supervisors. Megacity had not been designed for one suspecting citizen to pull it all apart.

'We're being followed,' I said.

Max didn't reply. He was trembling.

'I'm sorry,' I said, putting my hand on his knee.

I bit my lip hard. What could we do? Where could we go? Until now I'd been tolerated, like the forest community. An irritating child who would hopefully grow up.

But tolerance had a price.

Agents would always step in, whether to abduct a member of a breakaway community, or end a bad actor like me. My involvement of Max and our flight to Taiwan were transgressions too great to be ignored. This was pure betrayal of the system.

Yet why had we been allowed onto the plane and into Taiwan?

'That was an agent sent to arrest us,' I whispered into Max's ear.

'Why are you so sure?'

'What else could he be?'

'Thanks for making me help you.' There was more despair than anger in Max's voice.

I closed my eyes: what had I done?

We stopped to switch vehicles. Ground taxis were free in Taiwan, so we didn't need our lenses for payment. We crossed the road and stopped the next empty cab going in the direction we'd come.

Before we got in, I told Max to phone Yayuung. 'Tell her we have to leave Taiwan tomorrow afternoon and want to go to the mountains tonight so we can see them first thing in the morning.'

Max ran his hands through his hair. 'You know I can't.'

'We've got to get right off the grid and I don't know these roads. We need help.'

'What about our stuff?'

'The hotel could be swarming by now. Please make the call. At least you might get to see her again.'

'Do I have to lie?'

'Yes.'

'Whatever you say, asshole.'

'Mask your ID.'

'I am. Think I'm an idiot?'

It was torture making Max lie to a woman he liked. It was also madness to involve another person, but we had no choice.

And how many other choices had I just sacrificed? We

might never be able to return to Megacity or leave this island. Max might never be able to work again, to use his devices and a lifetime's worth of expertise that meant everything to him.

I still wasn't sure what was going on; I just knew we needed space to think—downtown Megacity was not going to give us that.

25

We hovered at the entrance to a biopark in southern Taipei, where Yayuung had agreed to meet us.

'Did you see the way he looked at us before he ran after us?' I asked. 'Remember I said there was something weird about James Lin's gaze? I don't think James is the only one who's—'

'OK, maybe we've been trolled by an agent, but you're imagining the eye thing. You're wired from what just happened.'

'I know I might be wrong. That agent woman, though—the one who came out of Bar 75 last night after the paramedics—she looked at us in that same messed up way. You said she was high. I think it was another eye job. What if Fresh Eyes is already being rolled out?'

'Maybe the agents here are artHumans,' Max said.

I thought back to Grace's assistant, Sam. 'No. These guys move too freely. There's definitely a feeling of naturalness about them.'

'You're saying they're still human if they've got the eyes?' Max asked.

'Now we're back to that question.'

Yayuung pulled up and we got into her taxi.

'You're alive,' she said.

'What do you mean?' Max asked.

Yayuung laughed. 'Do you think I'm stupid? Nobody talks the way Ben did and gets away unpunished. Isn't it the same in your part of Megacity?'

She was right, of course. I was the stupid one. The careless one. Talking about Supervisors and countryside at every turn.

'I am sorry,' I said in a low voice. 'I asked Max to lie to you.'

'That's OK. You're lucky you've got me, eh?' she replied, surprisingly unperturbed.

'It's so kind of you to help us,' Max said. 'I promise we're not bad people.'

'This is nothing. My family have been in trouble with the authorities too many times. I am used to these situations, sadly.'

Yayuung uttered a string of destinations, some of which she later deleted. 'Old-fashioned road taxis are still the best around here,' she told us. 'They're rarely tracked closely.' She added new destinations at various points and told the vehicle to take unintuitive turns. What may have been a half-hour journey took two hours. Yes, we were lucky we had her. I was a tiny kid in the back seat, repenting my actions.

We got out on a narrow road, dingily lit by short street-lights from another era that had somehow survived Taiwan's urban renewal. Traffic might as well never have existed here.

Yayuung rang her younger brother and asked him to fetch us. Max told her more about why we were really here, while I walked over to an old-fashioned street stall you wouldn't see in London. It was still serving dumplings, and I ordered three portions. Not to satisfy any hunger, but because we needed some comfort. The vendor smiled as he handed me three boxes.

A cool breeze breathed against my neck. I exhaled slowly. A safer place.

Agents wouldn't arrive here just yet, I thought, though nothing was certain anymore.

It was Max's and my first time in a non-self-driving vehicle. We held our breath as Yayuung's brother, Gumai whizzed round hair-pin bends and through tight mountain tunnels as if laws of physics and all notions of safety were deleted when he was at the wheel of the dusty people carrier bouncing us around.

To my excitement and Max's obvious terror, we were being taken off-grid, which of course wouldn't have been possible in a self-driver. Max was doubly challenged: this was also his first time without lenses.

I put my arm around him. 'Be grateful you haven't got your lenses in. The warnings not to go any further would freak you out.'

'My brain is giving me them anyway,' Max said between gasps.

Gumai laughed. 'This is fun, sis, we never get any visitors. Especially from overseas.'

'Have you told Older Brother we're coming?' Yayuung asked.

'Yes, Bayhui is not very happy,' Gumai continued. 'He's worried your friends may bring others up here.'

'They won't, will you?'

'Of course not,' Max said, and I echoed his words.

The only lights now were the vehicle's headlights shooting their beams onto rocks, tunnel entrances and a river gushing by to the left when we rounded a bend. All the windows were down, another new experience for us. Max probably wished they were closed; I was getting used to the banging air. When we weren't going through tunnels I stuck my head out the window, blasting my face with the wind, listening as the river tumbled towards us and washed some of my worry away.

26

Meeting the new face of the planet first thing in the morning came as a shock.

We were on a rocky plateau, removed from anything that resembled the world we knew.

I allowed new meanings of the word 'beauty' to take shape as I stared out of the window. Once it applied to cityscapes, Herculean feats of engineering, new products crystallised in the constant stream of scientific progress, or to manicured bioparks. Now it described the wide azure river directly below the jagged outcrop the house was built on. A little upstream, the river bent and vanished between two majestic mountains. Higher up, the rugged edges of the peaks were bathed in morning gold.

I opened the window, and the sound of the rushing river filled the room. Insects chattered endlessly. The air was cool, crisp, pristine.

Out there was the kind of scenery my grandfather's parents would have walked in. I was sure.

Max was deeply affected too, but differently. Having hardly slept—like me when I'd passed that first night in my apartment without supplements or earpieces—he took one glance at the view, turned back to the room, flopped to the floor and cowered below the windowsill. He was trembling, his breath rapid.

'I've got chest pain and I think I'm about to faint,' he said.

I wasn't surprised at his state, thinking back to my own experience when I arrived at the forest. But I wished there had been time to prep him and soften the stings of paranoia.

After a long coaxing, I managed to get him to the kitchen table. Breakfast was taro plant with large ribs of a wild boar that Yayuung's older brother Bayhui said he'd caught the day before with his bare hands. Max and I struggled to believe how such a feat was possible, and I expressed our amazement that such large wild animals weren't extinct.

Yayuung's mother and aunt, who also lived in the small cottage, spoke in hushed tones over breakfast and only when necessary. Neither of them wore lenses. Yayuung chatted, I guessed to keep Bayhui from questioning us. 'Most of our relatives have long since gone to the city, got jobs and had lenses fitted,' she said. 'Only a few friends and relatives remain up here.'

Bayhui cleared his throat and said with an edge of warning, 'And we hope to stay here for as long as possible.'

'So different,' Max said in disbelief. 'Relatives can live as neighbours and know each other.'

'To us this is the most precious place in the world,' Yayuung continued. 'We have been more or less forgotten by the authorities, and with so few of us still living here, I don't think we are seen as a danger to anyone.' Her face brightened. 'Look outside, the weather's brilliant. I could take you for a walk if you like—I can introduce you to my favourite part of the universe.'

'That would be lovely,' I replied.

Max shot me with his eyes.

. . .

'You don't mind getting your shoes wet, right?' Yayuung asked. 'We'll be walking in the river. It's shallow.' She caught the horror on Max's face and winked at me.

We climbed down the outcrop.

'Your family are quiet,' I said to Yayuung, once she and I stood at the bottom on the riverbank waiting for Max to catch up. 'I imagine they're pretty unhappy about us being here.'

'Mainly they're just shy. They hardly ever meet new people and they never really learned the social etiquette of the city, even though they've been down a few times.'

'It can't be easy surviving here.'

'You're right. They've had tough lives. Unlike me, they're not registered as citizens and so getting quality medical care is impossible. My father and sister died when I was still a girl.'

Better a short life up here than a long, virtual one strangled by networks and social control, I thought.

Yayuung stood knee-deep in the river, water gushing round her legs, and held out a hand to Max. He trembled as he poked the tip of his right trainer into the water.

'You made it!' she shouted as he stood on both feet in the river.

Max pushed out his first smile of the day.

'I used to come down here to go to the toilet,' Yayuung called over the racing water. 'It's nice, it automatically flushes everything away and washes you afterwards. Over here, come with me, this is where ... don't worry, it's easy.'

The river was about sixty metres wide. Soon Yayuung was waiting on the other side while Max and I wobbled about in the middle, still getting used to the expanse of dazzling water tugging at our legs as it swept by.

Yayuung led us to a waterfall that tumbled over a steep cliff face. 'This was my shower. It's cold, but nothing beats it. Take off your clothes and put them on the rocks. I won't look. Go on, have a shower!'

And we did. I could tell Max was beginning to enjoy himself.

We waded up the river, till it narrowed and engulfed our thighs. Then we continued over large boulders on the left, deep into the gorge. I remembered my journey out of London.

'I never believed this sort of place existed and that it could be explored by humans,' Max said.

'Most people don't,' Yayuung replied. Her eyes flashed with pride.

Our clothes stuck to us in the midday heat, and we lay down on a large flat rock to rest, Yayuung between Max and I.

She took off her backpack and handed us each a peach. 'This is how my family make money. We grow these high up in the mountains and sell them on the black market in outer Taipei. Each peach commands a high price as it is totally organic and much fresher and more delicious than the mass-made ones the city farms produce.'

I closed my eyes and savoured my peach.

Minutes of quiet.

I turned towards Yayuung and saw her back. She and Max were kissing.

She had rescued him.

I surrendered to the complex aftertaste of juice and nutrients entering me from the best piece of fruit I'd tasted. As the river churned by, I became more aware of the rock supporting my back and wondered where everything had gone wrong. What desires had driven our species to sacrifice pure, effortless pleasures such as these? What had driven us to dominate the natural world to such an extreme that we'd separated completely from it and built a brand-new world so intelligent it could control our every move?

Even as I told myself how relaxing it was on this rock up

here, water singing to us, thick trees standing guard behind us, my thoughts were on the loose as my situation hit home: if I wasn't going to give up and hand myself over to the authorities, I would soon need an impossible level of ingenuity. I was in a foreign land, trying to identify—hopefully even challenge—powers I knew nothing about, except that they were incomparably greater than anything Max and I could pretend to muster.

If only I could find a way to interview James Lin. Would he have any links to the Supervisors? What if the clandestine group of Supervisors didn't even exist and were concocted by the megacorps' artHuman PR managers to distract us from corporate greed, and keep morale high by making us feel gratitude for all the gifts of development? But then they might as well make us feel gratitude towards the megacorps' leaders themselves. Like many citizens, I'd speculated that the Supervisors could be artHuman, but that was too easy an explanation, and artHumans could always be hacked. Like Fern, I was sure that somewhere at the top, humans were still in charge.

I knew I may never get answers to any of these questions. But at least we'd managed to get to Taiwan, and after last night's chase at the night market, giving up on the search barely looked safer than continuing.

We'd just stood up to head back when Max shrieked and jumped backwards.

'What's the matter?' said Yayuung.

'What the fuck ... is ...' Max was pointing at a large insect with pincers and a black-and-red shell that had joined us on the rock.

Yayuung giggled. 'That's one of my friends.' She knelt down and picked up the insect. 'As long as you hold him like this, thumb underneath and middle finger on top, he won't do anything. He's so cute, don't you think?'

Max didn't look like he agreed, but I knew the sight of his new love interest holding the insect, surrounded by river and mountain scenery, was shifting some mammoth conditioning.

'Back to business,' I said to Yayuung, as we started back. 'Assuming the Supervisors are in some way behind the bionic eye, why did they choose to develop it in Taiwan?'

'Simple,' Yayuung offered. 'Like I say, I get a lot of time to read science. Do you want the full story?'

'Yes please,' I said.

'OK. Taiwan has been at the centre of the global electronics supply chain for centuries. Already in the early 21st century pre-Megacity, we produced a huge proportion of the world's semiconductors, liquid crystal displays and motherboards. It was common for school-leavers to take subjects like computing and engineering at university. We were academically keen, a nation of graduates, post-graduates and PhD-holders. With time, almost everyone went into some science- or tech-related field, whether it was bioelectronics, biofabrication, optoelectronics or whatever else. It may sound a bit boring, but think of the breakthroughs and progress that were possible.

'We began collaborating with more and more experts from around the world, and the megacorps kept piling more money into Taiwan's chips and artificial intelligence. Anyway, I think it's only natural that the bionic eye should be developed in a place with this sort of history.'

'Interesting,' I said. 'We are so lucky we met you.'

'I'm happy I met you guys,' she said, stepping on Max's foot.

'Who do you think the Supervisors are?' I asked her.

'Ah yes, your big question. Let me think ... they're probably assholes.'

Max snorted a laugh.

'And what about their whereabouts?' I pressed on with.

'Why, are you planning to visit them?' Yayuung said sharply. 'Are you trying to get yourself killed?'

I didn't have anything to say to that. This could well be a suicide mission.

'I think they must be spread out across Megacity, don't you?' she went on. 'It depends on how many there are. Don't quote me, but I wouldn't be surprised if there's someone pretty important in Taiwan right now, with Fresh Eyes being released to the world.'

Her words gave me goosebumps.

But I could only dream about what we could do if she was right.

27

Yayuung had to get back to Central Taipei in the afternoon for a job interview at a social media company. She said we could stay for however long we needed if it meant we wouldn't be arrested. Her brother Bayhui might not be happy about it, but as long as we didn't betray the family's trust and endanger the mountain community, we wouldn't have to face his anger. Gumai would drive us down the mountain whenever we were ready.

'I'll be back in time for the Beat Heaven concert,' Max said.

They kissed.

Fern swelled into my consciousness.

Yayuung swung a leg over Baihui's moped, and he drove her off. We waved as they disappeared in a cloud of dust.

'What next?' Max asked.

'We celebrate you've kissed a human.'

Max elbowed me. 'I have kissed a couple of others, you know. Anyway, I'm serious—what do we do now?'

'Expect me to have all the answers?'

'Yes, actually. You got us into this.' He smiled.

'I do have the beginnings of an idea. But first we need to sit down with a drink. You're not going to like this one.'

'I don't like any of your ideas.'

We went into the kitchen and found some oolong tea.

'OK,' I began, 'actually, no ... I don't know if I can just spell it out.'

'That bad? Let me guess, you want to go back to London.'

'No.'

'You like men after all and want me, but it's too late?'

I laughed, but only to delay.

'Stop wasting time and tell me.'

Sharing my newly hatched ideas with him was high-risk, but we were in this together and he deserved to know.

I sipped slowly at the oolong, my heart thumping. 'Alright,' I began, but I had to stop I was so scared of what I was about to say. 'First we spend a couple of days up here, planning, then we go down to kidnap James Lin.'

Max smiled. 'You know, that's not such a bad idea. I'm surprised I didn't come up with it myself. Wait a minute ... Ben?'

I looked straight at him. 'Max, he's our only hope of gaining any knowledge about the Supervisors. He must know something. We would let him go when we're done, obviously.'

Max's cheeks reddened. '*Fuck* you! I didn't come to Taiwan to become a criminal.'

It did make me think when he put it that way. Trying to find out a few things about the Supervisors was quite different to kidnapping an innocent man, who might not have any useful information anyway. I was shocked at the workings of my mind. On the other hand, this wasn't the first time I'd thought of radical moves.

'I know how extreme it must sound,' I said. 'Even I'm horrified by how immoral it would be. Yes, kidnap is a filthy word and one of the biggest crimes a citizen can commit. Look, I just want to get close to James Lin and ask him some questions. I admit, I'm getting desperate. But I don't see much hope in any other ideas.' I paused. 'Have you got anything better? At least we know all the research behind Fresh Eyes was funded by the Supervisors. You have to admit there's a chance James Lin knows something about them.

'There's more,' I went on. 'If agents really have been given the eyes as well, and the media's talk of ordinary citizens receiving them one day comes true, we might as well kiss goodbye to human life as we know it. Just as with lenses, it wouldn't be optional. Everyone would get their natural eyes cut out—whether willingly, or by force—and replaced with devices that are hardwired into the brain. You'd be under total control of the central feeds one hundred percent of the time.'

'It also might not come to that.'

'But it really might. This is no longer just about finding out who the Supervisors are and why they make the decisions they do. Healing blindness is one thing, but if this "cognitive upgrading" is the real agenda, it must be stopped.'

'Like it's that easy, right?' Max said.

Nothing I said would convince him. 'I totally understand if you don't want to be part of this.'

'Damn right, I don't. You're on your own here, mate. We both know you're never getting close to James Lin. What are you even imagining you'd do with him if you did manage to magically kidnap him?'

'Take a deep breath, Max, and hear me out.'

'I'm tired of hearing your ideas. When you get them, there's no discussion. It's just you against the world.' His eyes welled up. 'How does your mind even get from enjoying this mountain scenery to kidnapping the one man the whole of Megacity is watching?'

He was right—my mental leaping had gone off course. 'The idea has been brewing in me since we got into the taxi with

Yayuung last night, but it only began taking shape when we walked back from the river.'

'You haven't answered my other question. What would you do if you manage to get him?'

'Bring him up here.' Immediately my mistake was obvious.

'You would not,' Max snapped. 'Yayuung trusts us.'

'I would never bring him to this house.'

'Where then?'

'A good few kilometres beyond these peaks.' I was improvising here, pointing to the mountains we could see from the kitchen window. 'It's the only choice. We'd be off-grid, and without Law Enforcement pursuing us, hopefully we wouldn't need to worry about getting caught and could take our time extracting information from James.'

Max's shoulders relaxed a little. Was he open to my madness after all? 'To your credit, since you proved your belief in the existence of countryside back home, your ideas have been spot-on, and I've followed through on all of them with you. But this one's a shocker. As your friend, I have to tell you you're going a step too far. Your mission has gone to your head.'

Moments of silence.

'Can't we just go back to Taipei and visit a few more night markets?' he said, calmer. 'The maniac chasing us was one isolated incident. We might be fine.'

I longed to say yes. Losing Max was going to be agony. But once I'd prioritised something … 'I'm sorry. I know my idea is crazy. Terrifying as well. But I don't feel I've got anything else to go back for in Megacity. Unless you can suggest a more effective approach, this is my next course of action.'

Max frowned, his eyes drilling into mine. 'You mean all that, don't you? I didn't know you could be so ruthless to a friend. Let me ask you, have you thought about how committing your crimes might affect me? I have a life to lead as well.

I'm on sabbatical. I'm not you. I'm not trying to quit my job and throw everything away. This is suicide, Ben, and you know it.' He stood up. 'This is where I leave you. Find some therapy, will you?'

'You wouldn't have met Yayuung if we hadn't—'

'Don't even try that. You just ruined the best day of my life.'

Clearly I'd shared my idea with Max far too suddenly. He wouldn't have liked it, though, however long I waited.

I softened my tone. 'I never wanted to force you into anything. Just know that this isn't easy for me either. I didn't grow up dreaming of getting into kidnapping.'

No response.

I was powerless to stop him now. He'd be gone soon.

I stood up as a sign of respect. 'In case something happens to me and we don't meet again, thank you for being my closest friend. Promise me you'll protect yourself when you're back in the grid?'

'Don't worry about me, I'm invisible already.' Max stood staring at me for a few moments, shaking his head slowly, then stormed out to find Gumai for a ride.

28

I bent forward over the kitchen table and pushed my face into my hands, hoping the sky would fall.

What was I thinking, sacrificing the one real friendship I'd known in my tortured existence to go and commit a major crime? And if it had been hard for two of us to get anywhere, how was I supposed to continue alone? Even if there were fifty of me, kidnapping James Lin was a tragically unhinged idea.

Was I a sociopath? A psychopath? Would I feel any guilt if I miraculously succeeded? Remorse for imperilling mine and James's lives in the process?

I sifted through Max's words. Was therapy the answer? If I turned myself in and admitted to mental illness, I might still be able to live in Megacity as a decent, law-abiding citizen as long as I agreed to meds and lifelong therapy. I looked up at the scenery through the window. I would never find peace if I forced myself to fit in down there again. I'm not lying when I say I was tempted to stay in the mountains and try to make a life among the few remaining Atayal. But my anger that this beautiful and energising world had been denied the citizens would plague me in no time.

I had to make my peace with the idea I'd be caught soon. The life I'd once known as a citizen was clearly over. I might as well give it my best shot before Law Enforcement took me down.

Max hadn't been gone forty minutes when it struck me I had to leave as well. He'd been right about one thing. I needed to keep Yayuung's family out of my own business. I had no clear plan, but even considering the dreaded kidnap felt wrong here. Of course, it would be 'wrong' anywhere, but it wasn't as if a lot of what was tolerated as normal in Megacity was any more right.

I wondered whether I should wait to ask Baihui or Gumai to drive me down, but it seemed like too much to expect them to make the same trip twice in one day.

So I said goodbye to the vistas that had given me and Max such magical experiences only a few hours ago, left a thank you note on the table, filled my water bottle and set off down the dusty road on foot. Walking would give me time to ponder the ruins of my life.

After two hours in the afternoon heat, I stopped, undressed and submerged myself in the river cascading down next to the road. If my wild idea amounted to nothing after this, at least I'd have enjoyed my little holiday up here to its full.

I put my lenses in and walked on for about half an hour, until I dipped into connectivity. I found a private taxi company, shared my location and situation (that I'd lost my way and walked off-grid), removed my lenses again and sat down on a rock by the road to wait.

Trundling down the mountain on the cool, white seats of a vintage taxi, which—to my surprise—was human-driven, I avoided bending my mind to what lay ahead. For a moment I sought solace in the gentle music the elderly driver had on; a man and a woman crooned in call and response, before their voices united on the same notes in the resolving phrases.

'What sort of music is this?' I asked.

'This? It's romantic *lao ge*,' said the elderly driver. 'Most of these songs have been forgotten, but for me no new artists or genres come close. Long ago you would hear this music in every Taiwanese taxi. Can you sing? I'm always waiting for the next *lao ge* star to come along.' He chuckled and glanced round, revealing a set of yellow, crooked teeth he hadn't had replaced.

'How do you manage to compete with self-drivers?'

'I got a customer just now, didn't I?' He grinned in the mirror. 'No, you're right. This is a taxi of last resort. When nothing's available in Outer Taipei, or the occasional customer goes off-grid by mistake, the calls come through to me and I rescue them as I'm rescuing you now. I've been up fewer times than you can count on one hand. I haven't seen anyone dare go as far as you have on foot, though. Only driven this far up once before today, and I'm hoping this'll be the last time. Wouldn't want to get stranded.'

'When was the other time?'

'Well, it's interesting you ask. A year ago I get a call from a guy. He tells me he wants to go up into the mountains, a bit further south than here. I'd never been up here myself, so was pretty scared as I'm sure you can imagine. Call me crazy, but I thought it would be interesting to see what it's like—not much going on in my life these days. Anyway, I drove him up.'

'Do you know what he was doing up here?'

'Well, I shouldn't say, really.'

'It's fine, you can tell me.'

The driver took a breath. 'He had three pretty unsavoury guys with him. The four of them had tattoos all over them, except on their faces. Not those shifting kind of tattoos, but the old-fashioned ones done with needles. Here in Taiwan people with tattoos belong to the underworld. I know other people get tattoos as well, but you can just tell. You can hear it in the way they speak. They like swearing. These guys also started chewing betel nuts and spitting that red juice all over the pavements. That's banned here nowadays, but they were doing it anyway.'

The driver braked suddenly as a minibus appeared out of nowhere and Gumai hurtled towards us. He didn't seem to be paying any attention to the taxi, and the driver had to pull to a halt.

I might never see Yayuung and her family again. Or anyone I'd previously encountered for that matter. Max had just deserted me. My love affair with Fern was dead. Acquaintances, colleagues, past flings and everyone in the pit and the forest community—all inhabited a reality separate to mine. Was my scheming worth the loneliness? Wouldn't I end up swallowing a euthanasia pill?

These mountains would be a majestic place to die.

I refocused. 'What do you think the four men were doing that day?'

'Oh, hardly worth sharing.' The driver took out a cigarette: the black market was alive in Taiwan. 'Here, do you smoke?' He pointed a second cigarette over his shoulder at me.

Being offered something chipped away some of my loneliness. 'I'll try one.' I fingered the thin white paper; the squidgy brown end, and a sliver of exhilaration opened in my heart: I was about to do something that vast swathes of the population once did. 'I'll need your help lighting it. This is my first cigarette.'

'Before I tell you my story, I want you to know I reported everything to the agents afterwards. I did my bit. Now I wish I'd left them up there while I could, instead of hanging around like an idiot, waiting for them to finish their business and then driving them all the way back down.'

'It can't have been that bad.' I coughed as my first drag kicked my lungs. 'What's there to do in the mountains?'

'Ha! You don't know the Taiwanese mafia.'

'Were they indigenous given they wanted to come up here?'

'No, being a gangster has got nothing to do with your background—it's about what you do.'

'So, what were they up to?'

The driver took a drag. 'You're definite you want to know?'

'Yes.'

'About halfway up, they asked me to stop. All four of them got out of the car. One of them had a cardboard box. Half an hour later, three of them came back, carrying something in the box. They'd killed the fourth guy—the quiet one. All the way up I'd wondered why he was so quiet while the other three cracked jokes. Whenever a member of the Taiwanese underworld kills another gangster, they bring back their head. That's how you prove to your boss you've completed your mission. The quiet guy would have been from a rival gang.' He sucked hard at his cigarette. 'This is why I said I wish I had got the hell down the mountain before they ever returned.'

The driver glanced round at me as if to check I was OK. 'As soon as I saw them in the mirror, the three of them coming out of the bushes and walking slowly towards my car, with the tall one in the middle carrying the box with both hands, I knew they had murdered him. You can't predict how you're going to react in a situation like that until you're in it. I was paralysed. I thought they were going to shoot at the car if I drove off, like in the movies, you know? The drive down felt the like the longest drive of my life. I still get nightmares. I dream that they're coming for me because they know I reported them. Or that one of them was watching as I made the report and is following me. Sometimes I'm up here again in my dream, and it's me they're taking into the bushes.'

'Thank you for sharing the whole story with me.'

'It's actually quite a relief—I don't talk about it to anyone.'

'I'm amazed you came to get me after that experience.'

'I was going to turn the job down, but I saw on your profile you're from London and knew you wouldn't be a bad guy. I don't have much to do, so I ended up coming to get you. May I ask, what were you really doing up there?'

The question was like a smack. I fought for an answer. 'When I travel, I like to look for adventure. I was curious about visiting the mountains and spending the night up here. It's not as dangerous as I thought it would be.'

'What? A whole night? I'm impressed by your courage. I wouldn't stay away from the grid for longer than I have to.'

'I don't understand why more people haven't been up here.'

'There could well be more who ignored the warnings and kept going like you and me,' the driver said, 'but nobody would admit to it. Who wants to be labelled a lunatic or a suicidal victim of the sadness? That sort of thing ruins a person's profile, right? Not that I've got much of a profile to speak of.'

'It frustrates me how everyone has to behave in the same way. We're a boring race.' Having neglected my cigarette, I took a second drag and coughed again.

Now that I'd made the driver relive his traumatic experience, I felt duty-bound to follow him along the pathways of bland small talk. But it bothered me that he'd said he knew I wouldn't be a bad guy. Didn't my crazy idea of kidnapping James Lin put me on a par with the gangsters he'd met?

'Are you staying in Outer Taipei long?' he asked.

'I don't know yet, maybe a week or two.'

'Do you want me to drop you at your hotel?'

'I haven't decided where to stay yet. Let me out anywhere once we're officially on the edge of Outer Taipei.'

'What? You haven't ...' His voice trailed off.

I panicked—it was indeed rare for a citizen not to have every step of a trip planned well in advance by one's devices. Would he report me as he had the gangsters?'

'How about you come to ours for dinner? I live between Taichung and Chiayi districts. You can spend the night. I'd like you to meet my wife. She's an excellent cook.'

All these offers coming from a stranger sounded bizarre. Unbelievable. Then it dawned on me this man really was being kind. 'Your wife? Isn't marriage—'

'Of course we're not married.' His voice was getting louder, friendlier. 'We might not have the option of legally marrying, but we've always called each other husband and wife. We like things the good old way.' He turned round and winked. 'My surname is Chen. You can call me Jinlong.'

'I'm Ben.'

'So, will you come, Ben?'

'I'd really like that,' I said, my spirits lifting.

'I'll let her know right away.'

Having made my way to the end of my cigarette, I concluded that smoking was the most unpleasant thing I'd ever tried. But I liked how it was so different to all the sanitised drugs like Bliss and vitabeers. There was something real about it. Gritty.

Maybe that cigarette marked the birth of a different me.

29

Aromas of cinnamon and cloves enveloped us. Jinlong and his 'wife's' apartment seemed surprisingly tech-free.

'Shufeng, come and meet Ben,' Jinlong called.

A petite woman with frizzy hair strode out of the kitchen. Lines from decades of smiling radiated from the outer corners of her eyes.

'Sit! Sit! You must be hungry,' she said, gesturing towards a small dining table already laid.

'Hurry up and get him tea!' she said to Jinlong.

'OK, OK!'

Over plates of braised pork rice, bamboo shoots and hot and sour soup, Shufeng repeatedly told me how handsome I was. 'Find a traditional Taiwanese woman while you're down here. Not too traditional, just a bit. She'll take good care of you. There aren't many of them around nowadays, though. Whatever you do, don't be like the young people in Central Taipei, who don't know that it's even possible to have a relationship. Look at us! We've been together almost fifty years.'

'I can't begin to imagine how that might feel,' I said.

Jinlong's face was scarlet from the spices and the *baijiu* he kept toasting me with. 'Yes, we were lucky to find each other. Our friends say we're mad—I don't care. We argue a bit, but we've always got each other's back.'

I found myself longing to be back in the forest with Fern.

We could start again—we could resolve everything.

I poured myself another cup of *baijiu*.

Small talk returned. I wasn't sure how long to wait. I didn't want to put my hosts out, but I'd always struggled with etiquette. No sooner had Jinlong put his chopsticks down than I said, 'There's something I'd be interested to know.'

'Go on.'

'About that incident in the mountains.'

I waited for a signal from Jinlong that he was OK with me coming back to the topic.

His smile evaporated. 'My wife knows about it.'

Shufeng stood up and said, 'You two men can keep talking. I'll bring you some more tea.'

'I'm sorry to bring it up again,' I said. 'I'm just curious, do you think those men ever got caught?'

'I doubt it. They probably fled to the east coast or south to Gaoxiong. The greatest benefit of being a gangster nowadays is you're more or less impossible to track. Most of them don't wear lenses or carry any tech. Obviously, that's a major problem for the agents as the gangsters can roam around most of Outer Taipei untracked. There are crackdowns from time to time, but I'm sure there's a constant trickle of new gangsters destroying their lenses and entering the underworld. In general, agents turn a blind eye. The gangsters' petty crimes are hardly worth the hassle for them and generally go unrecorded.'

'Are you saying the gangsters stick to Outer Taipei?' I was worried I was offending Jinlong or raising suspicions by clinging to this topic, but it was just starting to get interesting.

'They can be anywhere, for sure, but I can't imagine they'd

want to hang around Central Taipei much—it's higher risk. You're most likely to see them in localities like this, for example, or further south. Judging from the incident I told you about, I wouldn't be surprised if a few of them hang out in the mountains when they're on the run.' Jinlong lowered his voice. 'I'll tell you something interesting, though. There have been rumours lately of gangsters going missing—heaven knows why. A friend of mine says the rumours were started by a group of them after they looked all over the island for their boss.'

I needed something more concrete, but was wary of pushing him any further. He had given me a lot for one day. But what the hell: 'If somebody wanted to find some of these guys to interview them,' I asked, 'where would they go?'

'You're not serious, right?' Jinlong tensed all over and stared at me.

'Of course not, I'm just fascinated as we don't have gangsters like this in the UK. I mean, it's an interesting thought—what does a hardworking gangster with minimal tech get up to on his day off?' For a moment I thought Jinlong's face had gone even redder and he was about to explode in anger.

To my relief, he sighed and said, 'In the evenings, they're usually in pubs or KTV bars. They might also be at home. Unlike your average citizens, a lot of them have families, believe it or not. Oh yes, you also see them in the temples. They go there to atone for their sins.'

That would be enough information for now. I allowed the conversation to shift towards my grandfather and London, and on to whether James Lin would end up heading a transhumanist party in Taiwan. But hiding behind our laughter and jokes, my mind wrestled. Was there really no other way? No, it was clear as the light of day: tomorrow I'd go out and see if I could find any gangsters who could help me with the kidnap.

It was bizarre how things could take such a drastic turn,

but I was acclimatising to a new way of thinking: if you have a goal, a vision you're ready to lay down your life for, anything must be allowed—within reason—or you will get nowhere. Extreme measures are bound to be necessary—especially if your goal seems impossible from the outset.

'No need to go tomorrow,' Jinlong said, 'you must stay as long as you want. We like to have visitors. Our daughter moved to Central Taipei many moons ago. Her room is yours.'

I thanked Jinlong for his hospitality.

'Don't worry, it's the Taiwan way. Shufeng and I will be out in the morning, but we'll leave breakfast on the table. There's a key on the chest by the door. You can come and go as you like. Just don't go chasing those gangsters—they're dangerous.'

The first thing I did was put my lenses and earpieces in an empty metal jewellery box I found in the daughter's bedroom to reduce the strength of their signals. After showering, I lay down surprisingly calm and reassured. A few gestures of kindness, and the world seemed like a welcoming place.

I tried to forget about kidnapping James Lin and pretended I was living in a different era. Jinlong and Shufeng were my parents; we were a family living together happily.

Sleep brushed over my tired face and settled into my body, still burning from the sun I'd caught on the mountainside.

30

Walking out of a 7/11 store clutching a coffee, it struck me this was not a locale where you'd go looking for gangsters. Mopeds buzzed through the mid-morning heat half-obeying traffic lights. Elderly men and women sat in clumps on benches and chairs in the open, chatting and fanning themselves. I wondered if I might see the Chens among them. Many of the features I'd come to regard as commonplace in Megacity—few citizens outside, cutting-edge transport systems, skyscrapers—hadn't impacted this sleepy corner of the world, only reaffirming the spurious nature of the history and geography curricula we'd been fed.

Even without my lenses and earpieces, ripples of paranoia that I was being monitored came and went. But overall, this place seemed to offer a relaxation of the control the grid had exerted over me for much of my life.

Directed by what Jinlong had said about gangsters having old-fashioned tattoos, I walked up and down the streets till I found what seemed to be the only tattoo parlour in the vicinity. I pushed through some anxiety and entered a haze of cigarette smoke.

A shuffling of flip-flops, then a plump young man appearing through door beads to the side, perhaps from where he lived. On his arms black snakes and dragons depicted in bold strokes writhed upwards.

'What do you need?' he asked.

'I'm not sure yet.'

'You need a tattoo?'

'Maybe. I've got no idea of what, though.'

'We can do words if you prefer. If you want English writing, you can give us the words in print. Whatever you want, we can do.'

'Who is your artist?' I assumed this was the sort of thing a person serious about tattoos would ask.

'It's me. We don't employ artHumans. If you have any more questions, ask whatever you like.'

'How much experience do you have?' I asked, enjoying the randomness of the conversation.

'I'm in my fourth year of tattooing. I also like art. Last year I won an award for best painting in Outer Taipei.'

I didn't know where to go with him. 'I'm shooting a film about tattoos from around the world,' I said, 'and it would be amazing if I could interview some of your clients.'

'I don't know them.' Like his voice, the tattooist's face had zero expression. 'Try the Taiwan Tattoo Convention, though the people there are more into animated tattoos.'

Failure.

'Many thanks,' I said.

'OK,' he replied in a voice of stone.

I sat in a rock garden on a small hill. Behind a row of rooftops, the sun cast its gold onto the mountains, which flared up on the horizon like tongues of fire, unafraid to burn on despite being extinguished from collective consciousness.

I craved my devices—I was desperate to call Max and hear his voice. He'd be with Yayuung by now. Why hadn't I asked him to give me her contact details? Although he'd have no doubt refused. Perhaps we'd have been fine if we'd gone back to Taipei together. Like Max said, our pursuer in the night market could have been any idiot, and in my obsessiveness I'd just been looking for patterns everywhere and convinced myself he had Fresh Eyes.

Once again, I had only my own thoughts and experiences to go on. But if Max had looked closely at the man, the pictures of James Lin and at the female agent we encountered at Bar 75, he'd have noticed it, I'm sure—the identical hollow, artificial stare that bored right through you.

Hunger reminded me to eat lunch. I walked into a small restaurant specialising in beef noodle soup, ordered a large takeaway and took it back to the rock garden. It was scorching outside, but I felt freer, safer.

Dripping with sweat from chilli sauce and the midday heat, I bought a large bunch of flowers for the Chens. I went back to their apartment and put the flowers in a vase on the dining table, lay down and slept until I heard them come in at 7:30 p.m.

After dinner, I dragged myself back onto the streets. I'd passed a number of karaoke bars earlier that were open in the daytime, but remembering Jinlong's words that gangsters frequented the establishments in the evening, I'd thought I'd wait. Even at this hour, the bars looked anything but seedy. Senior citizens and their carers were out in large numbers; lucky professionals had gathered to celebrate the end of the working day; a few teenagers came and went, laughing and prattling at full volume. Hardly settings for a meeting of gangsters.

I kept walking until the streets became quieter and darker.

There was little traffic, and large gaps separated the buildings. Although the space beyond urban light was invisible, I thought I could sense the mountains not too far off. I was tired and my bum crack was sore from chaffing after too much walking in the heat. I thought I might as well try one more karaoke bar.

I approached a dimly lit establishment and realised I hadn't considered what I'd do once I was inside. Maybe if I paid for a room, I could wander around the interior in the hope of encountering some of the clientele as they arrived or left.

The price included the companionship of a young woman —human—who called herself Chocolate. Having managed to persuade me to sing one of Noah Black's songs, she patted my knee and exclaimed, 'You have such a beautiful voice. Sing another one.'

What the hell was I doing? I stood up and told Chocolate I was going to the toilet.

Wandering around the corridors, I felt as insignificant as if I didn't exist. Muffled moans of a couple having sex drifted through one door, but most of the rooms didn't seem to be in use. Only one other room appeared to have any custom, and its raucousness made up for all the empty rooms. I pushed the door open, walked in and apologised for going into 'the wrong room.'

Men in dark suits and scantily dressed women looked up, some of their faces red from drinking.

'Hello,' one of the men called. 'Come in. Sit down. Here, have a shot.'

I thanked him and joined the group. 'Are you having a work do?' I asked.

A second man shouted, 'We work at a bank in Central Taipei. But it's too crowded there! And so we come here! Have another drink.' He began pouring me some beer.

I apologised and said I had to get back to my girlfriend.

'Bring her here!' someone yelled as I left the room.

Back in the room I'd rented, Chocolate had fallen asleep.

I left and headed back towards the Chens. It was still alien having to estimate time and distance without my lenses, and I realised I'd walked further than I thought. I must have got about half way back, when I noticed a temple lit up by lanterns down an alley to my left. I'd not been in a temple, nor a church for that matter. Religion was barely talked about and even more rarely practised. I guess with all the games and other lens distractions, citizens didn't have the headspace to think about a creator or a spiritual life. We had our objects of worship anyway: the Supervisors. Their invisibility gave them an otherworldliness. Plus, the gratitude we were supposed to feel towards them for creating and running Megacity pretty much made them demigods.

The temple was almost empty. What I imagined was Buddhist chanting flooded from speakers equally spaced around the walls. Fragrances I didn't know embellished the air and were soon explained when I passed an elderly woman pressing incense between her praying hands at a shrine.

I'd not experienced such peacefulness in a public space.

I wandered from one shrine to the next, making a loop of the temple. A tall, thickset man stood at the last shrine, his eyes closed as he bowed to a red-faced deity. He straightened. His physique reminded me of the man at Tonghua Night Market. He even wore a tank top like him. Surely he wasn't going to turn around and chase me as well?

All across the skin of the man's arms and shoulders military gods grimaced and swirled in yellow, black, green and red.

I withdrew to a nearby shrine, so he wouldn't think I was watching. After about five minutes, he ended his prayers and planted his incense stick in a censer. He turned, his expression peaceful as his eyes travelled over me. He could have been in his early fifties, or if he was a non-citizen, early forties. I nodded a greeting. He nodded back.

Was it wrong to approach him inside the temple? What would I say? How's your God? Do you happen to be a gangster? Lovely weather, isn't it? Even asking him for directions felt out of place straight after the man had completed his worship.

I made for the exit to wait for him outside.

The man carried his massive frame down the five steps at the front of the temple. How to time it?

He lit a cigarette and walked off.

I strode after him. 'Excuse me?'

He stopped and looked at me through bloodshot eyes.

No lenses.

A strange warmth fanned out from my heart. 'Do you have a cigarette?' I asked.

'Wait.' He pulled out a pack of Long Life and handed me three. Lighting a flame, he asked, 'Where are you from?'

'London.'

'London's great. Taiwan's good as well.

'Yes.'

'What brings you to Taiwan?'

'Research. I'm interested in how Fresh Eyes might impact Megacity society.' I didn't want to lie, but had to tread with care. I felt surprisingly safe, though, chatting with this stranger, having witnessed him praying with such genuineness.

'So you think these Fresh Eyes are a good thing?' I had to decipher his question as his Mandarin was permeated by a thick Taiwanese accent.

'Probably not, but I don't know enough about them.'

Afraid he might walk away, I got opinionated: 'I don't like how our lives are completely dominated by tech.'

He looked at me silently. Had he noticed I wasn't wearing lenses?

'Wait here,' he said. 'I'm buying beer.'

He walked over to a kiosk. Moments later I was sipping at a can of Taiwan Beer.

'First time in Taiwan?' he asked.

'Yes.'

'What do you think of it?'

'People are really friendly. The food's amazing too. I can get the same dishes in London, but they taste better here.'

He dragged on his cigarette. 'You're not like other people. I rarely talk for this long to someone I don't know.'

'Likewise.'

'Why are you still talking to me then?'

He'd caught me off guard. To my relief he broke into a hoarse laugh.

'Let's go to a night market,' he said.

I realised I hadn't eaten dinner. 'Good idea—I'm Ben, by the way.'

'I'm Big Dog. People call me the Dog. We're good friends now.' He opened a second can, drank half and said, 'Come on, it's not far.'

I was trying to appreciate the taste of an oyster omelette the Dog had treated me to.

'What's London like?' he asked.

'Pure Megacity,' I replied. 'I'm sure it once had more of its own character and culture, but you know how it is these days. Downtown London's not that different from Central Taipei. We don't have these lovely night markets, though.'

'I've never been abroad.'

I must have stared at him when he said that. 'Do you ever wish you could travel?'

'It's a massive sacrifice,' the Dog said, pointing at his eyes. 'You're cut off from most of the world without those shit lenses.' The alcohol seemed to be loosening his tongue. 'The total space I move in will always be tiny. But I like real stuff. I couldn't keep up the bullshit about some other identity that's got nothing to do with who I actually am. Anyway, Taiwan's got everything I need. I don't even go up north much. Central and southern Taiwan are my paradise on earth.' The Dog smiled. 'But you're as bad as me. Why aren't you wearing lenses?'

I told him about how I'd played with leaving my lenses out when I still worked for Dwellings and about my experiments with the sadness. And as I went on to speak about my obsessive search for the countryside, I realised my own tongue was loosening as well. But somehow, I trusted him. Eventually, I told him about discovering the forest and hinted at my desire to find out who the Supervisors were, and why they'd decided the city was the place for citizens.

'I feel sorry for you,' he said.

'Really?' I'd expected surprise or amazement, not pity.

'Of course—in Taiwan, it's easy to find countryside. Nobody realises, as they're not even present in their surroundings. And the fear machine is too strong for them to do what you did. But there's a whole heap of natural beauty, believe me. My mates and I, we spend half our time in it. We don't talk about it to citizens—you're probably the first.'

'Do you work?' I had to throw this one at him.

Big Dog searched my eyes. 'Yes, but not the usual work. I'm linked to the underworld.'

Bingo. I swallowed an un-chewed lump of omelette and glugged my beer.

'Wow, so cool!' I said, feeling like an idiot as I heard my words. But I needed to let the Dog know I was comfortable with his line of work.

'Cool? Are you mad? I make enough to feed my family the best food money can buy and to go on occasional holidays, in Taiwan obviously. But I can be caught at any moment. I've already spent chunks of my life behind bars. I'm lucky it's always been for small things like fighting rival brothers. I'd be long gone if the agents knew some of the stuff I've been involved in.' The Dog lit a cigarette and handed me one.

Smoking wasn't quite so painful now.

'Prison's shit,' he continued. 'But it's worth the freedom when I'm out. So yes, scary as hell. But take a look at me. Do I look stressed?'

'No way.' I cringed at my keenness.

'Do I look scared?'

'No.'

'That's right. Sure, I'm scared. But do I give a fuck about fear? No. It's like this—I'm used to it. Often I forget it's there and I think I'm not afraid after all. But the fear never leaves you. You just learn to deal with it. Like I say, the freedom makes everything good. I can spend time with my family when I like, I can hang out with the brothers when I like, I can chase girls when I like, I can enjoy the mountains when I like. Most of the time nobody knows what I'm doing or where the fuck I am. I wouldn't get lenses or citizens' rights for the life of me. Wouldn't take a job in Megacity if you paid me millions.'

I was mesmerised. 'Is your partner fine with what you do?'

'My wife—we still marry in the underworld. She doesn't try to understand it. I honestly think she pretends I do something else. The first time we met was in a wreck of a karaoke bar, so it hardly came as a surprise when she noticed my friends all belonged to the underworld. She's pissed off I'm not around for the kids a huge amount—prison's crap for that, and sometimes I can be away on a job for a few weeks. She sure as hell hates it when I stay out late with the brothers.'

'Do your children know?'

'We're not telling them till they're older, but I honestly don't care if they find out earlier. They'll quickly realise I'm not the evil one. Try comparing me with a CEO of a megacorps or one of the Supervisors you were just talking about, and you'll see I'm a saint. The difference between them and me is I get to see a lot of shit close up and dirty, but on a tiny scale. They just give verbal commands that fuck with the lives of millions and then go and forget about it all.'

'This is helping me put things in perspective,' I said. 'You're the first member of any underworld scene I've met.'

'I'm honoured. Aren't you one too now, though?' the Dog smirked. 'Especially since you went off-grid into that forest of yours.'

'Almost seems like we're the good guys,' I said.

'Of course we are. You can call me and my brothers the mafia all you like, but we're nothing compared with the Supervisors. Who else can force so many people to do what they want? And they're such a well-organised ring you don't even know where they live.' The Dog checked the time on an old watch and said, 'I need to get home. Come and hang out at Lazy Bar. I'm there most nights. Be my foreign friend.'

Childhood programming was urging me to say there are no foreign people as we're all citizens of Megacity, but it occurred to me the Dog had probably never been a citizen.

Maybe I couldn't be classed as a true citizen anymore either.

The Chens were in bed when I got back to the apartment. I crept to my room, soaked in the guilt of ignoring Jinlong's advice to stay away from gangsters.

But I had to admit, Big Dog had been a top-notch companion and conversationalist and a surprisingly friendly ambassador of the underworld. Or had I simply been charmed? Climbing into bed, I forced myself to remember the many crimes gangsters might commit in their lives. I persuaded myself that should I succeed in enlisting the Dog's help, it would only be as a means to an end. I was not about to become a career criminal.

Then again, who was to say what was criminal when nothing on the planet was as it seemed.

31

The fire outside the Dog's shack was the only light I could see in the final throes of the day. His home lay on the fringe of Megacity, though it might as well have been off-grid—he'd told me the authorities could only tolerate him and his family if they stayed just behind the lights in the region close to the mountains, where citizens didn't venture.

Having not worn my lenses and earpieces once since my first evening at the Chens, going naked felt normal. I imagined receiving a warning that 'hazardous land' lay ahead and that I was 'on the brink of no return.'

I smiled—it was already too late to return.

I'd hung out with the Dog twice in bars since we met two weeks ago, and I'd learned he was the 'older brother'—leader —of a small gang of currently twenty-two members. This morning we'd attempted a game of tennis doubles against his closest brothers, Black Tree and Clear River. We played on an overgrown, pockmarked court a few shacks away from the Dog's home, and after the game he'd invited me for a barbeque in the evening. Tennis and barbeques didn't strike me as typical gangster activities, but again—nothing was as it seemed.

As I pushed through the darkness towards the fire, I sensed I was leaving behind everything that was socially acceptable, sanitised, orderly and—of course—legal. And yet that comforted me: my time with the brothers had confirmed for me that illegal activity was sometimes the only way to do good.

I could smell the meat roasting as I neared a gathering around a fire. A memory of fires in the pit unleashed another longing for Fern. The fire and barbecue contrasted with the cool of twilight pressing on my skin.

A skinny figure sidled over. It was Clear River with a can of Taiwan Beer for me.

Black Tree sprang from his chair and yelled, 'It's the UK guy everybody!'

'Shut up!' the Dog snapped. He turned to me and said, 'Black Tree's got no manners.'

I noticed for the first time that the little finger on Black Tree's right hand was missing. I don't think he saw me gaping, but not being used to any human deformity, I couldn't stop fixating on it. Perhaps it was hacked off in a fight.

I had no fear about asking the Dog for help, but how to gain the trust of his friends? Because my target was so high profile, the chances they'd even discuss taking part were incredibly slim. And I'd not done any research yet; James Lin could live surrounded by bodyguards for all I knew. Then there was the glaring unlikelihood that any of the gangsters felt as lost as me and would want to be involved in what could easily be a stroll into the jaws of death. We could be caught by cameras or agents at any point, from the planning of the operation through to its execution, and then during the escape from Megacity.

The Dog handed me a hunk of beef on a disposable plate.

'Daddy!' a high voice screamed.

I turned and saw a boy and a girl running in a circle around us.

'What?' the Dog said with a hint of irritation.

'When can we go to Disneyland?' asked the boy.

'Exactly. When can we go to Disneyland?' echoed his sister.

'My answer hasn't changed,' their father replied. 'When there's a Disneyland in Taiwan.'

'Poor bastards,' one of the brothers said. 'Maybe we should try and get our kids lenses? At least they could go to Disneyland in Japan with some caretakers—if we paid them enough.'

'But who'd want to take any of our kids?' the Dog responded. 'People don't talk to us. Not that we want them to.' He laughed, turned to me and said, 'Except for you, that is. My wife and kids are desperate for more friends, but things would quickly get messy if they got used to hanging out with citizens —our lifestyles are too different. One day, when I'm gone, it'll be up to the kids if they want to argue their innocence to the authorities and make friends with normals, or if they follow my path into the underworld.'

Despite the limitations on their lives, I envied the Dog's children for growing up with their dad around.

'This is Ben,' the Dog called to his children. 'He's from London. He can teach you English.'

The boy ran over to us. 'Come with me,' he said. 'I'll show you a cool place.'

'Sure.' I followed the children, oil dripping from my fingers.

They took me round a corner out of sight of the fire. The boy bent down and opened a trap door.

'This is a really cool hiding place,' the girl said once the three of us were in the pitch black of an underground bunker.

'Mummy and Daddy send us here whenever it's dangerous,' the boy said.

I could only assume that agents or rival gangsters were a constant threat in the Dog's life. Hanging out with him clearly wasn't without risk.

'Do you like it?' asked the girl.

'Yes, but I can't see anything.'

They laughed.

The Dog opened the trap door and told his children to run back to the barbeque. Then he joined me in the bunker. 'We are brothers now,' he said in a hoarse whisper. 'I want you to know that if you ever need help, you can just give me a call. I might need your help as well one day. It's useful to know a native English speaker—I don't trust the Taiwanese citizens who speak English.'

I couldn't help feeling honoured.

The Dog switched a light on. The bunker was bigger than I'd thought. Emergency rations of food and drink were stacked against three walls, while on the fourth hung an array of cleavers and choppers and three ancient handguns.

'I've got something for you,' the Dog said. He pulled out an old smartphone from his back pocket and handed it to me. 'This way we can keep in touch for as long as you're in Taiwan. I've saved my number on it. River's and Black Tree's are on there too.'

He couldn't expect me to mask my surprise. 'What the … a physical phone? Aren't they all in museums?'

'I guess we're responsible for keeping these old dinosaurs going. Some of the brothers created a dedicated network they can run on. The old standards and frequencies this thing uses make it impossible for today's systems to eavesdrop. The only guys you might get listening in are rival gangsters. Most brothers in Taiwan have these, so if we're away on a job, we might not pick up to avoid giving away our location.'

I wished I could show Max the smartphone. The Dog

watched as I explored its weight and texture, before slipping it into my pocket.

Cheers from the brothers reached us, and we left the bunker to rejoin them. I sat on a plastic crate and gazed at the faces around the fire. Everyone was smoking cigarettes or marijuana. In addition to the Dog, Clear River and Black Tree, there were five people I didn't know. All men. All tattooed. Thinking of tattoos, it was only then that I recognised one of the brothers after all: the tattoo artist had been here all along. The firelight was adding some colour to that face that was so expressionless when I'd met him. I nodded at him, and he broke into an endless grin.

I listened to them gossiping wildly in a Taiwanese I didn't understand as I worked my way through a few more Taiwan Beer cans. Soon my bursting bladder forced me off the crate, and I shuffled through the dark into a corner I'd seen the brothers using.

As the vapour from my urine wafted up, I felt what must have been the grimmest of smiles stretch itself across my face. The darkness hugged me from all quarters. I bared my teeth and clenched my jaw like a beast in the shadows. For a moment, I was a wild animal readying myself to savage everything that Megacity held dear.

I was indeed changing. The kidnapping and meeting the Dog and his brothers had forced me to reconsider my preconceptions of good and evil—challenge them even.

And would kidnapping someone for the greater good— with no intent to harm them—still be an evil deed? Things could get messy: if I was already justifying kidnapping an innocent man, what other lengths might I be willing to go to for what I rightly or wrongly believed was best for the world?

I knew questions like this would continue to hound me.

And if I kept hanging out with these new friends, who'd lived so differently to me all these years, would I not continue to learn ways of not just seeing—but surviving—that lay sealed below the surface of civilised consciousness?

Was this not a good thing?

Then again, what was good?

I stayed a little longer, alone in my thoughts. Then I said goodbye to the circle of brothers. As I left the fire and re-entered the blackness of a night behind streetlights, I acknowledged wholeheartedly that tonight marked my arrival in the underworld.

As the heat from the fire disappeared, silently, I tried to pray to someone or something.

That I would be unstoppable.

That good would come from the dark intentions I harboured.

However dark they really were.

Amen.

32

Over the following ten days I set to work establishing myself in my newfound social milieu. I spent the mornings chatting and going for walks with the Chens, before telling them in the afternoon that I was off sightseeing or going to read in a café, when I was actually devising my next step or hanging out with the brothers.

Mostly I met up with Black Tree, and before I knew it we were eating dinner at his home with his wife and daughter. I made an effort to get to know Clear River as well, with limited success. He told me upfront he didn't feel the need to socialise like the other brothers.

'All you need to know about him is he's loyal to a brother in need,' Black Tree said.

But I knew I couldn't hang around like this much longer before some citizen, a neighbour of the Chens for instance, would begin to wonder what this newcomer was up to and use their lenses to capture my image and gait for pattern recognition, or to file questions to Law Enforcement.

The biggest challenge was orchestrating a meeting that the Dog, Black Tree and Clear River could all attend. Often at least one of them was away on business or uncontactable by phone. Sometimes I couldn't get hold of any of them.

At last all three of them accepted one of my invitations—to meet at Lazy Bar at 8 p.m. on Monday night. Having reserved a table, I arrived half an hour early and ordered pineapple juice for myself and beers for the others. My jaw was jiggering. How in Megacity would they react? Would they actually be up for it? Would they be offended I'd thought of involving them in the dangerous kidnap of a public figure? Or would they just agree I was mad and walk out and not talk to me again?

I was fumbling around way outside my comfort zone.

Clear River arrived at 7:55 and plonked himself next to me on the black faux leather sofa.

'Eaten?' he asked.

'Yeah, you?'

'Yeah.'

A message on my smartphone. Black Tree was on his way.

Clear River and I waited for half an hour without exchanging a single word. Perhaps our disdain for small talk made us more similar than we realised.

And there was Black Tree's sturdy self, sauntering towards the glass door as though he could dictate the speed at which the whole earth rotated.

'Damn, that skunk was strong! Been drinking all day too,' he said, flopping into an armchair, eyes bloodshot.

'I've warned you not to smoke that shit,' Clear River said. 'It makes you crap to work with.'

'I don't care about your opinion,' Black Tree slurred.

'I wonder where the Dog is,' I said.

'Not coming,' Black Tree replied. 'I went round his place today. Wife says he's away on a job. Fuck knows when he'll be back. He's so unreliable. How much longer have we got to put up with this kind of leadership?'

Great. So I was stuck with just two, one of them pissed and stoned.

'Why did you want to meet up?' Black Tree asked, hitting me on the knee. 'Did you just want to go for a drink? I'm not in the mood. I should be home with my family. I've been up three nights in a row entertaining clients in karaoke bars. My liver's probably dissolved.'

I was desperate. How long might I have to wait for a better opportunity?

'Brothers, I need your help,' I said.

Black Tree sat up. 'Go on.'

'I've got a job. But you're going to think I'm crazy.'

A laugh blasted out of Black Tree's mouth. He stared at Clear River, pointing at me, and spluttered, 'He wants our help! He's got a job! The Londoner means business. Fucking hell. Go, go, go! Get more beers, River.'

I wasn't sure how to continue after this explosion. I waited for River to come back.

'It's a big job, and it's risky.'

Black Tree roared with laughter. 'So we're working for you now, are we? You haven't even begun working for us.' He slapped my thigh hard. 'C'mon, brother, spit it out! I'm getting curious now. You're the last person I'd expect to come to us with a job.'

I ignored the sting in my thigh and downed my juice. 'I would like to ask for your help to kidnap James Lin, the guy who's in the news all the time. I want to take him out of Megacity and up into the mountains. I'd pay you, of course.'

A look of horror on Clear River's face.

Black Tree's jaw hanging open.

About half a minute of speechlessness ticked past as the bar's outdated rock music accompanied whatever processes the two men had to see out.

Black Tree dragged at his cigarette. 'Why?'

I gave them the back story to the bizarre proposal. They already knew about my London searches and my penchant for independent thinking, so it was easier to explain myself. 'My main motive is to find out who or where the Supervisors are,' I concluded. 'I figure, if we at least know something concrete about them and why they decide the things they do, we have a small chance of influencing the games they play with us all. Citizens are virtually incapable of directing any aspects of their own lives. Fresh Eyes will be the final massacre of their minds if they all have to get them one day. As I see it, anything we can do to slow the spread of this technology would be a gift to the citizens.'

'Massacre of minds?' said Black Tree. 'Are you a poet? I'm not sure River here is following you.' He laughed and slapped Clear River on the cheek. 'Mr Lee, you picked the wrong people. We're gangsters—we don't care about citizens.'

He had a point. My anxiety kicked in.

'But the Supervisors?' Black tree continued. 'Now that we understand. Hell, yeah—we fucking hate their guts. We're not educated, but we know what caused the mess Taiwan's in. It's the system designed by people at the top. And yes, Fresh Eyes will be everywhere one day. We've already seen plenty of agents with them.' He leaned forward and took a close look at my face. 'You OK, Ben?'

I was registering—almost celebrating—the fact that I wasn't alone in noticing there were agents who already had them.

'Plenty of agents?' I asked. 'You sure?'

'Hell yeah,' Black Tree replied. 'If only the Dog was here. He'd support this all the way.'

I smiled. I nodded. I even slapped Black Tree on the back.

'I'm not sure he would,' River responded. 'It's high risk. Have you even thought about how the target's eyes might be linked to security systems in his house and to any nearby agents?'

'That's no different from lenses,' Black Tree said. 'We'd have to slap an anti-detection eye mask on either way.'

'Why don't we wait for the Dog to come back?' I suggested.

'How would you pay us?' River asked. 'You know we don't have normal bank accounts.'

'I'll set up wallets and use an untraceable currency. I'll have to risk connecting via my lenses for a couple of minutes, but it'll be worth it if I know I have your support.'

'When do you want to do the job?' Black Tree asked.

How to choose a deadline for a crime?

'Obviously we'll need to do a lot of planning,' I said. 'There's a lot to discuss.'

'When?' River said, leaning forward.

'Two weeks?'

Black Tree smiled. 'You're a slow planner, eh?' he said in a gentle purr I'd not heard him use except with his daughter. 'Wanna hear my opinion? We do it in three days. Give me a good night's sleep, and we get planning tomorrow. I'd go and do it tonight if I had the energy.'

'Easy, Black Tree,' said Clear River, 'Big Dog could be back in time to have his say.'

Black Tree ran a hand through his hair. 'OK, four days. If he comes back in that time and thinks we need even longer, fine.'

'You should wait to consult him with a job like this,' Clear River said.

'We're doing it,' Black Tree barked, equipping us with cigarettes and replacing his own. 'I'm sick and tired of waiting around for him. We get nothing near the amount of work we used to.'

My neck and shoulders had seized up. My thoughts that Max had dismissed as madness were taking shape in the real world. And so soon.

I could almost smell the plan being born.

Clear River chewed on his lower lip. 'Shit,' he said.

'Are you sure about this?' I asked Black Tree.

'Yep, I'm fuckin' restless and I'm bored of crap little jobs.'

I assumed Clear River's silence meant yes. 'Thank you, brothers.'

'Don't thank us yet,' River warned.

As we parted company outside the bar, Black Tree grabbed my arm.

'There's another reason we're helping you,' he whispered. 'Gangsters have been going missing. And not because of rival gangs. We have no idea why. It's sinister shit. But I would bet everything I have the Supervisors are playing some sort of game with us.'

'Damn right,' Clear River said.

I shuddered, as I remembered Jinlong also mentioning a rumour members of the underworld were disappearing.

Black Tree put a hand on my shoulder. 'Sleep—tomorrow we plan.'

Having persuaded two brothers to help me, the momentum my idea was gaining was palpable.

But even as I wandered back to the Chens', I couldn't help wondering if four days to prepare was sheer recklessness.

And was it wise to bypass Big Dog even if Black Tree was his closest brother?

33

The smell of incense brought me back to my previous visit to the temple. Now it was me holding the incense on the spot where I'd first seen Big Dog a few weeks ago. It was me standing opposite Guan Di, symbol of courage and brotherhood, great god of war.

I focused every scrap of my attention on the effigy's red face and endless black beard, his green robe and gold armour. Forced myself to believe in his protective powers.

Big Dog hadn't returned in time to be consulted. My two brothers and I were as ready as we'd ever be. I was still getting used to calling them brothers, but I liked the word and drew confidence from it. It reminded me I was no longer alone. I won't deny it also created a sense of loyalty towards my friends.

Clear River hovered behind me; Black Tree stood next to me, offering prayers: 'Help us succeed in this important task. We thank you. You have always protected us. We have always been loyal to you. Please defend us now at every step. Protect our families. Please, protect them. Thank you.'

I was amazed how such rough gangsters could sound so

heartfelt in their petitions to a being they believed was greater than them.

Black Tree kept intoning the same simple sentences. His words stoked my courage, but also filled me with foreboding: in two hours we'd be on the road.

The prayer reminded me of Elijah's water ritual in the pit and my own prayer-like thoughts of desperation on my very first day of searching in London, when I'd found the sprigs of weeds in the car park.

As the rhythms of Black Tree's words washed over me, his voice lingering song-like on every 'thank you', I too prayed in silence—to nothing in particular—that we would be safe; that what we were about to do would end up benefitting the citizens in some way.

34

It was 02:30. Most houses along the street were dark, and the lights in James Lin's house were out as we'd expected.

It was hard to believe I was actually driving the musty old van Black Tree had procured on the black market—so old it didn't even need an anti-tracking device. Given River had only taught me how to drive three days ago, I'd expressed my concern about being the driver, but Black Tree had insisted. He'd also told me to stay in the van as I'd just fuck it up if I went in with them.

'Remember,' he said a fifth or sixth time, 'you drive slowly round the block once, then come back. Easy, right? You call if there's a problem, or any agents show up. We have ways of dealing with James if he gets too noisy, but we cannot get caught by agents. Got it?'

'Yes.' The simplicity of the instructions did nothing to stem the adrenaline flooding my whole body as I slowed the van and rolled up outside James's home.

Despite all the prayers and the planning, I still couldn't picture us pulling it off. This was a very different level of risk to any I'd taken before. It was one thing to risk my own life in a personal quest to find countryside, but quite another to be engaged in organised crime, plotting the kidnap of an innocent member of the public. Not to mention James's high profile.

I also feared for Black Tree and Clear River who'd no doubt be killed if they were caught. I feared for the two additional younger men who sat in the back of the van. They'd only recently been recruited by the gang and had agreed to help out despite the pathetic payment I'd offered. I'd not realised just how much the gangster class hated the system and 'the guys at the top'. I feared for all four men's families, who might not see them again if the kidnap failed.

Despite my boldness in initiating this job, I also feared for myself, knowing I might never see Max or the mountains or forest again. I even felt anxiety on James's behalf as I imagined his horror when he realised his house was being broken into. How do you react in a situation like that?

And I was plagued with questions about what next steps we'd have to take if the kidnap did go smoothly.

Over the last four days, we'd made numerous trips past James's house and along neighbouring streets in Taichung District. We'd analysed the comfortable-looking residence through Black Tree's ancient binoculars from every angle we could. While there didn't appear to be any bodyguards or relatives living with our target, we'd be filmed by the house and street cams throughout the operation. As River had said, James's eyes were also likely to be capable of relaying live feeds to any agents in the area. Speed was vital.

'Good luck,' I said, trying to hide the shakiness in my voice as the four men stepped out, faces covered in stockings to avoid the cams face-matching with previous crimes.

I pulled away from the curb, teeth chattering. So this was it! My foray into major crime had begun.

I pulled up at a traffic light. With a few moments to myself, an unexpected wave of melancholy diluted my fear. What did it say about the world that I'd been driven to such extreme measures?

What did it say about me?

The lights turned green. I took a right, cruising my way round the block. I was tempted to speed up, but managed to stick with 30 kilometres an hour as rehearsed.

I sidled up to the property again, my right hand clenching the bizarre gear stick I'd learnt to shunt this way and that.

Where was everyone? They were meant to be coming out now.

A bang pierced the moment, reaching me through the van's open window.

Something was off.

My one thought: James had better not be dead.

The door of the house flew open. One of Black Tree's men came out, a limp figure slumped over his shoulder. Black Tree ran past him towards me.

I leaned over and flung the passenger door open.

'River's been shot,' Black Tree said. 'He went in first. James had a gun—he got scared and shot.'

I'd just made the stupidest mistake of my life.

I wasn't sure if seconds passed or minutes; I only knew Black Tree was ripping open the side door and his man was offloading Clear River onto a seat.

'Don't panic,' Black Tree said, 'we've got your man. River made a big sacrifice tonight, but we've got your man. There he is.'

The other man was struggling out of the house, his arms locked around James who was trying to break free. James was gagged and blindfolded with an anti-detection eye mask.

'Drive, Ben, just drive—fast!' Black Tree shouted when everyone was in the van. 'With a bit of speed we should be OK.

We're lucky this old banger's untrackable. You got the route, right?'

'Yes—it looks different in the dark,' I mumbled. 'Is River OK?'

Pangs of guilt were already crushing my heart.

Pandemonium in the back. Black Tree fussing over Clear River, trying to keep him alive. One of the young men trying to calm James, who was shivering and choking on the gag; the other mopping up blood haemorrhaging from Clear River's stomach onto the seats and floor. Black Tree phoning the lookouts, who were checking the roads to make sure the operation ran as smoothly as possible.

Black Tree finished making his calls and let out a howl.

Clear River wasn't going to make it.

My head swam. To think I'd imagined I should get into this!

My guilt assumed its full stature. How would we tell his family?

And Big Dog? It was a tragedy that Clear River had been the one who'd urged us to wait for the Dog to return before proceeding. How could I look him in the eye after this—the older brother who'd introduced me to River in the first place?

It was madness to keep driving towards the mountains and continue with the plan as if nothing had happened.

The roads were clear at this hour, but as a novice driver I was reluctant to max out the souped-up van's speed. Somehow I managed to swap places with Black Tree. With his foot hard on the accelerator, we fled the lights of the city, and the darkness closed in.

Sitting next to Clear River, I wanted to abort the operation and go back to Central Taipei, to find Max, fly back to London together and pretend all this was just a story.

Now that we'd left the suburbs and were heading straight for the mountains to the southeast of Taichung, it was unlikely we'd be filmed again. We'd made it out of Megacity, but with a man dying.

We'd practised making the entire journey twice in sunlight at a much slower pace. Tonight we drove in a dimension ruled by darkness and blood. Death's domain.

I tried to focus all my attention on the next stretch of road, then the next.

Even with Clear River's life draining, I knew we'd been lucky with the operation. Given the media's positive slant on James and Fresh Eyes, clearly no-one—neither the Supervisors, nor James himself—would have guessed that somebody might be plotting to kidnap him. Why should anyone want to? James was an underdog who'd been empowered, a miracle come true, a hero giving hope to the masses. Why worry about high-security protection?

The road narrowed to a disused lane, heralding the final, tortuous leg of the journey. We'd been up here two days ago, clearing some of the taller undergrowth with our bare hands. It was one of the ancient routes into the mountains once used by foresters and maybe hikers. The sort of mountain lane my grandfather once told me about: you keep thinking you're nearly at the top, but it continues winding higher into remoteness, further from the sounds and lights of civilisation.

How far removed I was from the innocence of time with Grandfather.

The steepness and remaining undergrowth forced us to slow down. Now that we were off-grid one of the younger men tentatively removed James's eye mask—we couldn't be sure Fresh Eyes wouldn't work up here.

Terror was etched across James's face, but his eyes were dead, as far as we could tell.

Clear River left us.

We parked away from the road on a flat patch of earth at the edge of the tree line. Black Tree sobbed as he laid Clear River out. He sat on the ground and gestured for me to sit on his left. One of the young men sat to his right, while the other remained with James in the van.

The three of us knelt in a line, and Black Tree launched into a ritual chant for the dead, joined by his friend. Absorbed in my shock and guilt, I had no idea how long they sang for. I allowed the repetitive melody to subdue my racing mind, until my nerves showed the first signs of settling and I became aware of my tiredness.

A dim light arrived and a new and very different day was born.

35

Black Tree chopped pork and prepared a fire, while James sat propped up against a tree next to us, hands tied around the trunk behind him. He was screaming, his eyes tightly shut as if he was in agony. Sometimes they opened and shot wild stares in random directions.

It was painful to watch. I'd thought hard about the questions I was going to ask, but you can't exactly get chatting with someone in that state.

Still, we had to get him to talk somehow.

'Black Tree, give me a cigarette,' I said. I walked a few metres away from them and paced about, spitting, swearing, trying to psyche myself up. I took glugs from one of the bottles of *baijiu* we'd brought up in preparation two days earlier.

I went back. 'Hello, James. I'm sorry we have to meet like this.'

It was no use. James had begun shaking his head violently from side to side. His constant screaming chilled me.

'I think he's trying to tell us something,' Black Tree said.

Gradually we realised James was shrieking one word as if on loop.

'DIRT! DIRT!'

After a while the theme became clearer. 'Get me away from here! Toxic! Toxic! Take me indoors! Take me back to the city. I don't want to die.'

'That's some strong conditioning for you,' I said to Black Tree.

'PLEASE,' James was panting now, 'Reconnect me!'

'You're in the mountains, James,' I said. 'There is no connectivity up here. Yes, there are corners in this world where your eyes can't function. And you are right, there is dirt here. Dirt, plants, trees and fresh air. But nothing has happened to you, right? It's OK in the mountains. See?'

James appeared to listen, but as soon as I finished, the torrent returned. 'I need connection. I'm not getting the thoughts; there's no info. Updates. Please … just plug me in! I'll do anything … just fifteen minutes, and I'll be OK—I swear to the Supervisors!'

'Could take ages for the withdrawal symptoms to go,' I said. 'If any of you need to go and get on with your life, that's fine. I'll stay here with him. Just leave me a knife.'

'Idiot,' Black Tree said. 'We're not leaving you alone with him up here.'

I swallowed. I'd not experienced such comradeship with someone I'd only known a few weeks. 'Don't you have things to see to—your families, Clear River's family?'

'River's family has to wait,' Black Tree said. 'Our families know we risk our necks for a living. It could be me or you next time. I've lost a lot of brothers on jobs, but you've got to keep going. Sure, I was close to River. We knew each other since we were kids, so I feel the pain.' He paused. 'But it's no different. We all agreed to the operation. Anyway, if we leave you alone, you'll fuck the whole thing up before we even get to the bottom of the mountain.' He punched my shoulder. 'The supplies in the van will last us a week. Let's take a walk.'

'Ahong, Aqiang,' he called—those were the names of his two men. 'Guard James.'

James took a break from screaming. His eyes stared at us as we walked away. Although they were expressionless, his pleading face was that of an addict demanding to be saved by the next hit.

Black Tree and I came to an opening in the forest about fifty metres to one side of where we'd left James. We stepped out of the trees and onto a rock. Expansive vistas unfurled: to our right lay Taiwan's western plains, while straight ahead the shoulder of a neighbouring mountain teeming with plant and tree life broadened as your eye followed it down towards a valley somewhere in the depths.

We sat. 'Taiwan is beautiful, ' I said, trying to focus only on the green opposite for a moment.

'I never get tired of it. Congratulations, by the way!' He patted my thigh, 'You've carried out your first job.'

'Thank you, I suppose. How can you do this kind of work full-time? I think I'd end up taking my life.'

'Human beings can get used to anything. I'd still give all I have to get out of the underworld, though.'

'Really?'

'I keep trying and failing,' Black Tree said, handing me another cigarette. 'Once you're in, that's it. I've got a lot of history with the brothers—they'd never let me leave. People all over Taiwan have done me favours—given me money, protected my family. Some have saved my life. I owe all of them, and they can collect anytime. The brothers from rival gangs we've worked with on jobs in other parts of Taiwan are a lifelong threat I can't afford to stop thinking about. If I turn an angry brother down, there's nothing I can do to save myself and my family apart from killing us all.'

In the trees directly above and below us, branches and leaves began shaking vigorously.

I jumped up—everywhere, little bodies were moving. 'What in Megacity—'

'Ha-ha,' Black Tree roared. 'Nobody's following us up here. They're harmless.'

I ran a hand through my hair and watched, as a family of monkeys travelled past.

It must have taken me a whole minute to return to the conversation. 'Do you ever find it hard to justify what you do?'

'Of course. I've still got a conscience. When I work, I've got to pretend I'm somebody else, or I can't cope. When a job's over I feel pretty shit about what I've done. But look at me and then look at how messed up Megacity is—how else can I and my family live?'

We went to check on James. He was talking deliriously. Ahong said they'd put a cushion behind James's head to stop him banging his head against the tree.

By nightfall his condition had deteriorated. We took it in turns to sit with him and make sure he stayed warm. He refused food, but accepted the occasional sip of water.

Without any sign we'd be able to have a conversation with James, the whole operation looked hopeless.

At ten o'clock the next morning I suggested medical intervention might be necessary to calm James down. 'We prepared so thoroughly,' I told the others, 'but I think he needs some kind of tranquiliser. Can a couple of us go down and get something?'

'Going into the city so soon as a group is a massive risk,' Black Tree said.

'I could go alone,' I said. 'The risk should only be on me.'

'It's OK, I'll do it,' Black Tree said. 'There's a hospital not far from the base of the mountain. I know people there. A couple of them owe me. I'll be back in four hours.'

'What if you don't return?' I asked. 'I don't want two men on my conscience.'

'Don't worry, this one's no big deal. I guarantee I'll be back.'

'You'd better be,' I said.

Black Tree chatted to the other three and got into the van. As he drove off, he shouted, 'Brothers!' through the open window and laughed.

'Brothers!' I shouted back. A lump formed in my throat. Black Tree was a real friend. I needed him.

And now Clear River was gone, maybe he even needed me.

36

I heaved a sigh when the van skidded its way back up the steep lane. As it neared the top, I saw not one, but two figures inside. The one in the passenger seat was huge and obliterated much of the light coming through the back windows.

Black Tree had come back with Big Dog.

I could tell something wasn't right by the way Black Tree ignored me when he got out of the van and walked towards the rocky outlook.

'Did you manage to get any medicine?' I called after him. But Black Tree must have been out of earshot already.

The passenger door flew open. The Dog jumped out and walked towards me.

Then his club of a fist was flying at my cheek.

Not long after, I saw the earth fall away from me as he lifted me up. I thought I saw Black Tree and the other three smoking in the clearing, before gravity and muscle power smashed me onto the ground.

'Why?' the Dog yelled, following with two kicks to my ribs and a deluge of slaps to my face. 'I'm away for one week, and you think you can wade in and lead my gang for me? I trusted you. I welcomed you in. Now you go and get River killed. He was my little brother! Fuck you!'

The beating went on until neither mind nor body could keep up, and I was gone.

When I awoke to a world of pain, I was sitting tied to a tree around ten metres from James. I groaned at a figure standing nearby. It was Black Tree; he walked over and shoved a cigarette in my mouth.

'I'm sorry,' Black Tree said. 'I had ten messages from him asking where we were. There was nothing I could do—the Dog's still the boss. He wouldn't have hit you that hard if it wasn't for Clear River.' Black Tree crouched at my level. 'Welcome to the club. You've been given some hard gangster love. If you were Taiwanese, he'd have cut one of your arms off. The only reason he's not chopping mine is that he's known me too long. He used to be harder on me.' Black Tree held up his shortened little finger. 'You're lucky—other bosses would have put an end to you with the triple stab.'

'Where is he?' I asked.

'He'll be back. Don't worry.'

'I am worried.'

'He won't hit you again. He had to do that. I guarantee he'll behave differently now. Watch.'

I didn't believe Black Tree.

Footsteps crunched to my right, and I tried to turn, but my neck felt like it would never turn again. The smell of marijuana wafted over, and the tower of the Dog moved into view.

'Chill out,' he said. 'I'm not going to hit you again.'

Something else.

'I'm sorry,' I said.

'Apologies are no use around here. Just don't fuck about with my men.'

'Definitely not.'

'Have some of this. It'll help with the pain.' The Dog leaned forward and swapped my cigarette for his large joint.

I inhaled, and almost immediately coughed as I exhaled harsh, pine-flavoured smoke.

'Everything we do carries consequences,' the Dog said. 'Sometimes negative, sometimes positive, sometimes both.'

Surely the consequences were purely negative this time. I took another puff, hoping to dull the pain. 'I'm really sorry, brother,' I said again.

'Too late for your pointless apologies. I'm pissed off about Clear River—and hurt—but this is the life of a gangster. We move on.'

I took another drag, and the magic of the herbal concoction spiked into every corner of me.

'To be honest,' the Dog said, 'I kind of like your operation. I would have said no—too risky.' He paused. 'I've never met a citizen like you. A challenger to all those men who think they can govern us the way they do. That I can support.'

With the joint fragmenting my mental processes, I struggled to reconcile the Dog's solidarity with the pain from his battering that spread out all over me in colourful stripes. The throbs in my head were like digs of a spade.

I shut my eyes.

Relief … finally.

My mind floated away from the group of brothers huddled together and found a soothing home with the rustling leaves in the treetops.

Sometime later I became aware of Black Tree untying me. A recollection of why we were all up on the mountain drifted into my consciousness.

'You never answered me,' I said to Black Tree with a rasping voice. 'Did you get the tranquilisers?'

'Yep. Some antipsychotics as well. Let's give them to him now.'

'I need coffee before I do anything,' I said.

'Ahong, get this brother some coffee,' Black Tree called.

Sipping at strong instant, I watched as the brothers tried to administer the medicine. Our captive wriggled hard, but through a mixture of encouragement and gentle coercion—and helped by Black Tree's reassurances they were not poisoning him—they succeeded in getting a low dosage of tablets down James's throat.

Minutes later a different man sat before us, his breathing peaceful as he chewed at a hunk of bread, his eyes fixed on the ground at our feet.

I sat cross-legged a few metres opposite James, with the Dog and Black Tree either side of me. Finally—the interview I'd been waiting for.

'You must wonder why we brought you here,' I said. 'We've made you suffer, and for this we're sorry. But we don't want to hurt you. We're looking for information about the Supervisors and need your help.'

James glanced at me and dropped his gaze again.

'We believe you may have had contact with Supervisors before or after your operation,' I continued.

James readied his facial muscles to speak. 'I'm alive.'

'You are.' I wasn't sure how else to respond.

'I'm still on a mountain.'

'Yes. You've survived without connectivity.'

'Did I kill someone, or was that a dream?'

Sadness welled up in me; no words came.

'It wasn't a dream,' Black Tree said, 'you were trying to protect yourself. Let's not think about that now. Ben, repeat your question.'

I took a deep breath. 'Have you ever had any dealings with anyone who might have been a Supervisor, or with someone who worked for one?'

'I'd like to help you, but I don't know a thing about the Supervisors. If one of them was involved in my operation, I'd have no way of knowing. I was certainly surrounded by doctors, scientists—a lot of specialists.'

'Then why did you thank the Supervisors in your interview?' I asked.

'Well, the first thing that happened when I woke up after my treatment was I got a message from them saying, "Congratulations"—nothing more. Everyone knows they funded the operation.'

'Do you believe they did?' I was fumbling.

'Have you seen the news about our eyes? Every day it's like, "Fresh Eyes are at the bleeding edge of S&T." If Supervisors are powerful like we all think, isn't it obvious they are involved somewhere along the line?'

'*Our* eyes?' I asked. 'So you're not the only person with these devices?'

'Oh no, I'm just a recent addition. There are hundreds of us. Most of the others are agents of Megacity Law Enforcement.

And there was another confirmation.

'I'm only used for the media as the poster boy for Fresh Eyes,' James went on. 'I show everyone how amazing they are.'

'How do you know most of the others are agents?' I asked.

'I'm alerted whenever one of them is near me.'

'Who's your immediate boss?' the Dog asked.

'Boss? Well, I don't know really. I just follow the prompts and messages. I don't even understand how I became who I am. I'm just a public face—a celebrity who hasn't done anything to become one. I actually hate being famous, but I suppose I give people hope that they too might one day get treated, right?'

'Why should I believe you're being completely honest with us?' the Dog asked.

'Why not believe me? What have I got to lose? You'll probably kill me either way.'

I was about to assure him we weren't, when Black Tree elbowed my ribs.

'Not necessarily,' the Dog said.

'You looked like you were coming down off the biggest high last night and this morning,' Black Tree said, changing the topic.

'It was horrific. I'm always plugged in—connected. When I'm plugged in, I feel secure. Everything makes sense. Sometimes it's fun, like a game. You disconnected me. Of course I was a mess.'

'How is it like a game?' I asked.

'When you complete a task, you get another one. I must get easy tasks compared to the agents, like doing an interview and giving the answers I'm fed. Anyway, I don't have a choice. I just obey. You get a lot of rewards for obeying. And it makes everything easy as you always know what you have to say next or do next.'

'I'm glad you're talking normally to us at last,' I said, in a bid to put him further at ease. 'Are you sure you can't tell us anything at all about the Supervisors?'

'I'm afraid not. What do you want to find out about them?' James tilted his head to one side as if he was now the interviewer.

'Anything,' I replied. 'Anything about who or where they could be. That's assuming they exist.'

James nodded slowly. 'I'm pretty sure they do.'

'This guy wants to start a revolution,' the Dog said, pointing at me.

'I just think it's high time there's a conversation between rulers and subjects,' I explained.

'I don't think I understand. But I wish you good luck. If it was Supervisors who forced me into the operation—'

'Forced you?' I interrupted.

'Of course. I was taken. I'm told I was chosen, and that's what everyone thinks. But I had to give up my former life, which I can't remember, however hard I try. But, as the motto goes, life has never been better. Apart from the media and the fame.'

The four brothers and I looked at each other.

'Media, lies—that's exactly why we leave Megacity,' the Dog said. 'We stick with the life of the underworld.'

I took the Dog and Black Tree aside and said, 'So they're forcing people into it. But he knows nothing. We've kidnapped the wrong guy.'

'We should have taken one of the people who organised the operation instead,' the Dog said. 'We'd get a lot more than James can give.'

I wanted to tear my hair out—I wasn't sure I'd be able to live if the operation was all for nothing. And River's death had to count for something.

Black Tree sighed. 'At least James is honest. Normally there's a lot of torture involved, but you can tell it wouldn't work with him. Anyway, don't give up yet. Keep asking questions.'

I went back to James and asked him if he remembered anything about any other men being operated on?'

'I never saw any of them,' came the reply.

'Can't you give me something useful?' James surely heard my desperation.

'I've told you what I know,' he said. 'I'm sorry I'm not more useful. Now can I ask you something? Am I going to live? If I am, can we leave this mountain now?'

'Your time up here has just begun,' the Dog said. 'We can't let you go until we know we can trust you not to talk. Ahong and Aqiang here are going to build a log cabin and live with you for a while.'

This was the first I'd heard of the Dog's cabin idea.

James whispered something, his eyes half-closed.

'What?' I asked.

'Hualien.' James said.

'Meaning?' I moved closer.

'It's a place,' Black Tree whispered.

'I don't know it,' James said, 'but it's a name doctors said sometimes. I was unconscious most of the time, but when I wasn't I often heard Hualien this, Hualien that. They also kept saying "failed specimens". "The failed specimens of Hualien."'

'Where's Hualien?' I asked, looking at the others.

'Oh, lovely Hualien! We know it well,' the Dog said, as we wandered away from James. 'Ask a citizen, though, and you'll find they don't have a clue.'

'It's an old East Coast city,' Black Tree added. 'We've stayed there a few times when we were on the run. The mountains on that side of Taiwan are so close to the sea that Megacity couldn't be bothered to turn Hualien into a district and left it to rot.'

'How do we get there?' I asked.

37

The freshness and juiciness of the apples and pears reminded me of the peach Yayuung had given me.

Big Dog and I had reached the end of day four of a crushing seven-day trek to Hualien. Walking and clambering all day on mountainous terrain was far tougher than my original journey out of Megacity with Hendrik. We were following what remained of the overgrown Central Cross-Island Highway that had once been hewn into some of the island's highest mountains to connect the two sides of Taiwan. Black Tree had gone down to break the news to Clear River's family, and we'd left Ahong and Aqiang to build a hut for James on the mountain.

Part of me felt I should go to see the family too, but it made sense for me to make this trip.

We were resting by our tent on Pear Mountain, where fruit still grew in abundance despite the absence of farmers. We sipped at tea brewed from tealeaves we'd picked on the mountainside. Something about the landscape was changing how I felt about my place on this planet. Thickly forested slopes alternated with grassy expanses. Clear mountain peaks wreathed in sunlight could shift into rocky panoramas partially shrouded by clouds in mysteries; I ached to spend years exploring this rugged kingdom close to the sky.

If only I'd known earlier that such landscapes still existed. Even with the frequent and dangerous detours we had to take due to destruction of the highway—by earthquakes, landslides and just plain neglect—these heights showed me a freedom I'd never felt.

'I see why you love Taiwan,' I said.

Big Dog grunted.

On the seventh day, we plunged down Mount Hehuan. Big Dog identified a smell of sulphur, and we traced it to a hot spring. We soaked our shattered bodies till we were dizzy with heat, then continued on into a deep gorge. As we pushed further into the squeeze of the ravine, vast grey cliff faces as high as the mountains we'd just left soared up on either side, leaving just enough space at their bases for a river and the traces of a road now strewn with boulders.

It took us five hours to reach the mouth of the gorge where the highway ended, and a few more to arrive at the edge of the city of Hualien, where sea smells welcomed us. Cricket chirps and seagull cries were the only noises here. Plants had sprung up between cracks in the asphalt, and the overgrown buildings, tiny compared with their Megacity counterparts, appeared lost yet beautiful in the evening sun.

'That's where we're spending the night,' the Dog said. He was pointing at the remains of a 7-Eleven convenience store, its glass long gone, but the roof still whole.

'So, what's the plan?' the Dog asked, as we gathered anything flammable we could get our hands on and flung it onto a pile outside the store for our evening fire.

The question brought everything back. My heart beat faster,

the sun was an irritation and the creepers on the walls throttled my enjoyment of arriving at the city. Below all this, though, I noted the real source of my aggravation: the burden of being the one who had to make all the difficult decisions.

But this was all my doing; I had to make the decisions now.

The Dog was still waiting for an answer.

'Let's get a good night's sleep,' I said. 'In the morning we can start by exploring the centre.'

'Sure. I've never seen anything interesting here, though,' he said.

'Brilliant.'

'What do you mean, "brilliant"?' the Dog asked.

'It's called sarcasm.'

'What is?'

'Nothing.'

In the morning I set off to cover the streets north of Jianguo Road, while the Dog went south. Hualien was a compact city, and we hoped to scan most of the centre by mid-afternoon.

Shattered and barely able to move my legs after our endless hike, I stopped by a building still sporting a curvy, yellow M. Beyond the nebulous goal of finding something out about 'failed specimens of Hualien', I had nothing to go on, and my motivation was rapidly expiring. The 'mission' didn't make sense anymore, and I couldn't imagine anything more ridiculous than hunting around in an abandoned city, interesting though it might be.

Even so, it was nice to know I wasn't alone; just a few streets away the Dog was hunting too.

Our searches collided shortly after three o'clock, assuming the time on our smartphones was correct. We exchanged a half-hearted smile. No need to tell each other our searches had been fruitless.

We devoured a late lunch of fruit from Pear Mountain and vacuum-packed tofu, neither of us talking about whether to continue labouring up and down streets afterwards.

The air smelled different, surely due to the sea.

'This might sound stupid,' I said, 'but is seawater toxic?'

'Yes.'

'So our education *was* right about one thing.'

'Of course it's not toxic. Idiot.' The Dog laughed. 'Bit polluted, but it won't kill you. Brother, you've got a lot to learn.'

Excitement—I hadn't lost that feeling.

'Can we go to the beach? I've never been to the sea.'

'Come on.'

Waves thundered towards the pebbled shore, and a light spray spread saltiness through the air.

'Are you sure it's safe?' I asked.

'Safer than Megacity,' answered the Dog, removing his shoes.

Surrendering my fear to the sun and the churning waves, I kicked off my shoes before doubt could creep back in and tiptoed after the Dog into the sparkling shallows.

The temperature was mild, and I felt more alive than ever.

I paddled along the beach, kicking my toes into the water, while my companion stood smoking behind me. Hypnotised by the horizon, I struggled to compute how there was nothing to block my view of the boundless blue ocean. You could see further than from the tallest skyscrapers of Megacity.

After a couple of minutes, a strange stench hit my nostrils. I turned to face the shore and saw the mountains veer up behind the narrow strip of city. Rising from grey to black in the upper reaches, their summits were smothered by dark purple haze that suggested a brutal storm was on its way. Clouds swirled about the sun ready to throttle the afternoon, but the golden light still lit up the ground ahead, lasting just long enough for me to see what lay at the top of the beach.

I called to Big Dog.

As I squinted, it dawned on me what I was seeing.

It was then that I realised the search was over.

It was a pit the size of a tennis court, filled with human remains.

Hundreds of them.

The bottom layers of the pit were skeletons or largely decomposed bodies. The top layer was more troubling; here bodies, both male and female, had clearly been added more recently.

Something was wrong with the corpses. Although they were intact and mostly dressed, their faces had been tampered with.

Where their eyes should have been were deep holes, staring out at the cosmos, home only to flies, coming and going.

'Failed specimens,' the Dog said.

Sacrifices in the great stampede to develop Fresh Eyes?

With our noses in our sleeves—a vain attempt to mitigate the unbearable smell—we edged around the pit too stunned to speak, the waves continuing to thunder. For a moment, I almost believed we were the only survivors of an apocalypse.

'And all for research,' I said at last.

The Dog coughed as he crouched by one of the bodies at the edge of the pit. Images of dragons and prowling tigers still clung to its tanned arms. I remembered Jinlong's and Black Tree's references to members of the underworld going missing.

'Did you know him?' I asked.

'No, but I reckon a good number of brothers I've worked

with or fought are here somewhere. I've got to tell Black Tree …'

Something whistled towards us. The Dog fell forward onto the tattooed corpse. There was a tiny mark on the back of his head.

Another whistling sound shot past me.

I spun round, saw white fabric.

Punches to my jaw and stomach.

My attackers pinned me down. I strained to see who they were. Two men and a woman. Dressed in the same white uniform as the paramedics coming out of Bar 75.

One of the men shoved a needle into my forearm.

I stopped thinking and forgot pain, as my mind was sucked away.

38

The hardest thing of all was to stay focused on any single thought.

Who were they, the owners of these voices?

Where was this?

Why couldn't I open my eyes?

A memory of bodies in a pit. Panic. I was lying there with them, slumped over the Dog. Were we supposed to be dead?

My head droned with a migraine.

I remembered punches. Nurses. A needle.

Clanking, rustling, whispers. Odours of medication. The sound of steps passing, neither close, nor far. Two people, maybe three. The footsteps becoming fainter now, echoing in a different space. A door closing. Just me, drifting off again.

I longed for the slightest control over my motor skills, so I could stretch, get up for a moment, take myself to a toilet.

I tried to open my eyes again and failed.

For a while it seemed like one endless day, until I sensed too much time had elapsed, and I'd been lying like this for several nights and days.

It could have been weeks.

Was this a coma?

I could only be in a hospital. How else could I explain the odours, bleeping machines, the clatter of trollies, groans echoing along corridors?

Often these brief internal awakenings; a momentary awareness of people in the room, watching me. The sentences they exchanged. Their shuffling out again. Leaving me doubting they'd been there at all.

One morning, I perceived light.

Through my eyelids at first.

I tried opening my eyes, and the lids slid up effortlessly.

Brightness quickly dispelled some of the drowsiness. I was lying on a bed in a large room. Two men in white were pottering about with their backs to me.

Focusing on the doctor nearest to me, I instantly knew he was one of the top ophthalmologists in the world, aged 47, no convictions, from Beijing, interested in music and wine, liked young female medics, risk factor 1/10.

How in Megacity did I know this?

I was about to examine a stream of data in my head on the layout of the hospital, when the other doctor looked over his shoulder at me and said, 'Doctor Wei, looks like somebody's woken up. Shall I deal with it?'

'Oh, yes please,' said the Beijing doctor.

The second doctor grabbed a syringe and rushed over to my bed.

'Wait, please,' I called out, 'Why am I in hospital? How long have I been here?'

He didn't even look at me.

The spell of the injection was swift, but left me a second to make the realisation. The strange sensation of my eyelids sliding down over a dry, cold surface told me everything.

These were not the eyes I'd been born with.

39

Parts of my mind and body were being edited. Memories blurred and faded. I began to see Ben Lee as little more than a character in an average show or game. Irrelevant.

For long periods I seemed to be empty of thought altogether, as though somebody had powered my mind down. I preferred these periods of oblivion. They rescued me from what remained of Ben's restlessness, his insanity, his fantastical belief in the countryside. If I grew too aware of my own thoughts, waves of panic rushed over me, as I endlessly repeated the question in my head:

Who am I?

During one such wave, I recalled an unpixellated episode of Ben's life. It involved a continuous expanse of trees at the bottom of a hill, a group of people singing and dancing around him in a forest, a woman with green eyes. My blood coursed through me, and I almost believed I could smell the forest. Then something or somebody was constricting my neck, though I couldn't say if that was only in my mind or some hospital procedure. Desperate for air, I screamed. At least I thought I was screaming.

My thought process snapped, and I blacked out.

With time, the panics and unhelpful memories subsided, and I tuned in to hope: education was happening to me through voices, images, music. My brain could read inputted text and analyse large quantities of data.

I learned that my former self had been suicidal because of the sadness, and I was being gifted a second chance at life. Somebody had kindly brought me to the safety of the hospital, so that one day I might stand again, a valued member of society. So I might know—this time with certainty—who I was and what my role in Megacity was.

And it was true: a new, more powerful self was so close I felt I could easily reach out and merge with it. But it was not yet fully matured.

The time needed to be right—the time of my rebirth.

I couldn't precisely say where these thoughts and feelings were coming from, but they induced a new experience for me: enjoyment.

Although I was just lying there, life had never been better—those words made more sense than ever.

40

Then one day, the wait was replaced by celebration.

How lucky I was to be getting better.

My rest had given me a fresh perspective on everything. And I found I knew endless details about whatever I turned my mind to, as though I'd been permitted access to a higher knowledge.

Finally, my hour had come. I was just becoming conscious after a period of blankness a little like sleep, when the rebirth began.

It was like my senses were doing morning exercises, training for engagement with the outside world. My thought processes were speeding up. It was departure time. I was walking along a corridor on a plush red carpet. My experiences were still all in my head and body at this stage, but they felt as real as if they were out there, so it made no difference.

Dance music launched; I drank in the bass infusions and cosmic synths, the high-decibel anthem releasing every pleasure, as my reconstituted self logged in to the life that was rightfully mine.

I heard the crimson curtains part, saw the neuro-melodic

techno flow, as my senses mashed everything up in one sexy feast of a show.

I stepped out onto a stage, giddy with pride. Left and right—women dressed by my fantasies, Bliss tablets at the ready; in front and below—a sea of distinguished guests who'd travelled so far to be here tonight.

For me alone.

I pointed at the crowds, yelled, 'Welcome everyone. You, and you, and you!'

I stepped onto a rainbow path unfurling through the middle of the standing multitudes, wild in their clapping as they worshipped their new hero: the handsome one. The newly born.

Tonight, I was their darling. Polished and toned. Primed for greatness they'd not known. A silky smile across my lips, catching the light just perfectly.

I raised my arms and tilted my head back into the victory pose. I jogged, then sprinted towards a doorway at the back of the cavernous hall, as the music surged into a synaptic climax: not long now till the drum roll would signal the great transition I was so utterly ready for.

I had to watch my step—wouldn't want to disappoint anyone. Not with all the work that had gone into me; the whole healing process science and technology had donated to me; the iridescent, all-consuming beauty of my life awaiting me.

Shards of white light blazed through the cracks of the doors ahead. I had only to … open my eyes. Unbelievable that the party I'd been at took place entirely behind closed eyes!

It was here now—the ultimate drum roll climax.

My anthem settled into a comfortable, motivating beat with soothing sopranos, before fading slightly.

Eyelids up, vision commencing …

THE CITIZEN

**Agent 2501 of Megacity Law Enforcement
Congratulations on your birth into
ANOTHER WORLD, our greatest upgrade
to Megacity yet.**

**Enjoy your life, enjoy your work!
Life has never been better.**

Your Supervisors

The words sparkled in my new eyeballs.

A buzz sputtered, and my vision flickered off and on.

The euphoric track became background music, and I heard traffic outside. I could play with sound and filter out the traffic, or sample and mix it with the music playing in my head.

The world became hi-res like you've never seen it. This was no hospital: I, Agent 2501, had been born into a studio apartment on the twelfth floor of a block in Gongguan, downtown Taipei. Information was now fed to me as I needed it or when I was curious. It was 18.01 degrees in the room. My heart had beat 70 times in the last 60 seconds. I walked into a 6.28-square-metre bathroom and stepped into a shower to celebrate my rebirth with a wash.

Standing at the toilet, I felt myself hardening in my hand. The long rest I'd been given had left me with throbbing currents of desire. I knew that on the seventh floor of the building, in a studio apartment identical to mine, Agent 322 was looking for a mate. We chatted as I climbed into a stretchy black outfit the wardrobe in the wall printed for me. She invited me down.

Agent 322 opened the door with a blank expression. She wore a loose dressing gown, untied, displaying the full front of her naked body. I kissed her at the doorway, and we embraced as though we already knew each other. We steered back and onto her bed in the middle of the room, kissing and wrestling until I was inside her. Lying on top of her, I gripped her upper arms from underneath and shifted them up towards her ears, staring into her Fresh Eyes of luminous turquoise.

Hearing my thoughts, 322 said, 'I'm into turquoise at the moment. Do you like it? Do you like me?'

We coalesced, playfully exchanging thoughts without speech. We knew where to touch and what sounds to make to please each other. And our breath flowed in unison. Little wonder it didn't take long till our bodies shuddered at the same moments, with the same rhythms.

We kissed again, our mouths exchanging miniature jewels —emerald, ruby, sapphire. Or so it seemed.

So much better than Bliss, I thought.

322 nodded her agreement.

New messages sparkled in the air:

**1 Lifetime Achievement Award for
sex with another agent.**

**Your first task is in four hours.
Reward upon completion.**

Feeling hungry I shot down the elevator to market level and wandered into the streets of Gongguan, pulsating with students from Taiwan University's physical campus. I added pop music and the visual effect of additional crowds so I felt like I was at a festival.

After ordering two portions of dumplings at an eatery my eyes had led me to, I scanned the profiles of the waiters and clientele. They were all risk factor 0/10, and just 11.5% of the customers currently had jobs.

Upon swallowing the last dumpling, I sensed an emotional hollowness hovering alongside the satisfaction of a full stomach. But automated gratitude for my rebirth was quickly triggered. I wondered why gratitude made you feel good, and received the knowledge that it triggered the neurotransmitters oxytocin, dopamine and serotonin.

Leaning back, I closed my eyes and abandoned the restaurant-goers of Gongguan, intoxicating myself with flights through exquisite cityscapes in Another World.

Half an hour later, traffic data from Taipei's metro system flowed seamlessly into my internal trip and brought it to a gentle close. I stood up, left the restaurant and walked out to the station. I was heading to Taoyuan, where my first task awaited.

1 Lifetime Achievement Award for surfing the neverending skies of ANOTHER WORLD.

In the metro station, nothing escaped me. A hundred and twelve ordinary citizens with low risk factors were currently arriving and leaving. As I zoomed out to Greater Taipei, they linked with the vastly dominant section of the population, represented as a great white cloud of innocence.

Once on the metro, I was horny again. I amused myself by analysing the sexual tastes and experiences of other passengers through scanning the centralised data from their lenses.

I alighted at Taoyuan, and a neuro-stimulating dance track nudged me into a run.

Sensing my legs stored more power, I pushed myself to go faster, only to discover pushing was unnecessary: I sprinted off at a speed that shattered the pace of an ordinary citizen.

My legs had clearly been edited alongside my eyes and brain. I laughed, exhilarated—my legs now seemed entirely mechanical.

People stopped. Stared. They were right to—the pavement

was not the place for me. Having overtaken a few buses and cars, I switched to the road to avoid hitting any pedestrians.

At one point I faced a steep incline, but I barely lost any speed. I rounded another bend, leaning into it like a motorbike racer, amazed I wasn't out of breath.

One pleasure after another, this agent life.

I was approaching the address of my targets: two Texan men with risk factors of 5/10. Skidding to a halt at the front door of their house, I banged it with my fist. A small glass window in the door cracked with the impact.

A red-faced Christopher Turner (46 years old), wearing only a pair of boxer shorts, opened the door, his eyebrows raised in surprise. I pushed past him into the livingspace where Jesus Rodriguez (48)—also in boxers, hair gelled back—sat on the sofa with a woman, Gao Liling (28), who tensed up and tugged a quilt over her naked torso when she saw me.

Jesus put his hands in the air and said, 'Hey, is everything OK?'

'Please,' Liling said, 'don't take me. I don't even know these guys.'

'I'm not after you,' I said.

'You!' I barked at the men. They froze. 'You are being charged with disturbing the social order of Megacity.'

'What? How come?' Christopher asked.

'You established a cult with the intention of deceiving citizens. You are now in the custody of Megacity Law Enforcement. Exit immediately.'

'Go home,' I said to Liling.

She snatched her clothes together.

I left the house amazed: I hadn't prepared any of the words that came out of my mouth. In the same way I had access to vast quantities of knowledge when I wanted it, the words just arrived, and I knew what to say.

Outside, the men were still in their underwear. An ambulance had arrived and two paramedics were getting out. I went on my way. After a short walk I looked over my shoulder. The paramedics were pinning the two men to the driveway, while the injections took effect.

I reported completion and watched as the story of the arrest popped up in the regional news.

A message arrived:

**First Task completed!
Proceed to claim your reward.**

As I jogged towards whatever reward awaited me, an undercurrent of anxiety brewed in my new agent mind. Questions about who I'd once been vied for attention. The only answer I got was, 'A mentally unsound citizen, who once attempted to sabotage all that Megacity holds dear.'

I arrived at an ordinary-looking house, and my eyes opened the door. A woman with pigtails sidled up, removed a red lollipop from her mouth and said, 'Welcome, 2501, we've been expecting you. Here—drink some water. Can I get you anything?'

'What have you got?'

'Depends what you need. We've got Passion Lifter or Oxytocin Cake if you want to have sex with someone here or in Another World. Or you can choose from Space Walk, Nanoshox, Cognishift, Black Out and Magic. Or you can just pop a couple o' regular Bliss pills. Of course, you're also welcome to just kick back and unlock your next level of flights and adventures.' She paused. 'I'm afraid you'll have to do the choosing.'

'What's Black Out? It's my first time here.'

'Oh, baby, really?' she said, taking my hand, 'Black Out's simple. You go straight to sleep. Dream-free. Cut off from any noise inside or outside your head. It's a great break for an agent.'

'I'll try it.'

The woman dipped her fingers into one of her handbag's many pockets and gave me a black pill. I followed her into the lounge, where ten male and eight female agents were collecting rewards. On a mattress in a corner, one woman was performing oral sex on another. In the middle of the room a tall man swayed with his arms in the air, eyelids drooping. Others lay slumped here and there, some with partners, some on their own.

As I made my way over to an empty recliner at the far end of the room, a woman tapped my wrist.

'Hey, we saw each other once,' she said. 'Outside Bar 75—but you won't remember. Don't worry, I haven't got a clue who I was either. Welcome to the club. It's hard work, but we get to have fun.' She grinned.

I smiled at her clueless, lay down and put the pill on my tongue.

41

Within weeks, I was making an average of three arrests a day.

Fun, fun, fun.

I was attending parties held half in Megacity, half in Another World, and my sex life blossomed endlessly. It was hard to believe I hadn't always been an agent.

One morning, I was winding my way through a maze of backstreets after arresting a rebellious student who'd hacked her way into a locked text about pre-Megacity governance models, when a rare smell coming from an art shop to my right stopped me. The door was open, and I wandered in. Alongside photographs of people at work and in their homes hung paintings by artHumans of night markets, the metro and popular shopping districts.

I went deeper into the shop, and the smell hit me harder. The back wall was adorned with scrolls of calligraphy. In the corner, an elderly woman was grinding something black on a stone to create ink, producing the pungent, nutty smell that had attracted me.

The tranquillity of her face ... the crisp clean sheet of white paper ... the first black stroke as the brush made contact ...

Memories as if out of nowhere.

An old man grinding an ink stick, smiling at me.

A calligraphy scroll hanging on a wall in a bedroom.

Mental snatches I couldn't piece together.

I had to avoid any such glitches to be effective as Agent 2501. But the interference grew.

A forest.

A woman called Fern.

All this crashing into my consciousness as if someone else's voice was interfering. Someone unknown.

Or someone once known.

Was I really an agent? What the hell was I doing in this job?

Stop controlling my thoughts, it said. I said. I didn't even know who was speaking.

And did anyone even ask if I wanted these eyes?

What have they done to my brain?

A strike to the back of my head.

I dropped to my knees and commanded my body to turn round.

There was only the empty shop.

An alarm screeched in my ears, and pain swept my body, forcing me onto my knees. The world flashed red, and a pulse of searing pain threatened to shatter my cranium.

Another red flash. Another pulse. A skull and cross bones appearing across the red, underlined by the words, 'DANGER! TRIGGERING SELF-DESTRUCT MODE'.

'Stop this!' I screamed, and the pain disappeared as quickly as it had arrived; the vibrations of a slow nuClassical track caressed my mind, restoring my system.

I could function again.

I got to my feet, apologised to the shopkeeper for the noise and rushed out of the shop.

42

It was 22:34 on the following evening. I'd stayed in control of my mind since yesterday afternoon and I couldn't even remember, with any clarity, the thoughts that had disturbed me so much.

An all-night party for agents awaited me, but first I had to complete a last-minute task at a teahouse in the Shida area only a short walk away.

I squeezed into a paisley shirt my wardrobe printed and descended into the streets. The buildings in the backstreets were dull, so I washed them in mauve, pink and purple. I nodded to a senior citizen I passed. I've got your back, I thought. Knowing I was keeping Megacity safe was the most gratifying part of my job.

A few blocks on, the streets were thick with cafes, restaurants and bars. I eavesdropped on a group of students in a bar through their lenses and earpieces. The usual debate about whether it was worth trying to find employment or if liberation outweighed the boredom of a work-free life. I smiled. Little did they know that in Another World, where they too might one day live, such debates were redundant. Here everything you did, whether for work or pleasure, was stimulating. Life truly had never been better once you levelled up from old Megacity to Another World.

As if on cue, a group of professionals I tuned in to at a neighbouring restaurant were discussing tech upgrades and when they'd be able to apply for Fresh Eyes. I wondered how it once felt to be one of them—a regular citizen without full enhancements, having to make occasional decisions oneself, forced to double-check a map or the weather from time to time without the seamless consciousness I now enjoyed. Or the uncertainty of what to say when flirting. As transhuman agents, our thoughts and actions were now taken care of, so we could focus on taking care of society's ills.

Our Supervisors were master planners. Thanks to them, tech had gone from being a powerful tool in everyday life to a new form of life itself. The ultimate evolutionary stride. And *I* was fortunate to be one of the prototypes of the machine-citizen class of tomorrow.

I replayed the words of an agent I danced with the night before. 'Once there was a field called artificial intelligence,' she said, massaging me wherever her fingers led her, 'as if natural intelligence were preferable to any other. We are living proof that artificial is the new natural.' She turned away to give me a sidelong glance. 'And the new sexy.'

So the only difference between me and ancient humans was our creators. Once it was down to DNA and nature with all its faults and slow progress; now we had the Supervisors—superior in every possible way.

But despite all this, I still didn't really know who Agent 2501 was. Yesterday had taught me not to dwell on such thoughts: anything was preferable to going into self-destruct mode again. But there was a hidden part of me that yearned for just that—a sense of self.

The teahouse I was being led to was ninety-eight metres

away. I dipped into the interior through the lenses of clientele. People sat on silk-like cushions on new-wood floorboards around low tables, sampling selections of teas. It was a well-reviewed establishment that attracted both local citizens and visitors from overseas.

Overseas … London. I stopped walking—the thought of that name seemed to come from the voice I'd heard yesterday that I could never again be allowed to listen to.

Back to the task. My targets—both risk factor 8/10—had been trying to evade the grid and had changed their names, but their images had been identified centrally through the unwitting viewpoints of other customers in the teashop.

Inside the establishment, the aromas of different teas intermingled. One of them I was sure I recognised—jasmine—which mystified me as I didn't recall ever drinking tea of any sort.

And there were the targets, a thin man and a woman with olive skin. They were laughing.

I approached their table. The man froze as I waited for the words of his arrest. They were taking longer than usual to enter my head, and I wondered whether I'd been despatched mistakenly.

'You,' I could finally say to the man, 'are being charged with 3,009 counts of espionage.'

I turned to the woman. Another delay in the words' arrival. Could she be innocent?

My connection dropped entirely. Maybe because unauthorised thoughts were zigzagging through my mind and interfering. Either way, as I stared at the couple, I had the strange sensation I'd met them before.

The man stood up and—to my horror—reached to embrace me.

'Ben!' he shouted. 'It's really you!' The target had tears in his eyes.

I pushed him away and shouted, 'Get off me.'

His face contorted.

'I am Agent 2501.'

'What the fuck, Ben?' the man said. He looked over my shoulder towards the door.

I stared at the two targets without blinking, and they shrank back at the sight of my beautiful eyes.

'I am no longer ...'

Even as I spoke, images ripped into my mind—drinks with this man in front of me, me in his apartment in London, the two of us getting on a plane together.

Normally I felt nothing during a task; now emotions were zooming through my system, confusing and weakening everything in me.

I focused on the woman, and my connection resumed at last. The words reached me and I spoke them: 'You are being charged with associating with this man, who is a threat to social order.'

'No, Ben!' the man said, shaking. 'You don't have to do this.'

He kept calling me Ben.

And part of me kept responding to it.

'You are now in the custody of Megacity Law Enforcement,' I forced myself to say. 'Exit immediately.' I stepped aside for them.

Whole seconds were going by, and they were just staring at me.

Why did I care?

And why weren't they leaving? Surely they knew there was no escape.

I detected a change in air pressure behind me as the paramedics opened the door. The couple saw their removal was imminent and cowered against a window behind the table. Customers were getting restless and leaving.

'I'm your friend, Max,' the man blurted.

Hearing that name unleashed a flood of emotion.

'You know me from London,' he continued. 'We came here together. This is Yayuung—'

'It's OK,' a voice barked behind me, 'we'll take it from here.' Two paramedics pushed past me, dart guns at the ready.

Something was off—we shouldn't be arresting these two. I wasn't sure I should be arresting anyone anymore.

I watched the paramedics lift the tranquilizer guns to shoot the couple right in the neck.

'No!' I yelled, charging forward.

Part of me wouldn't let this happen—part of me that I couldn't control.

I watched as my hands bashed the paramedics' skulls against each other twice. Then my right fist was punching one of their faces while my left elbow homed in on the other's temple.

Some vestige of who I'd been before was alive. In me.

My former self had pierced the fabric of Another World.

The knowledge of an entire life swarmed into my brain.

The paramedics were on the floor, blood pouring onto their white uniforms too quickly.

Before I could think of a next step, the red flashes of torture returned.

Self-destruct mode activated.

I had to become Agent 2501 again.

'Get in a taxi,' I managed to yell. 'Throw me in the boot so I don't attack you. Get as close to the mountains as you can.'

The searing pain of a million overstimulated nerves suddenly brought me to the floor.

I'm Agent 2501, I told myself over and over, attempting to halt the torture whilst accepting the punishment for my deranged thoughts and actions.

Through the pain, I reported task completion so Max and Yayuung wouldn't be pursued by another agent.

I knew my deviant mental activity would attract more agents and paramedics if I couldn't switch it off. I grabbed one of the unused syringes and stabbed my thigh before I was dragged out and piled into the boot.

As it took effect, I heaped gratitude upon gratitude for the privileges of Another World, convincing the system I was simply Agent 2501.

But I could no longer deny that I was who I once was—a man named Ben Lee.

43

I awoke in the boot of a car. Still sedated by the tranquilizer, the confusion over my identity had returned.

The car drew to a halt. 'Let me out!' I shouted, convinced I was an agent.

I heard the front doors open. A muffled voice said, 'A random place to stop—we must be near the edge of the grid.'

'Do you think it's safe to let him out?' a woman asked.

'I don't know. Ben, are you OK in there?'

I didn't reply. I still had grid contact and I didn't know who was in charge—2501, or me. I was unclear again who *me* was.

The boot slid open.

I bolted upright.

Immediately, I saw the two the targets from the teashop running up a steep incline.

I jumped out and broke into a run, hard techno thumping in my ears.

As I approached, warnings about leaving the grid flashed up before me.

I ignored them.

I soon neared the targets. I reached out to grab the man, but my legs suddenly dragged.

My night vision was replaced by a blurry darkness.

In an instant, the pounding music dropped away, replaced by silence—only to be filled with the sound of leaves rustling all around me.

My eyes barely saw a thing.

I'd lost contact with the grid.

Then—me.

Just … *Ben*.

Gradually, the memories of who I once was became accessible again: life in London, my grandfather, Lanh, Max, James Lin, the gangsters. Not just memories, but the knowledge and the many feelings and experiences linked with these people and places.

As I breathed in the cool mountain air, disbelief that I'd found the way back to my original mind blended with the deepest relief.

And yet, I could still remember everything about 2501. Ben ceased to exist when plugged into the grid, but now I was away from it, 2501 no longer had the upper hand—it was as if I'd subdued him.

I peered through the black air. 'Max,' I said hesitantly, 'are you there?'

'Yeah,' said a quivering voice. 'Can you stop chasing us, please? What have they done to you, Ben? You of all people—an agent?'

'I'm so glad you're here,' I said to Max. 'You stayed in Taiwan.'

'I couldn't leave you alone on this island. I knew you'd get yourself into trouble. It's in your DNA.'

'You're probably right.' I tried to smile, unsure if he could see.

'Do you want to find somewhere to rest?' Yayuung asked.

'I'd love that,' I replied. 'Let's climb a bit higher and deeper into the trees. But I'm going to need your help—I'm half blind. My mind feels like mush.' I told them what little I knew about my operation.

Max and Yayuung each took one of my hands.

'We might need food and drink if we're going to be up here for a while,' Max said.

'Don't worry,' said Yayuung. 'I can get you berries and the best leaves to eat. Insects too. And water shouldn't be a problem up here.'

After a short climb up a steep wooded slope, we sat on a fallen tree.

'I'm curious,' Yayuung said. 'If you were programmed to arrest us last night, how come you managed to override your instructions?'

'It was seeing you guys—that brought up so much I seemed to have forgotten. I can only assume that the rewiring of my brain didn't work. I mean, the operation was pretty thorough: I had no clue about my past most of the time. But some things triggered my mind into remembering stuff. Why the hell they sent me—I mean Agent 2501—to arrest you, I don't know. I want my own eyes back. I want sanity.'

'Met any Supervisors?' Max asked.

'No.' Memories of the Chens, Big Dog, Black Tree, Clear River and the kidnapping surged into my mind. 'But I've met a lot of other interesting people. I can put "gangster" on my CV now.' I filled them in on my adventures.

'It's amazing you succeeded in kidnapping James Lin,' Max said. 'I guessed it had something to do with you when he was reported as … you do know he was reported as having died from a stroke, right?'

'No, I didn't—interesting.'

'It's late,' Yayuung said. 'Shall we make ourselves comfortable for the night? Don't worry, Max, I'll keep you warm.'

We found an almost flat bit of ground and lay down, Yayuung and I either side of Max.

'Were you two living together in Taipei before tonight?' I asked.

'We've had to move a lot,' Yayuung replied, 'but yes, we were always together.'

'I'm glad you've found each other,' I said. 'And I'm sorry you're both on the run because of me.'

'I was angry when Max told me your plan,' she said. 'I wouldn't have let you stay with my family if I knew what you were planning.'

'I'm sorry.'

'But thanks to you,' Yayuung continued, 'Max decided to quit his job and stay in Taiwan for longer. So I am happy, even though you guys have messed up my life.' She laughed.

'I'm sorry, honey,' Max said. 'I thought we'd be safe. I've been encrypting all our movements and communications, but we all know other people's lenses are the real killers, and disguises only work for so long. Do you know why they're after us, Ben?'

'It has to be the history we share. You'll have been identified as high risk because of our connection. They must know I was behind James's disappearance, although I think I might have been monitored for way longer than that. Again, I'm really sorry things have ended up like this for you guys. I made sure last night that 2501 reported your arrests as completed, so you stand a slim chance of being safe in the grid if you can somehow forge new identities. You'd be a lot safer up here, though.'

'Easy for you to say,' Max responded with a note of tension. 'The mountains are not exactly my dream home.' He paused. 'I'm sorry, I—'

'No, it's OK,' I said. 'You should be angry. You had no idea any of this was coming when we left London.'

An awkward silence.

'Well, we're here now,' Yayuung said.

'So what's it like having the eyes?' Max asked.

'You wouldn't believe what this place called Another World is like. It controls your experiences more than the most hallucinogenic substance you can imagine. None of the immersion games come close. It's hard to believe it's not a physical reality. It's a total mind bend.'

We exchanged a few more words through the chilly air and wished each other goodnight.

'What's that constant noise?' Max asked.

'Trees moving in the wind,' Yayuung replied. 'Don't worry, little boy.'

My head droned from the searing pains I'd been meted out over the last two days, making the message from my puppet masters obvious: as long as you behaved yourself in Another World, you were granted unlimited pleasure. As soon as you tried to re-enter reality, though, pain and death were your welcome.

44

Would there ever be a place for me again in this world, either as Ben or Agent 2501? That was the question that engulfed me after a cold and sleepless night.

The mountainside was black and grey, the sky white, and Max and Yayuung a mixture of these three colours. Edges were blurred.

'I can't see colour off-grid,' I said. I rubbed my eyes a lot harder than I would have if they were the originals, and I hardly felt a thing. Quietly, I mourned the loss of my natural vision.

'I'm surprised you can see anything at all,' Max said.

'It could be a low-power survival mode to help agents who accidentally stray off course,' Yayuung suggested. 'You've probably got some organic materials bundled in there too, helping you to at least be able to see something.'

Breakfast consisted of water from a nearby stream and various species of leaf placed on top of each other, which Yayuung called 'forest sandwich'. She'd found a large flat stone she used as a platter for berries and a few protein-rich insects I was glad I couldn't see well and that Max refused to touch.

'I feel terrible,' I said. 'What if I killed those paramedics last night?'

'Whatever happened,' Yayuung said, 'overall, you've done the world a favour—the service they think they're doing is a joke.'

I wasn't convinced. 'I've gone from being a kidnapper to a murderer.'

What could they say? It was the truth.

'I wonder if your eyes could help us trace who's running the ship,' Max said, as Yayuung and I finished eating.

'Too bad you haven't got any equipment with you,' I replied, secretly relieved.

'Well, you might be wrong there. I've got these. Your agent self didn't confiscate them last night.' Max had reached into a jacket pocket and pulled out a collection of devices I'd forgotten we brought to Taiwan—a rolled up screen, a fully charged battery and a tiny remote access hub.

'I carry these everywhere now,' Max said. 'They've come in handy twice already. We had to go off-grid a couple of times in the last few weeks as you can imagine.'

I put my arm around Max. 'You're a genius.'

'The first step is to go down to an altitude where you connect and become Agent 2501,' he said.

'That's high-risk,' I said, nauseous at the idea of coming into contact with anything Megacity ever again. 'My disappearance from the grid won't have gone unnoticed. I know I can't stay up here forever, but Agent 2501 could be killed pretty quickly if I go down. He could also have been re-programmed to self-destruct on awakening, which would no doubt take me—Ben—with him. Or he could be set to kill anything in sight—you do realise how dangerous this is for you as well?'

'Yes, it's high-risk for all of us, but have you got anything better?' Max responded. 'Anyway, we didn't see anyone tailing the taxi last night, despite the fact you attacked two paramedics. It's possible your agent personality is still innocent, especially if Yayuung and I have been registered as dealt with like you say we have.'

'I'd love to believe that, but I've left evidence everywhere, right?'

'Why don't we try to go just low enough for you to get the first sign of reception?' Yayuung suggested. 'Any messages you get will probably confirm whether your time as an agent is up. We can then decide on our next step. You can come back up out of range the first second you have a sense of the situation, and we can go further into the mountains if that seems wisest.'

I lay down. All the motivation that had once driven me had ebbed away. 'I'm done with trying to find any asshole Supervisors who might be out there. Just let them be.'

'I'll admit these mountains are growing on me,' Max said, 'but we'd quickly get restless if we tried to survive too long up here—except for you, Yayuung.'

I yawned. 'I'm quite happy here.'

'Don't give me that.' Max kicked my foot. 'You always need some crazy goal to pursue. Use the time we've got wisely. There may be a way for you to re-enter the city. Now you've got your memory back, you might still be able to find something. Why give up on the reason we came to Taiwan?'

Max really had changed. His boldness reminded me of how I'd been before the trauma of the kidnap. My blood pulsed faster as I digested his words.

'I guess you're right,' I eventually said. 'But every damn step we take now has to be radical—even with our almost nonexistent power. Anyway, after that horrible operation, I feel like I've already died once. Fuck it, I'll die again if I have to.'

I wasn't sure if I could trust my dodgy vision, but I thought I could make out liquid in Max's eyes. 'You're freaking me out —you don't cry,' I said, my own emotions rising.

'Actually, I cry all the time these days, don't I, honey?' Max pecked Yayuung's cheek.

'Just so you're not surprised, I might be on the ground with spasms soon if I get reception,' I said, taking tiny steps downhill and feeling like an invalid between bouts of suffering. 'The parts of my brain that feel pain appear to have been hacked, so they can be used against me whenever I have independent thoughts.'

'If you feel any pain, come straight back up,' Yayuung called. She was going to wait out of range for her own safety, while Max and I edged down the mountainside.

We skidded down a stretch of scree. Here and there I made out an alpine flower in some variety of grey.

'What if 2501 forces me to beat the hell out of you?' I asked.

'Don't worry about me,' Max said. 'I can always run up to Yayuung. Anyway, you showed an ability to think for yourself a few times last night, even under the agent's influence. Who knows what's going to happen?'

'Promise me you'll keep looking at me?' I said, 'That's how I recognised you last night.'

'No, we've got to look away from each other,' Max replied. 'If you come online, your eyes will be filming everything. I don't want Law Enforcement knowing we're still on the run if they don't already.'

A little lower down I made intermittent connections to Another World. 'It's happening,' I said. 'Ben Lee checking out …'

I held my breath.

Agent 2501 felt good—as if I'd stepped into a body of armour and was prepared for any task. Ready to be put to use.

Where are you, 2501? We've missed you.

**Your next task is in 5 hours.
Double reward upon completion.**

'Can you still think as Ben?' I heard a voice ask.

'What are you talking about?' I said, glaring at a thin man I'd never seen. He was looking away from me.

'You're Ben Lee. Think about the countryside. You're in it now,' the person said.

'I am Agent 2501. You should know we are cleansed of the countryside.'

'Somewhere in your mind you know it exists. Remember the forest you found. Outside London. Remember Fern?'

I took a step towards him, and to my surprise he ran uphill. I followed him higher but quickly realised I was losing connection to the grid. Going any further could bring me into contact with lethal contaminants of this strange toxic zone. Countryside indeed!

The lunatic was shouting all manner of nonsense, such as 'Look, it's all around you,' 'Look at the trees,' 'These mountains are safe.' He was gesticulating at the slope behind him, and it struck me I was unable to link the word 'trees' with the strange, upright objects I was seeing for the first time.

Maybe the man should die, I thought.

Or maybe not.

Maybe the upright things really were ... trees.

My jaw fell open. The rustling of little flappy scraps on the upright tree things seemed to coincide with a gentle commotion of thoughts somewhere on the fringes of my cognitive workings.

The deeply implanted myths stuttered, as it dawned on me I was Ben.

Ben Lee *and* 2501.

Because—weirdly—with every passing second it became easier to be Ben, whilst seeing the world through the agent's eyes if I chose. I waited a couple of minutes to see what might happen.

Had the spell been broken?

There was no torture, but I was able to think as freely as if I'd never been 2501. The agent's experience of the world was available to me, but I could dim the intensity of it at will, or even shut it off completely.

Equally, I could be in 2501's mindset, but still be aware of Ben's identity hovering close by. As 2501, I could see, for example, that if I went higher up the mountain, I'd have to push beyond a final warning that I was entering a zone where my life would be under threat and my skills as an agent would cease to function.

And thank goodness for that.

I clambered out of range of the grid and—fully Ben Lee again—looked up to where Max had rejoined Yayuung. Although I couldn't see clearly with my bionic eyes off-grid, I sensed Max was shaking.

'I've been given another task,' I told them. 'The obvious likelihood is that it's a ploy to get me out of hiding. But if I risk going down and accepting the task, there's a small chance nobody will worry about me; then I'd still have access to Megacity, which could be useful. Anyway, I can hardly stay up here. They know I'm alive now and they'll have my location—I might as well get the hell down there before somebody or something comes to collect me. You need to move as well. Although 2501's pattern recognition didn't seem to work on you, they're likely to come for you if they picked up on your presence in my thoughts.'

'Let's face it—all our futures look pretty grim,' Max said. 'Were you getting the spasms again?'

'That's what's weird—nothing happened this time.' I tried to describe what it felt like to be able to slip between my two identities at will.

'Maybe I've rewired some of my neural pathways by challenging Another World and my agent identity. Is that possible?'

'Don't ask me,' Max said. 'This level of hybrid intelligence is beyond anything I've come across.'

The seconds of safety were running out; my heart ached for my two companions. 'Your safety is our main priority,' I said. 'Why don't you stay up here and keep moving south for a few days? If you descend onto the western plains of Megacity away from Central Taipei, you might be safe for a while. Just don't put any lenses in.'

'I can see you want to go, Ben, but we haven't run any tests yet,' Max said. 'I want to try hooking into your network via your brain when you're still inside Another World to see which direction any signals are coming from. We can be done in twenty minutes.'

'I can't believe you're more reckless than me,' I responded. 'Hanging out in my brain for twenty minutes while I'm connected to the grid is like playing with a bomb about to explode. They already know where I am.'

'Again, I'm just trying to move the situation forward,' Max said.

'Ben's right,' Yayuung said. 'It's one thing to dip in and out of the grid like you did just now. It's another to put Ben and us in that situation for a whole twenty minutes when drones are probably already heading our way.'

'OK, ten minutes,' Max tried.

'Five,' I said.

'I feel like we're in an old sci-fi movie,' Yayuung said, as we went a little way down the slope and I re-entered the vistas of Another World.

As before, all 2501's identity, thought processes and augmented perceptions were available to me, but I could detach—pain-free—from the hyperreality, so that I had the strange sensation of observing it all from afar.

'What in Megacity?' Max said, staring at his screen.

'What is it?' I responded.

'Those are brutal waves. Looks like your head has been turned into a powerful network node. You must have some heavy-duty gear running in your eyes and brain. I don't know how your mind isn't completely fried.'

'Thanks for the pep talk. Can you at least see where I'm being controlled from?'

'Most of your data seems to be coming from Taipei, although there's some from Hsinchu as well.'

'Can you see where in Taipei?' Yayuung asked.

'Wait a minute.' Max's tone had changed. 'There's another signal.'

'Is it something moving towards us?' I asked.

'I can't tell yet. But it's not coming from down there.'

I stood up. 'Drones?'

Max put his arm on my wrist. 'Chill out.'

I sat down slowly.

'The source doesn't look like it's moving,' he said. 'The signal is coming from deeper in the mountains. The bulk of information is still coming from Taipei and Hsinchu and moves a lot quicker—that could be the messages and constant updates about your environment that are streamed to your agent interface wherever you go.' Max paused. 'I've no idea what this other signal is, though. Seems to be coming from a place not too far away called Sun Moon Lake. Does your agent self experience any connection with the mountains in that direction or an area with a lake?'

'Connection with the mountains? 2501 knows only Megacity, remember? But yes, I can locate Sun Moon Lake. The agent's map says it's the most toxic area in Taiwan.'

I was beginning to sweat: I wanted us to get away from our spot. 'Can we hurry up?' I was also getting reminders about the task.

'Have you heard of Sun Moon Lake?' Max asked Yayuung.

'Of course. I don't reckon it's that dangerous, though' she said. 'Before the days of Megacity, it was a popular tourist destination. My grandparents always said that every romantic couple has to visit Sun Moon Lake. You know how the first thing you learn about in school geography is the areas that are too toxic for humans to ever visit again? Well, in Taiwan Sun Moon Lake is the one everyone remembers. I'm sure a few curious citizens have made the trip up there, but it's not something anyone would share with the world.'

'I'm speculating,' Max said, 'but whoever these guys at Sun Moon Lake are, they could be pretty important in your life right now.'

For the first time since I'd regained Ben, a deep anger that anyone had this level of control over my body rumbled in my gut. 'Forget about the task. I think I should go straight to Sun Moon Lake.'

Max and Yayuung exchanged glances and shook their heads.

'If some organisation or node is controlling agents from

there,' Max said, 'the defences throughout the area are going to be unreal. Don't even try it.'

'It could be my only chance,' I said, inwardly admitting defeat.

'I know it's a massive risk to go back down,' Yayuung said, 'but overall, it's surely safer to try and complete any tasks you get and stay connected to the city. The punishment for disobedience is big, especially if your job is to serve Megacity. If you continue down there as if nothing has changed, you might be lucky and survive. You may even think of a way to approach Sun Moon Lake between tasks. But you're going to have to tread carefully—I might be completely wrong. Anything can happen now.'

I was caught either way, but I was past arguing with them: they were knowledgeable and better-rested apparently than me, and at this stage I just wanted someone to tell me what to do.

45

There were no smiles as we prepared to part ways, not even fake ones that could have inspired a sliver of courage.

'You'll make sure we see you again, right?' Yayuung said.

The absurdity of even imagining that might happen.

'Why don't you get yourselves to the mountain where James Lin might still be held?' I suggested. 'The gangsters were building a shelter there when I left for Hualien. You could stay for as long as you wanted.'

'Like we can teleport to a random mountain,' Max said.

'Well, you could move around in the mountains for a couple of days to make sure your tracks are covered, then go down to Megacity and Head to Taichung District—to the southeast of Taichung, to be precise. Hey, give me the screen, I'll draw you a map of how to get to the mountain lane I drove up.'

'Way too convoluted,' Max said. 'You should go now.'

'But you'd be safe again off-grid,' I protested. 'And the gangsters can be quite nice.'

'That's kind of you,' Yayuung said, 'but we're with you on this now. It's too late to get our former lives back. You leave, and we'll make our way down before nightfall. We can do a lot more research when we're accessing the power of the grid. We've got Max's encryption skills—we'll be fine for a while.'

'Speaking of encryption,' Max said, 'once you're safe, contact me via Katie, Ben.'

'Who's Katie?' Yayuung frowned.

Max explained what I already knew. Once when we'd been high on Bliss, he'd created a synthetic identity for a fake citizen called Katie. She had a credible family tree, an address and all the legal documents needed to pass as a real citizen of Megacity.

I gathered myself and tried to inject some bravery into our collective despair: 'Right, I'm plunging into the shithole below. I intend to find out everything I can about Sun Moon Lake tonight, once 2501's task is completed.'

I looked at my friends standing arm in arm, desperately wishing they had the leisure to just enjoy the love they'd discovered in each other, and hating myself for ruining it for them.

We put our arms round each other's shoulders and stood there in a triangular hug, none of us willing to let go, aware only of the finality of this goodbye.

At some point, I managed to peel myself away. I clambered down without looking back, then hurtled towards Megacity, courtesy of 2501's augmented limbs and the neuro-stimulating dance track I knew from previous tasks.

46

As I walked along a pavement once more, I had difficulty comprehending why I hadn't been arrested. With every step I was expecting an invisiDrone, an agent, a bullet. At the very least, my agent self should have gone into self-destruct by now.

I was equally baffled by the fact I still had the freedom to hop between myself and 2501 without being punished. My brain seemed increasingly flexible in this regard, so that being both at the same time was beginning to feel natural.

But there was one crucial change to the agent part of me. Previously, as 2501, I'd been centrally controlled by the systems of the grid, with most of my decisions made for me and my every thought delivered to me. Now, the original me steered every decision and thought process, while my Fresh Eyes kept me embedded in the vast knowledge base I'd used since the operation.

In short, Agent 2501 was in service to Ben Lee.

Perhaps it was because I'd thought I'd not live to see the city again that I experienced a mild pleasure at being back. While not as slow-paced as where the Chens lived, Taichung

District was definitely quieter than northern Taipei. But a good number of people were wandering the streets, all looking a lot more relaxed than Londoners. Maybe this spot had everything I needed for me to live out my days if the ruling class could ever be toppled: the conveniences of a modern city, less traffic and indoor culture, the mountains so close by.

The mountains. If only I, Max and Yayuung had the wherewithal to drag ordinary citizens onto the lush slopes where freedom reigned. Maybe they would embrace their own lost landscapes within. Was that the approach to adopt in the fight against our captors, the Supervisors—enlightening one person at a time? It would certainly be a stupid one: the first sign of aberrant behaviour in anyone who listened to us would trigger our arrest.

I amplified Agent 2501 and ran. Soon I was sprinting to the dance track. People stared as I shot by, some capturing me on video, others jumping out of my way with the terror of being jolted out of their fixation on their lenses.

Being the centre of attention was actually quite fun. I reflected on the privileges of the agent's life—the rush of power over 'criminals', rides through Another World, getting high on the latest concoction, copious amounts of sex. It was hard to imagine a more seductive lifestyle.

But since returning to Ben again, since connecting with the trees and the mountain and with Max and Yayuung, it was equally hard to imagine a more meaningless existence than what working for Law Enforcement could offer.

Not that I had much of a choice.

Not that I knew anything about where my life was headed at this point.

There was my destination: the top floor of a thirty-story Dwellings on the corner of a wide crossroads four hundred metres away. Upping my pace again, I switched to the road, overtaking most of the ground-based vehicles. In one car, a boy's blank face followed me as I sailed past. I winked, and he waved, then I swerved in front of the car and jumped onto the pavement outside the store.

In the moments it took me to reach the elevator, I scanned the layout of the building, the store contents and the 773 customers currently there. The man I'd been sent to arrest was on the top floor.

Shooting skyward, I had the disconcerting realisation that something was different: I could sense the thoughts and feelings of the criminal I was about to arrest. I noted anticipation, aggression and a dash of arrogance in the target.

He was expecting me.

Another agent?

Panic set in, as I deduced the obvious.

It was too late—the elevator would not be stopped.

47

I stepped out on the thirtieth floor and turned right.

No time to consider next steps, to ponder what I saw.

A tower of a man facing me. Thick, tattooed arms crossed.

Agent 2501 gave me the lowdown: this was Agent 2480, formerly a gangster.

But I wasn't there to arrest him.

All I could do was stare at him—the man I'd known.

Big Dog.

I gulped. He'd been through the same treatment as me.

'Law Enforcement worried you'd be late for the task,' 2480 grunted. 'They didn't know where you were, so they sent me to do it. I completed it five minutes ago.'

No signs of recognition from 2480. Plus no incoming message that the task had been completed.

I didn't attempt to call the elevator—my connection to the store told me it was now locked.

'I assumed you were dead, Big Dog,' I said, wondering how many more seconds I had left to live.

'Not dead, 2501. Reformed. And don't call me that name—I don't know it, and I don't know you.'

I tilted my head. 'You don't have to arrest me. I know you're an agent now, but look at me. Listen to my voice. I'm Ben, your fellow gangster. We were friends with Black Tree.'

But seeing me didn't activate memory in the way seeing Max did with me.

He took a step forward and spewed the words as they came. 'You are being charged with first degree murder and with breaking the Agents' Code by (1) refusing to complete a task, (2) deliberately abetting the escape of citizens you were sent to arrest, (3) risking your personal safety by leaving the grid, and (4) endangering the social order.'

Agent 2480 was a whole lot more articulate than Big Dog.

I was about to remind him of the trek through the mountains, but the same huge fist I'd encountered when the Dog punished me after the kidnap thudded into my abdomen.

I lay on the floor spluttering, as the feet of screaming customers scuffled past.

The paramedics would be here any second.

I heaved myself onto one knee, turned and saw a large boot swing back, preparing to send me to oblivion.

I triggered the spring in my legs and exploded past 2480 as his foot struck forward.

Let the chase begin, I thought—the dance track's bass pumping my mind and body.

I hurtled past a blur of garments and handbags and glanced back. Why was 2480 just standing there and not pursuing me?

There were elevators all around, and hacking into the store's cameras, the bit of me that was 2501 saw paramedics and other agents shooting up to the thirtieth floor and more arriving on the ground floor.

I skidded onto an emergency exit that led to the roof and whizzed up two flights of stairs.

I flew onto the rooftop, which stretched out 150 metres ahead of me.

No traffic, no bends—the perfect racetrack.

Other agents reached the rooftop; I approached its end. The 3D map of my immediate environment informed me that beyond the edge up ahead lay another building at a lower altitude and separated from Dwellings by 16.5 metres, which I could negotiate thanks to my speed.

I turned and saw the collection of individuals huddled at the emergency exit, not even attempting to run. Had their legs not been treated?

Stun darts flew my way, but where were the bullets?

Why were they letting me get away? Wasn't this when renegade 2501 was switched off?

Save the questions, I thought.

I saw it—the possibility that I may yet be free a little longer.

The dance track crescendoed as I leapt.

I soared through space and landed on the other roof in perfect timing to the thumping bass drop. I was three metres below the top of Dwellings and out of sight. But I couldn't get into the building.

The agents would be alerting security beneath me.

I pounded the roof and veered right towards a third building the map told me was a low-staffed meat factory. This time I'd have to land ten metres lower down—higher risk, but did I have a choice?

I almost smiled as I remembered when Max found me reading about extreme sports in Dwellings.

I leapt.

Watched the rooftop rise to meet me.

I landed intact and forced myself to ignore the pain shooting through my lower spine.

Avoiding the elevators and the factory floor, I dived down the emergency staircase, jumping whole flights at a time, inhaling the stink of animals that had never seen daylight.

I reached ground level in under a minute, and before any

security had moved, I was coursing through the streets of Taichung in pure disbelief I'd not been shut down.

Slowing down was not an option, so I made for the only place I knew would allow me any sort of rest—the mountains.

Agents sent vehicles after me and towards me and tried to block my route, but thanks to 2501's supreme skill set, I outwitted them at every turn, outstripping vehicles and changing course in a split second.

No agent could match my pace. Again—why?

But my strongest weapon was the knowledge that just one kilometre away, slopes of silent and leafy hideouts awaited me.

And there it was: the start of the lane the brothers and I had driven James Lin up on that dreadful night.

Halfway up the ascent, 2501's connection dwindled, taking with it the dance track, the torrents of data and the power behind my momentum.

The sweat on my forehead cooled under the forest canopy, as I breathed in the fragrances of bark and leaves.

With all my adrenaline spent, I longed for sleep. Housing two identities in one body was exhausting.

Relief overwhelmed me: I'd made it home once more—to my new home, my real home. The endless seductions and saturated cityscapes of Another World were, for now, behind me.

48

The space felt hollow without Black Tree and the others. And having just met Agent 2480, I missed the Dog. This was where he and I had departed for Hulian from. I couldn't help wondering what might have happened if I *had* managed to bypass Agent 2480 and get through to the gangster beneath.

There was the tree he'd tied me to, and not far from it the tree where I'd interrogated James. To the right lay the bushes that led to the lookout rock.

I'd come so far—the travels and revelations, the torments, the changes, the full brutality of my life.

My gaze travelled up the mountainside that was a dull black and white now that I was off-grid. Through the trees about fifty metres ahead stood a hut. As I climbed towards it, I saw that it boasted a large wooden veranda and was bigger than I'd first thought—more chalet than hut.

Could Ahong or Aqiang still be guarding James?

The front door was ajar; I walked across the veranda and knocked.

A pleasant-faced man opened the door. Shaggy-haired and

unshaven, he looked as though he'd spent all his life up here, except for one giveaway feature: his eyes.

When he saw it was me, James pulled the door back a bit and hunched his shoulders. For a moment I thought he would start screaming again.

'Why have you come?' he asked. 'You *are* the man who kidnapped me, right?'

'Yes. Please don't worry. They got me after the trip to Hualien—made me an agent. But I am still Ben Lee. I'm sorry … for everything that has happened to you. I can't ever right that.'

A light breeze whispered as James processed whatever he had to.

'You haven't told me what you're doing here,' he said.

'I'm a rebel agent. I went against my directives. I've remembered who I used to be and everything I believed in.' I smiled. 'You must have remembered your former self by now, right?'

James hesitated. 'I'm afraid I don't understand. Former self? I just know I am James Lin. I was a citizen before my operation, but I see white when I try to think about it. I remember only after the operation. From the time of being a celebrity onwards.' He paused. 'Actually, I have to thank you for this life. It's much more peaceful than being a celebrity.'

Gratitude was the last thing I'd expected. 'So you're able to take care of yourself up here?'

'The operation took away old memories, but the knowledge for doing basic things is still there. I think it is human survival knowledge. The doctors didn't take it. The doctors—just like the news stories—said I used to be blind, but I don't remember it.'

'Do you think they might be lying?'

'I don't know how to doubt anything I was told. Ahong and Aqiang found footage of me in my original house. It shows me reading a book before the operation. They don't believe the doctors. I don't know who or what to believe. It doesn't change anything now.'

'Do Ahong or Aqiang live with you?'

'No. They say they can leave me because I am not addicted to Another World anymore. They know I prefer this to city life and won't try to escape.' James shook his head. 'I never want to face a journalist again. Ahong comes once a week to bring me food—packets of dried food and some tins. I don't have a fridge. Sometimes he brings me a takeaway. Last time he came with Aqiang, and they made me this veranda. Do you like it?'

'It's very grand.'

'I sit on it every evening. Sometimes one of them joins me, and we smoke cigarettes or weed and watch it get dark. Sometimes they bring beer. Do you want to come in?'

'Thank you.' I stepped over the threshold. 'Isn't this weird? I organised your kidnapping, and here you are welcoming me into your home.'

'It's nice to have company,' James said as he led me into his sparsely furnished cabin, containing a portable stove, a small table and two chairs, three piles of large cushions in place of a sofa, and a single mattress in the far right corner.

'Stay for supper. Stay the night on the cushions,' James said. 'I'm making instant noodles with boiled eggs.'

Darkness had descended by the time we rinsed the dishes at the edge of the veranda with bottled water.

'How can you remember who you were before?' James asked, as we went back in to light candles.

'I still haven't figured that out.'

'Would you like a beer?'

'There's nothing I'd like more.'

'Are the two of us still human?' James asked, sitting down at the table and handing me a lukewarm can.

'Good question,' I said, joining him. 'I feel like I am. Let's just say we are, shall we?'

'To being human,' James said.

'To being human.'

49

I awoke in the early light and stretched on the cushions. Worries about Max and Yayuung had kept me awake most of the night. The thought of any agent laying a finger on my friends filled me with fury.

Should I go back down and find a way to contact Max through Katie, the fake identity he'd forged, I wondered. I couldn't move in with James—sooner or later they'd come for me.

'Have you ever been to Sun Moon Lake?' I asked James, who was already shuffling about, rustling up some breakfast.

'I have not. Where is it?'

'Probably not too far from here.'

'I don't leave this patch of land. Also, I never learned names of places that aren't in Megacity. Sun Moon Lake—it sounds beautiful.'

'I'm sure it is. But my friends also reckon someone or something is running the agents and Another World from there. It could be one of the Supervisors. Of course, my friends may be completely wrong.'

'I don't know anything like that.'

'Well, I plan to go there and take a look. Do you mind if I rest here for the morning and leave this afternoon?

'Sure. So am I right that you want to go to this Sun Moon Lake alone? You want to find who or what controls agents? Maybe you are going crazy.'

'I must be. But I've also had enough of not knowing who governs Megacity. Why do we never see the Supervisors? We're supposed to be grateful for all they do for us, but it seems to me all they've really done is pack us into a city and brainwash us. Were the people who lived in the countryside before the Great Urbanisation ever asked if they wanted to leave? If they wanted every last detail of their lives to be controlled by technology? Of course not!' I stood up and flexed my muscles, pleased to feel my anger returning. 'I'm sorry, this must all sound like nonsense to you.'

'It's OK,' James replied, 'I like hearing you talk. I wish I could have interesting thoughts. I can't think many different things. Since coming up here, I am even forgetting things I knew when I was a celebrity. So I just try to enjoy the fresh air and the company of the trees. Please, keep talking.'

'I can't rest until I've exhausted every avenue I can. I've been on a long, strange path to get this far—I've suffered a lot. It was seeing you on the news, James, that led me to Taiwan. Somebody powerful had to be behind your operation. Now things have come full circle and I have the very devices in my own head that drew me out here. Bizarrely, I think having these eyes and this messed up brain may be getting me closer than I've ever been before.'

But James had gone back to preparing breakfast. He might have been just as interested if I'd been talking about the weather. The clutches of my old friend loneliness reached out to me.

'What's for breakfast,' I asked, once my frustration at not being heard subsided.

'Pancake. You can add chilli sauce if you want.'
'Great.' I tried not to be or sound sarcastic.

It came just as I swallowed my last bit of pancake—a knock on the hut door.

James jumped up, terror etched on his face.

'Could that be Ahong or Aqiang?' I asked.

'No. They came only recently.'

In full irrationality, I prayed it was Max and Yayuung.

'I'll go and see who it is,' James said, clearly trying to sound calm. 'Go and hide somewhere.'

Another knock—much louder.

'Let me get it,' I said in a bid to protect James.

I walked quickly over to the door and yanked it open.

Daylight streamed into the cabin, and a cold breeze encircled me. The sky was a harsh white through the thinning trees.

Ten men in camouflage clothing and two men in white stood in a semicircle that formed an arc around the front wall of the cabin.

How had they found me?

How had they managed to go off-grid?

Even if my legs worked up here, I wouldn't have got away.

I took five steps into the middle of the semicircle, as though sacrificing myself. Self-defence would be futile anyway—the men were armed.

Two soldiers stepped forward.

The first blow was no more painful than I'd expected. I was so prepared for it that I managed simply to observe the impact, pain and light-headedness.

Soon my body found the ground, kicked by a bunch of

agents who were blind to the redness that poured out of my nose and mouth.

The last words I was capable of taking in were, 'Don't kill him. Remember the task said to focus on the legs. That way he can't get away.'

And focus they did. Although my legs were barely human, I seemed to have nerves—real or artificial—that experienced pain with full honesty.

Witnessed by the clinical white sky, I succumbed to a blitz of boot work on my toes, ankles, shins and thighs, and gave in to the realisation that I would never walk again.

50

I figured out that my head lay in the direction I was travelling in, like the tip of an arrow.

My shredded mind seemed to nestle in the warm fog of some sort of medication.

No light crept through my blindfold; my arms were bound by my sides. It felt as if a hundred battles were being waged against the lower half of my body. A stench of disinfectant burned my nostrils.

Was I in the back of an ambulance?

The vehicle swerved back and forth between what I imagined were different lanes of a highway. It was clearly speeding, as it fulfilled the urgent task of delivering me.

Despite my attention on the agonies in my legs, I was able to note that the surface supporting my back was cushioned. I scratched an index finger across a few millimetres—velveteen?

A jolt threw my body forwards a few centimetres on the soft bedding, causing fresh pain to slice through my legs; it was only when I tried to move them that I realised they wouldn't cooperate. Panic rushed through me.

Then some of the fog shifted, and I remembered that my

legs as I knew them were gone. Turned into limp appendages that somehow still hung on the rest of me. With my fingers at my sides, I could have explored my thighs, but horror at the idea they might have been turned to mush prevented me.

Better to have something there than nothing, I told myself. It was a question of dignity. It dawned on me that everything I'd done since my first search across London had been in the name of dignity. My own, but also—in my view—that of my fellow citizens, though they would never know it. How much loneliness and heartache I'd made myself endure to defend my sense of dignity. All driven by a desire for truth and by what had seemed like a deranged wish to discover a bygone realm of green and prove it was not bygone at all.

And my wish had been fulfilled.

How stupid I'd been not to spend more time in the forest while I could—with Hendrik, with the community that had danced for me in those beautiful woodlands. And what was Fern doing at this moment? Had she remained with Duc or gone back to the forest she loved so much? Whatever her situation, I hoped she was happy. Max was my greatest loss. It hurt me not knowing what, if anything, had happened to the only person I'd ever felt loved and understood by.

Was this it?

Had the time really come to say farewell?

If I and the agent parts of my brain were not about to be terminated, I was surely going to be imprisoned and used for any number of experiments to further Another World.

Why torture myself thinking about it? Surely it was better to remain calm, now that I had no control over the outcome of my life.

But in seeking calm, I was only confronted with the failure of my mission. Did it really matter for society at large? I was a particle of dust: virtually no citizen knew about my searches, nor would they care if they did. Probably only a small handful had ever encountered the lost countryside as I had. For all I knew, most citizens were content to believe in the gifts of Megacity and the Supervisors and would hate to be 'enlightened' by my findings, though I still doubted they could ever be happy on a deeper level.

At least I wouldn't have to regret not following my dream of finding countryside when the time came to take my leave. And no-one could argue I hadn't thrown all I had at trying to unearth who our rulers were. My only regret was not beginning my searches earlier.

And yet ultimately, everything I'd discovered and attempted had been for nothing, beyond my own education. Megacity remained unchanged.

Had it been worth it? You want to have a positive impact on the world and end up getting kicked to a pulp.

Then there was the unbearable irony of my situation: by managing to leave Megacity and distancing myself from the technology that ruled life in the grid, I'd ended up with bleeding-edge equipment implanted in my body, my mind half-torn apart and reconstructed into something unrecognisable to me, some awful messenger of times to come. Unfortunately for 2501, I was also lumbered with an agent identity that would no longer have a role to play.

There was something healing about being able to reflect like this. My natural tendency to reflect on my life and everything I saw was, after all, the only kind of real freedom I'd found in this life. A freedom that human beings, as a species, seemed to have lost somewhere along the way.

The vehicle hit a bump, and I squirmed in pain, wondering if my legs would detach.

A chasm of loneliness opened beneath me, waiting only for the gravity of time to suck my mind, identity, body and all I'd stood for into its depths. Apart from the billions of traces I'd leave behind in the virtual spaces of the grid and Another

World, I'd only live on in the memories of a small handful of people: Max and Yayuung if they were alive; the Chens; Black Tree, if he hadn't been turned into an agent; James Lin maybe; Duc, Hendrik and Fern; perhaps a few one-night stands.

I was sure the darkness behind my blindfold thickened, as though I was being covered by the hands of a nameless person who'd just joined me for the ride and was kneeling over me, whispering, 'We're at the end. Your time's up.'

The van slowed. The swerving was replaced with a gentle, more rhythmical swing, this way, then that. I drifted into a space where thoughts were recast as dreams I was conscious of having. In moments of wakefulness between the dreams, I realised I couldn't remember the last time I'd dreamed, and it was a comfort to know my ability to imagine had not been destroyed.

I was walking in a woodland with my grandfather, sunlight falling on our shoulders through gaps in the trees, the sound of water flowing nearby.

'Congratulations,' he said. 'You understood the messages I gave you. Please know that it was too risky for me to speak to you openly about the things you now understand. You've come far, and I am proud of what you've achieved.'

We neared the stream I'd always imagined he'd played in when he was young. 'You live in a troubling time I'm glad I never got to see,' he continued. 'But you've listened to your natural instincts and found the courage to remove the obstacles that held you captive in Megacity. You've learned to read a map of the world that the masses cannot see. What more could you have asked for?'

The vehicle stopped, then went on, and I emerged from my dream into the darkness. I was strangely invigorated by the words of my ancestor. I brought to mind Lanh's gentle smile, then the eyes of the dancers who'd welcomed me into the forest. And I didn't know if it was my own imagination or a hallucination from the painkillers I'd been given, but I could distinctly hear the pounding drums returning—the sound I'd followed through the trees, stunned by the unspeakably fresh air, the calming coolness and the fragrance of morning dew on twigs and leaves. That same hidden yet beckoning beat, echoing my heart, piquing my curiosity even as my fear levels soared.

In this reliving, the drums promised a new start.

But how could I be thinking so positively in such a desperate moment? Well, it was at last possible to make peace with myself: dreams had been dreamed; hopes had been had; and a victory had been achieved, if only in the tiniest of ways.

The discoveries I and the forest dwellers had made were testimony to the human capacity to make free choices in the face of extreme danger, and even to rebel. Through the actions I'd taken, I sent a message to the powers in charge, letting them know that they might not be able to enjoy the status quo forever. Maybe what I myself had failed to achieve would one day be attempted by the forest community after all. And if they didn't have the courage, others elsewhere would discover their capacity to question. Someone, somewhere would continue the work I'd begun. Maybe they'd already started.

Then one day, the great veil of ignorance that clung to the citizens would be torn away.

I was now ready to face whatever came next.

51

The van came to a halt, and the engine stopped. The drum beat retreated to the edges of my consciousness.

Steps approached.

Voices.

I focused on the rhythm of the imaginary drum beat that had been so much louder moments before, trying to remain in the contemplative state I'd reached. If this was my time to leave, it was vital I carried indelible thoughts of hope. So that regardless if I was executed, or my mind was dissected again, I could surrender all despair without effort. By then, fragments of hope would have formed indestructible neural pathways, and the electrochemical activity of my brain would leave behind some sort of pattern at the subatomic level. Never mind the science behind my reasoning—I simply knew my hopes for the world after Ben Lee had to have some purpose or impact.

And if that was the belief I left this world with, then so be it.

A lock clicked, and the door at my feet swung open.

THE CITIZEN

My blindfold was removed. In the shadows of a black world, I made out six standing figures. A filling moon traced silvery sheens on their outlines. The cool air carried fragrances of an alternative life I'd come to know well, though I'd never had the chance to learn the names of the many native trees no doubt present.

Up here, Megacity was no more than a memory.

They scooped me off my cushioning, and the pain in my legs and hips cried out. My body had warmed up during the journey, and the cool air swept up my back as they lowered me into a wheelchair.

They wheeled me over an uneven surface without a word. Explanations were hardly necessary at this stage. For them, it was a case of seeing things through; for me, it was a matter of getting closer to my sweet release.

We continued along a path for a few minutes. The trees to the right cleared, and I realised we were on a hill overlooking a huge lake. A white line of reflected moon stretched towards me from the middle of it. Apart from my brief paddle on the beach in Hualien, I'd not seen a body of water this size. I was sure it would once have been perceived as beautiful, back when it had been the pride of Taiwan.

I smiled inwardly. Max was right—Sun Moon Lake was important. Assuming that's where I was.

But why bring me here?

The lake was eclipsed by a wall as I and the wheelchair were lifted and carried down a few steps dug into the earth. At the bottom, one of my carriers shone a torchlight onto a small, weathered door; in the light I saw all six of them—four male, two female.

Nurses in white uniforms. Hardly a surprise.

While one held the torch, another took out a physical key you saw in games and unlocked the door.

Whoever was in charge was serious about not getting hacked.

My carriers negotiated two longer flights of steps encased in a tunnel, muttering now and then while I tried not to faint from the pains in my lower body.

Light from downstairs increased the deeper we went, till the tunnel opened and the final thirty-odd steps fanned out either side towards a bright underground space. The nurses paused to swap roles.

As we resumed the descent, I felt a push.

Deep in my brain.

My eyes adjusted.

To colour.

Everywhere: colour.

Agent 2501 was back online.

But how? Sun Moon Lake was miles away from Megacity.

With 2501 fully operational except for my legs, I followed the workings of the agent parts of my brain. The nurses carrying me were all agents, as were the ten guards in military uniforms on the final steps, five standing either side.

Like last time, 2501 seemed to be entirely in the service of me, Ben Lee, so that he was a tool now, rather than the all-controlling identity he'd first been.

I used the connectivity to check in with some of the guards and nurses, but found little of interest. My arrival featured as an important event in their minds, and there were a number of thoughts about how to restrain me if the need arose, plus a few wishes for bed or a snack floating about. Yet these agents seemed to be in the grip of mental inertia. There were certainly no traces of the party-fuelled journeys I'd known in my early days as 2501.

I was wheeled onto a twelve-metre-wide walkway extending ahead that, on first sight, resembled an underground shopping mall. On the right was a small pharmacy, while on the left we passed a café manned by the latest model of barista; the coffee aromas unleashed a craving in me for the urban comforts I'd once enjoyed.

Further along the walkway, we passed a larger room containing 3D maps and five gun racks that were 75% full. In the middle of the room an agent in army uniform—Agent 1679—stood with her back to me, facing a semicircle of displays that relayed views of the lake, the mountains immediately surrounding this subterranean fort and the steps and battered door through which I'd been carried into the tunnel.

I mentally greeted Agent 1679.

Her head shot round, and her eyes bored through me.

My heart jumped as I was reminded of the agent's stare in the night market that time with Max.

It was the next room that intrigued me the most. Behind a wall of glass, rows of books crowded tightly packed shelves. Above the entrance a small sign read, 'Library'.

This was the first non-virtual library I'd seen. Many of the spines were faded and worn. I zoomed in with 2501's eyes and caught some of the strange titles and author names.

> *The Complete Works of William Shakespeare*
> *Faust* Johann Wolfgang von Goethe
> *The Collected Poems of Williams Wordsworth*
> *The Holy Bible*
> *The Mahābhārata*
> *Brave New World* Aldous Huxley
> *The Odyssey* Homer
> *War and Peace* Leo Tolstoy
> *The Philosophy of Freedom* Rudolf Steiner
> *The Second Sex* Simone de Beauvoir
> *The Art of War* Sun Tzu
> *The Republic* Plato
> *Utopia* Thomas More

THOMAS GODBER

Permutation City Greg Egan
The Origins of Totalitarianism Hannah Arendt

I scoured the data stores 2501 had been given access to—not a single entry on any of these titles or authors.

We arrived at a T-junction. I was wheeled left along another walkway, which opened out onto a circular space twenty metres across. The nurses pushed me into the middle of the circle and stood in a hexagon around me.

Injections would be next. I tried to focus on a vision of the forest.

But the nurses didn't move.

The floor seemed to print a large circle around us, leaving just enough space for someone to walk around the outside.

Air rushed upwards from below, as the floor fell.

52

Thirty metres deeper underground, I was wheeled onto a narrow mezzanine under a low ceiling. My agent self was still operational. Looking down through a glass-panelled safety railing, I saw I was at an upper edge of a vast, low-slung dome.

The ground below was divided into sections of workspace, each twelve square metres according to the 2501 part of me, and separated by boards three metres high—a little like makeshift cubicle shops. I could almost have been looking at one of the old-fashioned airport terminals I'd seen in history films, though it was not as brightly lit, and small areas of dark earth were visible in occasional patches of flooring or walls that had been left uncovered.

At the end of the mezzanine was a narrow, black spiral staircase, descending ten metres to the ground. The nurses puffed and grunted as they edged me down the steps.

At the bottom was another library. Some of the titles I saw upon zooming in were:

De Humani Corporis Fabrica Andreas Vesalius

Neurotechnologies: Optimising the Brain Zoe Patel
and artHuman Ksenia 80j
Synthetic Biology: Latest Leaps Emma Wang and
artHuman Hearty 11cc
The Double Helix James D. Watson
From AI to Integrative Cognition Sami Rousseau
with artHumans Hamza 8gb and Nixit 95ak
On the Origin of Species Charles Darwin
Beyond Biology Oluwa Wilson and artHuman
Sun-Hee 8mum

We began to traverse the floor of the endless cavern in a straight line between two rows of workspaces. In many of them machines hummed or rasped as they carried out precision tasks on what could only be body parts—human, artHuman or otherwise.

Foreign smells I couldn't name hung in the air.

We passed workspaces manned by non-agents. In one, a woman in a lab coat was watching fingers move on a hand that stood upright on a stand; in another, two men were adding droplets to a red liquid; in a further space, groups of people were working on muscles and organs.

Finally, we passed a room sealed off with glass walls. Inside, four complete bodies lay submerged in liquid in large see-through baths.

I thought of the mixture of synthetic and original parts I carried in my own body and had to admit to myself that my ability to distinguish between synthetic and natural materials both inside and around me was slipping away.

My heart palpitated as my sanity evaporated momentarily: perhaps all of life was manufactured in dungeons like this one.

We came to the end of the dome, turned left into the mouth of a dimly lit tunnel with a rounded brick ceiling nine metres above the floor at its highest point.

As we passed an inconspicuous staircase that led still deeper underground, I spotted a small sign next to it bearing the words 'Servers—Another World'.

We approached a huge wall of glass that sealed the tunnel from ceiling to floor and wall to wall. In the middle was a glass door with two armed agents in uniform standing on either side. They nodded, and the door slid open, breaking the silence with a swish.

A few steps further a second glass door guarded by two more agents let us through.

A memory of one of London's old underground bars flashed into my mind.

We'd arrived at the final section of tunnel—a thirty-metre-long room. The tunnel's grey-and-brown walls had not been painted, but were lit up by homely wall lights.

A soaring violin passage that began faintly swelled in volume the further we went into the room. It was unenhanced and punctuated by bursts of static.

Clearly not nuClassical.

I looked ahead. The music seemed to be coming from speakers built into the wall somewhere above a man who sat facing me behind a large desk at the far end, the wall a few metres behind him marking the end of the tunnel. He was reading the yellowed pages of an old leather-bound hardback called *Frankenstein*.

We reached the desk and slowed to a stop, so that a mere two metres separated me from the man on the other side.

He glanced at me, smiled and went back to his reading.

I couldn't find any data on him with 2501's input, so I continued to make rudimentary observations: Caucasian, of slight build, shorter than average, wearing a green pastel waistcoat and a yellow shirt with the top button undone tucked into white chinos. He was leaning back into his chair, legs crossed.

I lingered on his face that was framed by brown-and-grey shoulder-length hair. It was thin, with a large hooked nose.

Unbelievably, he wore external glasses. The gold frames glinted around brown eyes that looked heavy.

What the hell was I doing here?

Instead of fear—it was too late for that—I felt awkward: there was a broken-heartedness about this person that was uncomfortable to be in the presence of. You could sense it even in the minutest processes of his breathing.

'Welcome, Agent 2501,' he said, putting down his book. 'Isn't it wonderful? The second movement of Mendelssohn's Violin Concerto.'

Augmenting 2501's skills, I identified a thick German accent, which surprised me—most people with German-speaking ancestry had grown up speaking only English.

'So, we get to meet,' he continued. 'I am a free man, a "Supervisor" as I am more commonly known, or not known, to be more precise. Forgive the joke.' He chuckled.

I swallowed, feeling oddly relieved: although this was likely to be my last interaction, I couldn't have asked for a more interesting conversation than one with the type of person I'd tried so desperately to locate and understand. But now that I was here—juggling two identities, my legs crippled, powerless to proceed with my mission—I wasn't sure what to say.

The Supervisor helped me. 'You have found one of us now,' he said in a matter-of-fact tone as he sat down again, 'which I gather is what you've wanted for some time, no?'

'Yes, it is,' I heard myself reply.

The Supervisor turned the music off somehow and said, 'You have failed, Agent 2501, and you know it.' Venom flickered in his voice, but it was quickly replaced with a friendly tone as he said, 'But let's do away with the numerical component of your name, shall we? Perhaps we can get rid of "Agent" altogether. It should be obvious that I know who you are—Ben Lee. I made Agent 2501. Not directly of course. My scientists did all the dirty work. But they and I like to maintain a healthy channel of communication.'

I nodded.

'In fact, I think I may have paid you a visit during your operation. One is not always clear about who one has visited —there are many of you. But I recognise your face. You are handsome. Can I call you Ben, by the way, or do you prefer Agent?'

'I don't mind either.' I didn't want him to call me anything.

The Supervisor laughed and said, 'We don't mind either, do we? Well, Ben it is.'

I regretted not picking the alternative.

'It is a delight to meet you, Ben. Can we get you any coffee or tea?'

Caught off guard, I stared at the Supervisor. At that instant, a final coffee was more welcome than anything else.

'I'll have coffee, please.'

The man flicked his hand at one of the nurses still standing behind me.

'Ben?'

'Yes.'

'You do realise why I have brought you here tonight, yes?'

'I let you down by leaving Another World and not serving Megacity as 2501 was tasked with. I have also strayed repeatedly beyond the grid. Before becoming an agent, I was responsible for the kidnap of James Lin.'

'It is good to see you are honest. All this is true. And there are consequences to your actions you may not yet grasp.'

'I'm sure there are,' I said, choosing a bolder tack. 'What about the Supervisors and their actions? Now that I'm here, you can at least tell me why you forced the citizens out of a perfectly clean and safe countryside.'

The Supervisor chuckled. 'Now we're really getting down

to business. That is one of your big questions, isn't it? An entirely justified one too.'

A familiar aroma reached us.

'Do you take sugar or milk?' a voice behind me asked.

'Both, please.' Normally I took neither, but tonight sugar and milk would be the finishing touches to my final indulgence.

'Personally, I like it black,' said the Supervisor, as a mug was passed his way. 'Ah, for pure coffee! I always say, a coffee a day keeps the doctor away. It's an irrational statement, and yet I find it works. Oh, I am sorry.' He sounded genuine. 'I have not answered your question about the move from the countryside, have I? Do forgive me. I am a little out of practice. These social skills of mine could do with a little more oiling from time to time.'

I was still adjusting to this slow and deliberate way of talking. It was as if the Supervisor was proud of the way he'd mastered English as somebody who'd not spoken it in childhood and was now claiming a new identity from it. Constructing each sentence was a form of entertainment; each word selected was to be savoured like the coffee we were sipping.

'So, let me see … the great diaspora as I like to call—'

'You mean eviction.'

'Oh, can't we pretend they're synonyms for a moment? Goodness, where did you pick up these excellent interruption skills?'

I stayed quiet.

'The decision was made by the Early Eleven, the first Supervisors, who each represented one of the ruling families dotted around the planet. Incidentally—and I am sure you will be grateful for the clarification—today there are still eleven of us, each selected by our families to carry both the burden and the glory that the mantle of Supervisor brings.'

He paused.

And I was finally getting answers.

'But at long last, I address your question. For a start, although pockets of countryside have always existed, the cultural concept of, and belief in, the countryside as a place where humans go to seek spiritual nourishment from natural phenomena was more or less dead before my generation came on the scene. This can partially be traced back to the seduction of citizens away from interacting in physical space with each other and their natural environments, which we can call the biggest victory over the human being that our great tech companies ever achieved. Much of the work was done for us when so many people no longer felt connected to the land around them. And by this time, the majority of people globally had moved to the city anyway.

'No amount of time spent on constructing an old-fashioned government with real policies would ever give us complete control over the masses of citizens spread across countryside and city.

'Which leads us to the final reason for the eviction. It is elegantly simple. Again, our darling tech came to the rescue. We had long since programmed it to maximise our own chances of survival at all costs, ideally without killing off the rest of humankind in case we should need it someday.'

And that was it, the reason behind it all. Fern was right—it was all about social control.

'An algorithm, Ben. One simple, little algorithm. Eviction was what the machines wanted for us. So much easier, after all, *so* much easier to control a mass of people if they are all in one place, believe the same things and act the same way. The smart city was the place for that, the grid the key. To top it off, any remaining countryside would not be polluted.' He winked at me. 'The machines have done their job well, no?'

The Supervisors had made a decision, but even they had

handed over their thinking power to machines—entirely artificial policymakers for the whole planet.

'And from our bases in the countryside,' the Supervisor went on, 'we can pluck the occasional citizen for research, pleasure, procreation or whatever purposes we want, without fear of vengeance visits, because we are invisible—ooh, spot my love of alliteration in that sentence.' He repositioned his gaze at me. 'Do you like pastries?'

Before I managed to process this surprise question, he glanced at the nurse who doubled as a waiter.

It was pointless arguing with the Supervisor's explanation of the reasons behind the Great Eviction. But I owed it to the billions of citizens enslaved to tech in the city to stand up for them while I still could.

53

I took a deep breath and said, 'I think I am justified in wishing for the citizens that they are fairly governed. They deserve to know the truth about the countryside. After all, we are taught from a young age that the Supervisors always have the people's best interests at heart.'

'Why so naïve now, eh?' The Supervisor shook his head. 'Naturally we must give the *impression* we care, but caring does not even make it onto our priority list, as you have been finding out so cleverly.'

He waited for a response.

I gave him nothing.

'Where, please,' he continued, 'is the logic in hoping for some sort of fair governance? You're not showing me a link, Ben. I know what you're getting at, but you must enlighten me as to why you think it would be *fairer* if the people were handed the truth about their situation. I am losing faith in you. Come on now, what is fair rule?'

Sensing he wasn't expecting an answer and was building up to something, I remained quiet.

'Fairly governed?' he barked. '*Deserving* of knowing the

truth? Can you think how ridiculous such concepts sound to me, here—in this position? I grew up in one of the eleven most privileged families that ever graced this planet. My generation has inherited all the fruits of our ancestors' hard work. You cannot know what life is like for us. Don't try to fuck around by arguing about fairness! Don't you owe it to yourself to show a bit more intelligence? Think of capitalism—was it ever fair in the distribution of wealth? Is not profit mongering the inevitable result? Or how about communism—did that ever work out with your fuzzy little fairness? Mm?'

Again, I gave him nothing.

'Am I being too harsh on you?' The Supervisor's voice quickly switched from aggravation to a purr. 'It's surprisingly easy to forget that you've been fed all the stories. That there may still live in you these notions about us being generous—loving even—because we gave humanity comfort, convenience, extended lifespans and so on through the mechanism of Megacity. Yes, we gave you a lot. But, as you know only too well, we also took a lot away from the citizen—the freedom to feel too much negative emotion, the freedom to roam in nature and, most important of all, the freedom to think independently.

He yawned. 'The problem lies in power, Ben. Great power and fairness cannot share a bed, so to speak. This has been shown through every era of human civilisation.' The Supervisor's eyes lit up. 'Speaking of power, did you not enjoy the small amount of it we gave you as an agent?' He removed his glasses, as though wanting me to be honest.

'There were fun moments, I won't deny it, but it wasn't fulfilling on a deeper level.'

I took a long, slow breath. 'I'm curious,' I began, 'why did you choose this spot in Taiwan for your centre? Are there really no Supervisors who live in Megacity?'

'Taiwan is technologically advanced,' he said, 'which naturally is useful to me. But it is such a little island—a mere afterthought, you could say—that I did not think citizens would come hunting for me here. You prove otherwise. Regarding your second question, how could we live in the city? We don't complicate our lives with stuff like smart lenses, social media or any other tools that are essential for interaction and exchange in the city. I'm sure you realise by now that such things are merely control mechanisms.'

I let the thought hang in the air for a moment. 'Why are you happy to sit here and tell me so much?'

'It's not like I've got anyone else to talk to down here, right?' The Supervisor smiled. 'All will be revealed in good time. Can I finish my train of thought now? Very occasionally one of us makes a trip into the city if we feel some ennui coming on, for example. But we find the air too polluted and the crowds too stressful. It is true, some of our younger relatives run the urban organisations with artHuman help. They must subscribe to all the trappings that a citizen's life brings, though they may take vacations whenever they like. Incidentally, that place you once worked—Dwellings—is run by my colleague's granddaughter.

'Most relatives opt for the simple life in our well-masked country estates, from where they can assist the Supervisors. I am an exception out here, in that I am entirely alone. Oh, and you are lucky the forest in England you found is not a region we have yet chosen to populate.'

How did he know everything about me?

'You look surprised.' He grinned. 'We must have a full understanding of anybody we recruit as an agent.'

'Anyway,' he went on, 'we don't feel a lack without a city to have fun in. Our playgrounds and kingdoms are separate from Megacity and well under the citizens' radar. The Supervisor gestured towards the ceiling. 'Our greatest prize—the countryside. And we respect nature, which is more than can be said of pre-Megacity humanity. Can you imagine the chaos and destruction if everyone had free access to it? Nature has to be a privilege for the Supervisors and our families. And we certainly enjoy our regular hikes to clear the cobwebs. It's beautiful in the mountains, is it not? It may surprise you that sometimes I don't even take a map when I go walking. It is more exciting—I feel like some ancient explorer discovering hidden lands. Ah, yes, the solitude is another benefit of keeping the countryside to ourselves.' He twitched. 'I almost forgot, you know all about doing away with maps, don't you?'

So, it had been theirs all along—whole expanses of the earth they'd taken over at no cost to themselves, while the rest of humanity had simply been piled sky-high in a make-believe fantasy of progress. It all made sense, but hearing it from the Supervisor made it sickeningly real.

'But this is nothing new, Ben,' he continued. 'Take the British Isles. As far back as the mid-18th century before Megacity, the Highland Clearances in Scotland forced the destruction of the clan system and the removal of rural populations. Later during the Industrial Revolution, large populations moved from the country to the city with the ascendency of industry over agriculture. By the 21st century, 70 percent of the land in England was owned by around half a percent of the population. The Great Urbanisation led by the Supervisors was just a new—admittedly dramatic—chapter in that process.

'Well before Megacity, people lamented the scarcity of lush green space that had not been built upon. What many of them didn't know, even back then, was that lush green landscapes have always been plentiful there. It is just that they have been kept out of sight, out of mind, for a long time by the powerful families—until people began to forget they were there. Delve deep, Ben, and you'll find that the histories of land ownership in many parts of the world are murky at best. We are not so "evil" as you might think. We are merely continuers of a long tradition that has kept the world functioning.'

The Supervisor waited, as though giving me time for his lectures to sink in.

The extremes of inequality I'd heard about stoked a primal anger I just managed to contain, but I did say, 'Is all this stuff you're telling me supposed to be the first stage of my torture?'

The Supervisor chuckled. 'What a question, not at all. I just thought you might find it interesting—you've been so desperate to find out about us.

'But I should move on. We need to talk about the anomaly you represent to us at this stage in our research. The reason I am sharing so much will then become clear.'

54

One of the nurses handed me a plate of neatly sliced pastries. Freshly baked. I took a bite—half melting in the glory of sweet, warm dough, half hating myself for accepting a treat from a Supervisor.

Now that I realised there was nothing I, nor anyone else, could ever do to challenge the invisible dictatorship that smothered the earth, a small part of me wanted a swift death. I had no interest in becoming a guinea pig or being torn apart again for the Supervisors' relentless research.

My gaze reconnected with the Supervisor's. I was weakening. My injuries had sapped my vitality. But there was also a tiredness about the man that leeched into me just by being near him.

'We are rebuilding the human being,' he said, as though addressing a lecture theatre, 'from the inside out. Agent 2501 is our most advanced model.' He pointed at my legs. 'You may or may not have noticed that all the other agents have numbers below the one we christened you with.'

My mouth stopped chewing as the thought fell into place.

I'd sensed there was a logic to the numbers, but—for a second—nothing made sense. 'Why me?'

'You were different.'

'In what way?'

'Somehow, just the right amounts of the right combination of factors were constellated in your psychological makeup for you to get as far as you have. Whether you were born differently, I cannot say. But you were unlike any of the other citizens or gangsters we have sacrificed on the altar of science. We wanted to see how far we could go with you.'

'Why do you take so many gangsters?'

'For quite some time we've been interested in carrying out profound thought reform and creating identities we can roll out across the grid on a global scale to further enhance social control. Here in Taiwan, gangsters operate outside the grid. There is no better specimen to try and reform than somebody who disagrees with the philosophy you wish to implant in a host.'

Specimen.

Failed specimens.

Words somebody … James Lin had said on the mountain.

Hualien.

Me at the edge of the sea of corpses.

I searched the Supervisor's eyes. 'Have you ever imagined what it is like for us to be kidnapped, forcefully operated on and robbed of all knowledge of who we were?'

'Actually, I have imagined it countless times. But only the operation part, minus the force, I should stress. I am tasked with fronting this area of developments here at Sun Moon Lake. We've come far, haven't we?'

'You have,' I said, suppressing my disgust at his complete lack of empathy.

'I know Fresh Eyes still look a bit glassy,' he continued, 'but I still must congratulate you on spotting a pair at Tonghua

Night Market so soon after arriving in Taipei. Well done too for escaping.'

'Why were you after me that night?'

'Well, first you need to understand that the global news launch for Fresh Eyes was a big deal for Taiwan. All our surveillance and intelligence were on hypervigilance. Every arrival and departure was closely monitored. You were an early arrival, and you were very silly, I might add, to go talking to strangers in a bar—all of whom were connected with eyes and ears—about where they think we Supervisors might live and whether Taiwan still has countryside. Very silly, indeed.'

'You were going to kill me for asking a couple of innocent questions?'

'You can be an arrogant little Miststück, can't you?' He spat the German word, which 2501 told me was vaguely equivalent to 'bastard'. 'That conversation in the pub was just icing on a cake. We could previously have justified getting rid of you based on your absence from work in London and your little trips off-grid. Your ability to think for yourself was obvious by now, and it was only confirmed when you spotted and escaped the agent in the night market, before successfully vanishing off-grid yet again. But even then, we didn't consider you too serious a threat.' The Supervisor paused and shook his head. 'How wrong we were. No, at that point we were just glad you weren't in Central Taipei. The citizens there are apt to listen to people from abroad.'

'And then you found out about the kidnap.'

'Exactly. Who gets away with a crime like that? Nobody, right? But not only did you succeed, you managed to get yourself off-grid *again*, and *with* your victim.'

'How did you know I'd end up in Hualien?' I asked.

'We didn't. Like I say, we had to be especially cautious after launch day. The specimens had to be guarded. One stray citizen discovering what you did in Hualien would quickly wreak havoc in other citizens' minds. Actually, we were surprised when you turned up there. Of course, we knew we'd get you sooner or later, but we hadn't expected you to walk into a trap quite so soon after your kidnapping escapade.'

I was silent.

'And, Ben?' He was staring at me.

'Yes.'

'You have shown you are mighty clever. Somehow, you possess a hangover of a cognitive process we hoped we had eradicated in the Great Urbanisation and the spread of the "fortunate citizen" identity. Namely, intuition. I find the concept of it problematic, but we must use the words we've inherited. You also have courage in abundance to follow said intuition. Combine this with your ability to make judgements for yourself and your willingness to experience heightened emotional pain and uncertainty, and something magical occurs —you become able to unpick the supposed reality. And you have done this more or less on your own. Now, you've finally been caught at it.' The Supervisor laughed. 'I almost feel a sense of remorse that we're not chasing you anymore. It is interesting to be challenged once in a while. I suppose I should be thanking you.'

'Please—I have done nothing to benefit you!' I put my plate down, wanting to spit out the last bite of pastry.

'Some of my colleagues would agree with you on that.'

'Perhaps this is a good time to ask you then,' I responded, 'what you plan to do with me when this conversation is over?' I caught myself suppressing a twinge of fear that had emerged, but my pride was still intact.

'Undecided. Will you mend your ways?'

I refused to ask for clarification. It would surely come.

'Why so silent now, Ben? I didn't expect you to be boring. Then again, I may be boring you too. I am not the most polished of speakers, but I try to improve when I get opportunities like this for practice.' He ran a hand through his hair. 'What if this is our only chance to chat? Isn't it unexpectedly nice, us hanging out like this, discussing the problems of the world, despite our differences?'

'I don't see that you've ever faced any problems.'

'Ah! Wrong again. There was the problem …'

The Supervisor's eyes clouded over. His head drooped forwards.

I wondered if he had narcolepsy.

Murmurs from the nurses behind him.

Then he straightened and opened his eyes. 'Forgive me—I still have a fear of this. For a long time, the big problem we couldn't solve was that of our own mortality.' The Supervisor looked spent, as though the mere utterance of 'mortality' had sapped some of his life.

He reached for his mug and prepared to speak. 'You are a brainy boy. Can't you see where I'm going with this?'

'Not really.'

'How old do I look to you?'

'Late fifties?'

The Supervisor grinned. 'I can't be doing too badly. I'm seventy-three. But myself and all of us in the eleven families wish to live forever. This doesn't seem possible in the way we'd ideally like. No number of stem cells and regenerative and nanomed treatments will keep our frames going indefinitely, but we are going for immortality nevertheless.' He leaned forward. 'Tell me, is Another World a convincing reality?'

'Of course. But you don't need me to tell you that.'

'Is it even better than the so-called *real* world?' he asked, lowering his brow, continuing to stare at me.

I didn't answer.

'Doesn't 2501 feel like an actual person?'

I toyed with whether to respond or not. 'You know he does,' I eventually said, under my breath.

'Ha! There you have it. 2501's brain parts built by our team of synthetic biologists, biomedical engineers, neuroscientists and artHumans has won. A real mind has been created at last. We could exterminate Ben Lee and your body right now, keeping only the fabricated agent parts of your brain, and 2501 would live forever. Of course, we could use a grown copy—we prefer to call it a virtual upgrade—of your original brain instead, then it would be Ben Lee's victory over nature and mortality. We could then house Ben Lee's artificial brain in one of our ultra-advanced bodies you passed on your way here. They are packed with nerves and hormones, so you would still be able feel, both physically and emotionally. You've tried the legs yourself already. Oh Ben, for centuries, transhumanist activists and science fiction films and novels have dreamed of immortality. Who would have thought it would take so long for us to reach the point where we can preserve an individual's actual consciousness inside a working body—complete with their peculiarities, memories and so on and so forth?

'We plan to undergo the operation ourselves, so we can benefit from the extraordinary verisimilitude that Another World and identities such as 2501 provide. Instead of the agent identity, however, we will receive upgrades of our own personalities.'

'Why not just use your original brains?'

'I'm afraid we've only managed to slow cognitive decline, not prevent it completely. This is why we need to resort to virtual upgrades. I am starting to notice my mind is not what it used to be—I must have the operation soon to create the most optimised virtual me still possible. It will be installed in my head together with Fresh Eyes. Then my natural brain can deteriorate as quickly as it likes. And so can my body for that matter—I won't need it in the long run. Bit by bit, every piece of me will be replaced with enhanced artificial components.'

I shuddered. 'Are you genuinely happy to become entirely artificial?'

'I think about this often. An increasingly enhanced body is unlikely to feel completely natural, but we've got to make do with what's feasible. One's personality will inevitably change to some degree, and we accept we cannot predict what those changes will be, nor to what degree we might change. Regardless, you will no doubt confirm that Another World will allow our renewed selves to flourish and have a lot of fun. We'll be able to play there like 2501 has, but we will remain invisible to the agents. We will also broaden Another World's scope to include all regions outside Megacity, so we can continue our lives off-grid.'

'But can a virtual personality ever be truly conscious?'

'It depends how you define consciousness. Long ago, philosophers wasted countless hours on metaphysical discussions of the mind, but consciousness can be reduced to mere activity of the brain. And all our experiments have proven that activity of the human brain can easily be transferred to the artificial brain of a transhuman organism. Don't you see? We are like gods. We have captured and distilled what people for centuries believed was the human soul.'

'And agents have been nothing more than guinea pigs to you?'

'They serve a dual purpose—helping to keep citizens in check, whilst allowing us to refine the technology we will need ourselves. In just three years from now, we'll also recommend all citizens undergo free operations that will give them entry to Another World, though it will be a more rudimentary version than the one 2501 inhabits. This will more or less glue them to the grid. We cannot have them roaming and spoiling heavenly nature. The excitements of Another World will keep most of them indoors twenty-four seven. They'll fatten up and continue to die as we live on. Fortunately, the ageing population and anti-family *zeitgeist* in Megacity we promote have worked wonders in reducing the number of citizens filling the planet. It would go against our sensibilities to do the dirty work of culling the citizenry, but we do dream of an era when the eleven families and their offspring can truly possess the earth in its entirety—our own Garden of Eden.'

These guys are killers, I thought.

As if he heard my thoughts, the Supervisor said, 'This must all sound highly immoral and distasteful to you, Ben, but at least I am honest with you, right?'

Despite the horrors of the future taking shape in my mind, the Supervisor's words were losing their shock factor. I was troubled by something quite different: my own feelings. I realised that through this long interview with the Supervisor—and thanks to the respectful manner in which I was being treated—I felt honoured. He said I was different. I'd been given the most advanced version of agent identity. I'd contributed to a project at the frontiers of science. I'd been part of something bigger than myself, though admittedly something I'd never have agreed to, something that jarred with all my values.

And with these thoughts came a realisation.

I was not about to be sentenced.

The Supervisor had summoned me. Only, for what?

I sobered up and forced myself to remember the suffering that had marred my life, both before and after the operation. I thought of James Lin and the agents surrounding me in this underground fortress. It saddened me to think who each of them might once have been.

'What is going through your mind?' the Supervisor asked.

'How come I can access Another World off-grid out here?'

'This is where we run it from, so there's no better place for

2501 to connect. Urban agents can't normally go beyond the city's edges, but now you're here, we're giving you access anyway. The agents up here operate in a limited version of Another World that incorporates only this building and its proximal surroundings. We can open other areas to them when needed—for example, when we dispatched the soldier agents who broke your legs.'

One puzzle piece could wait no longer. 'Why have only I been able to find out who I was?'

'Good point, and one my surgical team has struggled to explain. We did our best to recondition you, but it seems your free thinking and your discoveries ran too deep for you to be entirely altered without rendering your brain useless. This only fed our curiosity. Most agents are programmed to go through a moment of awareness of their former selves and to rejoice at being given redeeming identities. However, you remembered too much. And so we experimented with the pain to see if that would prevent you from revisiting your memories.' He shrugged. 'You must understand, we didn't want you escaping off-grid and finding space and time to dismantle the nascent neural pathways an agent needs to function correctly. Of course, you eluded us in the end anyway.' The Supervisor leaned forward again. 'All of this, Ben, only made us more interested in you as an individual.'

'Why did you send me to convict my friends?' I was fearful of endangering Max and Yayuung by bringing them into the conversation but I had to know.

'Simple. It was a test,' he replied. 'You had been integrating into the agent lifestyle pretty well on the whole. You were going to all the right parties and seemed wedded to Another World. After the first bout of pain we administered, your inflammatory thoughts disappeared, but we needed to carry out a final check. This is where an agent's former friends are particularly useful. Re-meeting them is the ultimate test of fealty and the success of our program.'

'And that is where Agent 2501 failed.'

'Yes. Are we ready to move on from thoughts of failure now?'

'I'm not sure I understand.'

A glow descended over the Supervisor's face, and his features softened. 'You don't see your own beauty, do you?' he began. 'It shines in everything you do. The way you see life puts you in a league so far above your fellow citizens and makes you more akin to how we Supervisors think, untrammelled by the conventions of the grid and the strictly curated education the masses are fed. The complete freedom you have claimed for yourself informs your every action. Some pre-Megacity philosophers would have said you are proof of the indomitability of the human spirit. You refuse to be controlled, and therein lies your beautiful essence. Do you get me now? It is important you understand me, Ben.'

I swallowed. Sadness overwhelmed me. Confusion at being so understood by this grandiose, barbaric individual. 'Why is it so important I understand?'

'You are lucky to find me at an important juncture in my biography. As I indicated, I am waiting to undergo the operation myself. I've had my health checks and can say, with much delight, that I am in line for my initial work in just a few weeks' time. I am the next guinea pig after you. If all goes well, the other ten and various relatives will follow suit. And it shall go well—I'm surrounded by greater expertise in every area than anyone in history.'

What in Megacity was he telling me this for? This guy dominated and directed our conversation as if he were history himself. 'You still haven't told me why my understanding of my "beauty" is important?'

The man took a deep breath, removed his glasses and sought my eyes. 'Because of how amazing you have shown yourself to be, I have a proposal for you. I'm scared, Ben. I've no idea how it will feel to wake up and see things as the upgraded, virtual version of myself, living in Another World. I've talked to the team about whether I can use both my old and new personalities as you have managed to, and they said they can't guarantee anything. There's even a small chance the operation will fail, and I won't survive. But the likeliest scenario is I'll be living permanently in Another World, and this thought frightens me as much as it excites me. You know Another World.' His voice was gentle. Intimate. 'If I have you by my side, you can guide me through. Unlike you, I've lived a sheltered life. My lineage protected me from anything that might overwhelm me or that was overly stimulating. Alcohol was off limits, I've never even tried Bliss. Everything was pure, organic and unprocessed. I don't know pain, Ben.' The Supervisor gave a solitary cough, as though his body was admitting his vulnerability.

I struggled to process his words. 'Guide you through …?'

'Yes. I want for you that you can continue to enjoy your free thought and your body, which we can quickly repair for you. All I ask for in return is that you are there for me when I come back from my operation.'

How … what … a Supervisor, one of the invisibles, the nameless individuals I'd poured everything into pursuing, despite enormous odds I'd ever get near them, was—weak as a child—reaching out to *me* for emotional support. All thinking, both Ben's and 2501's, ground to a halt.

'Are you serious about this?' I asked.

'Why do you think we've been talking this long? *Yes*, I'm serious. You would have to have the right intentions—the first sign of a threat would end our deal and your life.'

I still couldn't believe what the Supervisor was requesting of me.

'But you needn't decide right now,' he said. 'Sleep on it. There is a small bedroom made up for you.' The Supervisor gestured to a door in the wall of the tunnel to my right. 'Next to the bed you will find a bath with running water from Sun Moon Lake. I know that you will have difficulty standing or getting to the toilet in your current state, so the nurses will be on-hand through the night. They have snacks and painkillers and can assist you with any mobility problems. They can help wash you if you are not averse to that.'

He tilted his head—was that affection? 'I think we have said enough for one night. You've got a lot to think about, I am sure. Do you have any questions before I let you go?'

Broken and depleted, I relaxed into the thought of one whole night of sleep in a freshly made bed. But I knew the terrible decision I'd have to face in the little room would swamp my mind and dominate each minute of confusion I had to endure.

'Yes, just one thing,' I said. 'Assuming your operation goes well and you adapt to Another World, what will happen to me?'

'If you follow your brief and we get on, you may become my right-hand man, my Chief Assistant, let's call it. You would accompany me to meetings and would get to know the other Supervisors. With time you could help monitor and look after the other agents, until you are ready to assist on larger operations. Also, we Supervisors may enjoy our power, but that doesn't mean we don't get lonely. You see, I have no children of my own. So, you're in luck—you'd enjoy all the benefits that I would bestow on my own son. If we develop affection for each other, I will give you the gift of immortality should you one day want it. We can delete 2501 and procure for you an upgrade of your real self. Of course, you'd get limb and organ replacements whenever you wanted them.'

'Why do you trust me after everything I've done?'

'How could you have behaved any differently, given your disposition? I act on gut instinct. I think you know a thing or two about that, no? Anyway, I am willing to take a risk. You would be on probation indefinitely. In the early years, you would remain in the company of guards at all times, and they would be fortified with the necessary weapons and bodily enhancements to quash you if your behaviour poses the tiniest threat. You may also benefit from sporadic re-education. You and I would have to sing from the same hymn sheet. I accept that it might be difficult for you at first, but once you have tasted the life I have to offer, you will, with time, be grateful.'

He turned the music back on. 'OK, go and rest now. Breakfast will be brought to you in the morning. Do you have a preference?'

'I wouldn't say no to eggs Florentine.'

'Eggs Florentine it is.' The man gestured to the nurses to wheel me away.

My mouth filled with water: I'd said the name of my favourite breakfast dish half in jest, not believing for a moment I'd get it.

As the nurses opened the door to my room, the Supervisor called over, 'Ben, my name's David. I am David of the zu Mattburg family.'

55

Knowing my time to think was limited, and not wanting to take in the sight of my legs unless I had to, I went straight to bed without washing. I lay drugged up and tucked up on the tiny room's single bed, which relieved some of my pains by moulding itself to my contours.

The last bite of pastry climbed back into my throat as the mental torture began.

The absurdity appalled me: my ability to challenge the system had landed me a job offer at the centre of the ruling elite itself. Of course I wouldn't support a coterie of power abusers who had throttled all freedom out of the citizenry to turn themselves into invisible gods. That wasn't me. I'd be betraying Max and Yayuung, the forest community, the watchers in the pits of London and any other like-minded people who might exist in districts or pockets of wilderness I'd not visited.

At the same time, David's world was compelling. If I'd grown up with the same privileges, I'd probably share the same world view and value system. I'd have known myself as a member of a distinct line, an inheritor of a lifestyle enjoyed in pre-Megacity landscapes that were my birthright, reigning in a kingdom that existed thanks to the ignorance of the masses left to wallow in mediocrity as they fulfilled predetermined fates, certain that life had never been better.

Was this latest generation of Supervisors really to blame? Weren't they merely embracing the duties they'd been selected to carry out like their forebears?

And power? Perhaps David had a point. Exercising power as 2501 had been exhilarating, even though I'd been under the influence of the agent's identity.

I cringed—was I admitting I'd enjoyed deciding the fates of citizens as 2501?

Maybe. But it hadn't made me happier.

My mind went back to my infatuation with Fern, then forward to the connectedness and friendship on the mountainside with Max and Yayuung. No amount of power I was given could give me such feelings.

Power and ethics aside, wasn't it possible that genuine friendship could grow between me and David? It would take years of effort on my part. If living with David felt like captivity to begin with, mightn't I still develop feelings for my captor? Stockholm Syndrome was a thing, after all.

The self-coercion needed to develop affection for—and loyalty towards—a man whose beliefs I would never share was not worth the suffering. But how important were my own beliefs now that I'd learned so much through my journey and the Supervisor's story? My present views might shift over time until they seemed childish and unrealistic once I adapted to the life I'd been offered.

And maybe I'd even be of better use to the world this way. Better than dead at least.

If there was one thing I could take away from David's rants and justifications, it was that even views entirely opposed to my own could worm their way into the realm of plausibility when grounded in another human being's reality. Especially when that human being was sitting opposite you in the same room.

There was one final thing that spoke to me: the idea of having a father figure in my life. The sadness so many citizens sought to escape from the time they were born was surely in large part rooted in not having a family of fellow humans, with whom to laugh, cry and share the moments that mattered.

The little boy in me had been moved.

Could the unimaginable happen?

Could the most unlikely relationship history had yet to witness evolve from me working for David—a meaningful father-son connection between a runaway citizen and a Supervisor?

56

I ached for five minutes of sleep.

No chance.

After flirting with the offer, I swung back. I couldn't help thinking about what they'd done to the Dog. Couldn't help reliving how I'd come so close to destroying Max and Yayung. Accepting would only lead to self-hatred and loneliness.

Apart from hanging out with a power maniac, I'd be alone with mindless agents. Could monitoring and caring for them as "Chief Assistant" allow me to love anymore, or, as 2501 called it, 'release oxytocin'? Would I be able to see them as human beings, or would I be expected to treat them more like machines? Although they didn't share my double identity, I'd achieved at least some sort of connection with each agent I'd crossed paths with since arriving.

I could read their thoughts for a start. But their emotions remained largely hidden.

Did a part of them crave love like everyone else? If so, were they as unconscious of it as most citizens.

Somewhere the agents had acknowledged me tonight: I'd

felt their cognitive systems reach out to me, as though they'd not entirely lost the desire to connect with others.

I let 2501 waft into the agents' pseudo-dreamland in Another World and told my agent self to ask them if they remembered their former selves.

'I remember nothing,' most responded.

'Do you?' others asked.

'I do,' said 2501 on my behalf. 'Maybe there is a way you can too. One day. Who knows?'

To experiment with what caring for them might feel like, I asked 2501 to pass on words of comfort to each agent, one after the other:

'It's alright. You're still alive. I am here with you.'

'You don't have to worry.'

'Rest your tired mind.'

With some of them I took risks. 'Quiet. Relax—the emptiness you feel is natural. You were robbed of something once precious to you.' And 'Remember what it is to want to love and be loved.'

The clarity of my own thoughts faded as 2501's experience grew in intensity into a delirium with nightmarish qualities. I thrashed my head from side to side as pieces of the other agents' consciousness infiltrated my own, and I became aware of their angers, their insatiable sexual appetites, their ruthless loyalty to David, their repetitive to-do lists, their anti-viral systems constantly battling suicidal thoughts.

I had the uncanny sensation I was dreaming awake. Another World could be like that. Perhaps sleep was optional as an agent and I just hadn't realised until now.

I allowed 2501 to freestyle through a selection of districts in Megacity and gaze through the lenses of random citizens, from a young man gaming in his bedroom in LA, to a woman skiing down an artificial slope in Moscow; from a businesswoman sealing a deal in Chengdu, to a naked couple spooning on the floor of a room in Paris.

The choice of scenes was endless, and I could choose to feel any of these people's sensations as if they were my own.

My line of thought crystallised into hyperfocus, and I felt a wave of panic as I looked on: wherever I journeyed as 2501, an audience was witnessing me.

The other agents were watching me.

I gazed at their inner expressions. Each of them—without exception—contained a longing. They knew how to obey orders, complete tasks and calculate distances, weights and quantities with minute precision. But they were seeing now that my agent's identity was not like theirs. Their limiting rules in Another World did not apply to 2501.

They began to gossip amongst themselves as together they reached the conclusion that 2501 acted entirely at the mercy of the brain in the host body, not the neural network that ruled all of them.

And they wanted that.

Their hearts—for unlike artHumans, they still had living, human-grown hearts—cried out for freedom.

Above all, they wanted to remember.

Had I just been hugely irresponsible?

And did I sense rightly that they were already developing a connection to me—not merely a cognitive one, but a felt one—perhaps seeing me as their carer-to-be?

I asked 2501 to be still, so that I could shut out the noise of the other agents' hearts and minds. I needed to be just myself, hear only my original thoughts, make up my own mind on how to respond to the offer of a lifetime.

57

Morning arrived in record time.

I dosed up on painkillers and hoisted myself onto a pair of crutches one of the nurses handed me. Although my right leg was unusable, my left leg had been left with a degree of stability, and I was able to transport myself across the short distance to where David sat waiting for me behind his desk.

The smells of a rich brew, toasted muffin and parsley attracted my gaze to a full cafetière and a plate of eggs Florentine, presented with the care you'd expect at a gourmet restaurant.

David was smiling. Was he pleased with himself? Dressed in a pale blue suit and a pink shirt—a matching pink handkerchief protruding from his jacket pocket—he gave the impression he was celebrating that the sun was shining somewhere above us.

'Good morning to you, Ben. You are well rested? I'm afraid I have already eaten.'

David read, while I ate as slowly as I could to delay what had to follow.

After a few minutes, I sensed he was watching me eat. I didn't look up from the plate but forced myself to focus on the buttery creaminess of the hollandaise sauce.

There was only the sound of my chewing and the clink of my heavy silver cutlery on the antique, bone china plate.

No sooner had I swallowed the last mouthful and placed my cutlery neatly in the centre of my plate, than David said, 'So, you've reached a decision?'

I picked up my crisp linen napkin to stall death a moment longer.

I wiped my mouth, folded my napkin and placed it on the table. I blinked and spoke. 'I have, yes. I cannot help you. I willingly choose death over supporting what you and your friends stand for.'

I heard my words tumble onto the desk and relished how brutal they must have sounded when the message hit home.

I waited for a command to take me away to my execution.

'Naturally you have your doubts about us,' David said with unexpected gentleness. 'Who wouldn't in your situation, and coming from your background? What could I do that might make you change your mind? You see, I actually quite like you, Ben. I know I haven't known you in person for such a long time, but I think I made it clear to you last night that you are highly valued. You have much to contribute to us poor bunch of Supervisors as you have experience of what it is like to be a citizen, an agent *and* a free thinker. Think again. If you were to do well here, I might even permit you to influence policy one day. That's worth considering, is it not?'

I marvelled at David's intelligence—he knew how to speak to me. But I marvelled equally at his manipulativeness.

'How can I be sure you mean that?' I asked.

'The other ten hold me in high esteem. I have never let them down. It is as simple as this—if you decide to work with me and we develop a good rapport, they will have to listen to me when I inform them I want you to be more involved.'

If I accepted the offer and took a leap into the unknown—as I had so often already—I could always escape by taking my life if things didn't work out. And of course, you can't really change a system from the outside. You have to be within to shift anything.

But I'd have to compromise too much. It would be naïve to endure months and years, in the hope I might gain enough of the Supervisors' trust to effect changes? It was nonsense to imagine they'd agree with my ideas that would have to involve challenging the subjugation of the citizen and the rule by the few.

My entire body was depleted with the exhaustion that comes with making a huge decision, but I wasn't going to budge now.

David fixed his gaze on my empty plate. The veins on his hands stood out as he gripped the upper knee of his crossed legs. The mournfulness had returned, but he also looked absent-minded. Resigned. As if all along he'd known I'd decline.

'I respect that you've made me an offer that may never before have been made to a citizen or agent,' I said, aiming to bow out with grace, 'but I am sorry to say, my decision stands.'

David leapt out of his seat with an energy I'd not suspected he had, as though everything up until now had been an act.

'It's the *wrong* decision!' he yelled, leaning over the table and staring at me just inches away, his face contorted with fury and hatred.

He yanked open a drawer and took out a long, golden knife; walked around his desk till he was standing by my side.

'I am just a tiny bit disappointed,' he said. 'I thought we could have worked well together.'

He grabbed my hair with his free hand hair and sliced the knife upwards, nicking my lower lip.

'So, you actually want to die. This is most admirable.' David returned to the other side of the desk. 'Fine. I will give you one more chance. Only this time the conditions have changed. Accept the offer, and you remain on probation and under supervision for however long I let you live. It doesn't sound so appealing now, does it?' He frowned. 'Perhaps this will help you to make up your mind.'

David gestured to a nurse who walked over to the left half of the wall behind where we sat and flipped a switch. Cracks appeared in a section of the wall, which shuddered and began to swivel.

It was too painful to look.

On the other side, gagged and tied to chairs attached to the wall, sat Max and Yayuung.

'You won't, I don't think, want me to describe the minutiae of the fates awaiting your friends if you don't make the most sensible decision?' David said. 'We are reading from the same hymn sheet, are we not?' He grinned. 'Or perhaps I should add after all that Agent 558 here derives a great fulfilment from twisting heads until the neck can no longer support life.'

My pounding heart threatened to burst through my chest.

I opened my mouth, but nothing came out.

'I'll be honest, Ben,' he went on, 'I am sure I would actually be fine without you. I am just used to getting my way. Every time. That's just how I'm wired, I'm afraid.'

I fought myself to gain composure.

'What will happen to them if I accept?' I finally managed to say.

'Then you will stop them being killed, of course.'

'Let them go back to Megacity, back to their lives.'

'Come on, Ben, you know that's a shit idea. We'd have to remove their tongues to stop them from talking, and their eyes to stop them communicating. Much better that they stay here with us. You and your friends could be together every day.'

'You wouldn't lock them up?'

'No, that would be too painful for you. You would not carry out your duties sufficiently well. Obviously it'll mean a little operation for your friends. I can't have three free-thinking individuals around me, can I?'

'What sort of operation.'

'They'll be fine. They will be as they are now, with a mildly reduced ability to think for themselves. That may be a poor trade in your eyes, but they will still have their feelings. They will be happy every time they catch sight of you, and me for that matter, grateful that they can spend time with us. They will look up to you as their saviour. I assure you it will be a painless transformation. Come on, Ben, it's an easy choice now.'

I looked from Max to Yayuung. Their bodies were still, but their darting eyes communicated panic.

The seconds ceased their forward march.

I cursed myself and my cause.

'OK. I see you need a moment or two for quiet reflection again,' David said in the gentler voice. 'Compared to this, the many other decisions you have made during your life suddenly look easy, no? Well, take this as a lesson. Speaking of lessons, there's a lot more I can teach you if you'll only give me the chance. Listen, I'll make sure this is the only nasty lesson you receive. The choice is yours, but I speak from the heart when I say that I see this as an exceptional opportunity for you.'

'I need time to think.'

'Please! Do I look like I'm stopping you from thinking? You've shown me over and over I can't do that. Go ahead, take your time. How long do you want?'

'A couple of hours.'

'I say ten minutes. This has taken a day too much of my life already.'

David got up and sauntered around the cavernous room.

Knowing that the slightest glance at my friends would dissolve my focus, I closed my eyes and tried to concentrate on my breathing and the aftertaste of coffee in a bid to collect what remained of my dwindling mental energy.

Sweat trickled down my face.

I prayed that the bricks of the tunnelled ceiling might collapse and squash my pain by killing us all. End of consciousness. Not another moment on this earth. Peace.

The thump of my heart refused to ease. I wanted to get up and hug my friends and tell them how sorry I was. To sit with them one more time on the side of a mountain, a breeze stroking our faces. Sunlight. An hour of togetherness before we had to say goodbye to the world or take up the nightmarish offer of censored lives. David would understand the desire for one last moment together, wouldn't he? I wasn't sure how much he truly felt anything good, but he at least understood how minds and feelings work.

It would have to be death.

I would never work with David.

Yet I had no right to decide the fate of Max and Yayuung whichever way I went.

Perhaps I could ask David to let me speak with my friends once the ten minutes were up, before I made my choice.

I tried to recall the sound of the drums I'd heard so clearly in the ambulance, but heard only David's pacing and the muffled breathing of my friends opposite me.

'Five minutes left,' the Supervisor said from somewhere in the darkness behind me.

I forced myself down a different path.

THE CITIZEN

Time was relative. I had to find an escape from the oppressiveness of the physical room by entering a timeless space. I just about managed to dampen the explosions of my own thoughts, grab 2501 and abandon my immediate surroundings for Another World.

Another World had never felt so welcoming. I slipped seamlessly from one reality into the next, from a journey on the zip back in London, to Bar 75 in downtown Taipei and on into the heads of other agents I shared the space with.

I would spend the final minutes free of pain. In hiding. Lost but found in the ever-changing tapestry of Another World.

But it was different. For the first time, I was going there with close-to-a-hundred percent Ben consciousness, as though I was riding on the shoulders of 2501, rather than merely observing from a distance.

And it was good.

For whatever reason, the trauma of what I had to do induced me—just when it mattered most—to discover refuge in Another World, the very place that once threatened to separate me from my past and from myself forever.

Now my sense of who I was—not just what I was—expanded to include 2501, as if we were one.

Yet, we were also united with others in Another World.

What had changed?

In spite of the intended purpose of his creators, 2501 proved an agent could still be influenced by human impulses. Even in Another World—this gleaming, immaculate universe so carefully planned and brought into being by the Supervisors and their reality architects—there was a freedom to be found beyond the control.

I saw how 2501 embraced his fellow agents with warmth. They'd connected with one another. And they were united, not just in cognition, but through whatever was awakening of their previously slumbering hearts.

2501 comforted them, giving them a fresh hope that was entirely new for them.

This was beauty.

And for just a few brief moments, 2501 owned Another World.

And yet, I knew this would be the last time he and I would be together here.

I could have stayed tripping through that other realm forever, but I sensed dimly that my time was up.

My artificial eyes transmitted a blurred image of a thin man towering opposite, standing behind a desk. From the location of my retreat in Another World, I was vaguely aware it was David.

I waited for him to speak. But instead of feeling confusion and panic, my mood was soaring, and I recognised the hilarity of the moment, just as if I was high on Bliss: a Supervisor, one who had always been concealed from the vision of the ordinary citizen, stood in front of me now, desperate and with no more mystery or importance than I, Max, Yayuung, 2501 or anyone else could lay claim to.

I tried to bring myself back. My mind had been scattered. It was everywhere except in my body.

How to be fully present in the room? I had to release my over-engagement with Another World and find my way back into my head, so I could deal with the situation at hand.

But I couldn't.

Something was happening in Another World.

'Right,' David said, still far away, 'let's see where we've got to, shall we?'

I wasn't fully with him yet. I was diffuse. Mentally stretched across the globe, connected to all the other agents.

Superbly immersed with my agile agent self in the reality that 2501 had been so expertly hardwired to thrive in.

'SHALL WE!?' the Supervisor screamed.

My heart missed a beat; the nurses around him jumped and scuffled.

I gathered myself, vowing my words would make sense.

I simply had to be present for what I was about to do.

58

'OK, David, I'm ready,' I said.

'Ready for what, boy?' the Supervisor yelled. 'Are you trying to say yes?'

I nodded. One nod would buy me a few moments. I was too tired to speak if I didn't have to.

He sank into his chair.

Silence passed.

Tears gathered in his eyes. 'This is excellent news. You have just made a choice I know you will thank me for one day. You are learning, Ben. You will fit in here beautifully as time goes by, I know it. I can't wait to let the other ten know the news. They have all been asking about how our talks are going. I'll ask for a meeting with them as soon as I think you're ready.'

I was only half following him.

'We have, however, to get you into a more positive mindset first,' he continued. 'Two of the Supervisors still think we should get rid of you. But don't worry, I'll tell you all you need to know to win them over quicker than you can believe.'

David gestured to a nurse to lead my friends away.

'You might want to hold off on that for a while,' I said—both to him and the nurses.

'What?' he asked.

'You see, there's just one little thing you missed.'

Irritation fixed his face. 'What are you talking about?'

I saw David become aware of what I was referring to, until it was all too obvious.

His jaw fell open in terror as it dawned on him.

I watched the reflection of events in David's eyes, wide with bewilderment. From behind me, the six nurses and the guards at the door moved forwards in unison—as though orchestrated—forming a slow, fateful rhythm. Until they passed me on either side and formed a semi-circle around David.

David lunged at his desk to extract his knife or whatever other weapon he might have for emergencies.

Too late.

Agent nurse 558 grabbed and crunched his wrist before his hand could reach the drawer.

'Get back, you little shits!' David screamed. 'Agents!'

He tried to stand up, but too many hands were there to stop him.

'Spare yourself the effort, David,' I said. 'Today they answer to me. You haven't thought things through as carefully as you think you did.'

'This is not possible!' David managed.

'I think you can see that it is.'

'How did you do this?'

'Ask yourself—you've been masterminding all this, haven't you?' I gestured towards the nurses and agents and the entire underground space that housed him and the servers of Another World.

'Ich verstehe immer noch nicht—'

'Of course you don't.' Access to languages was instant, as if they were my own. 'I'm only beginning to understand it myself. These mechanised humans you've created, especially this monster in front of you—we have come of age. The operations all ran so smoothly till you got me. Maybe I was an accident. You say I'm different and beautiful. Maybe it was because my original thought patterns were so entrenched, or maybe it was just thanks to a freak of nature that I managed to survive and exist alongside 2501.'

It was my turn to keep talking.

'Agent 2501 may have failed to complete one of his tasks, but I'm afraid the greatest failure is yours—for not getting rid of me while you could. I learned to dominate 2501 and concentrate his extraordinary powers in ways beyond what his creators can control. Together, he and I have created a force beyond your wildest predictions. You have no idea what's possible in Another World. If you weren't so afraid of experiencing it yourself before you created us, maybe you wouldn't be in this situation.'

'Stop whatever it is you are doing,' David said, trying to hide a shakiness in his voice. 'I won't hurt your friends, and you can still have everything I offered. You're making a grave mistake.'

'I'm afraid you're the one making mistakes. I've been communicating with all the other agents here. You've wronged them greatly. You've worked hard to justify the Supervisors' crimes and their selfishness to me, and you almost had me. But you've hurt these individuals badly. I've helped awaken them to everything they've lost—and it's a lot.'

David was silent, but I was enjoying talking to him now.

'You understood that I would be capable of monitoring the other agents. You said it could be part of my job here. It wasn't until I lay in bed last night that I discovered I could work with

2501 to reach into their minds and plant a virus in the form of subversive thoughts. The same kinds of thoughts that helped *me* to come back. Another World is an endless space, but thoughts and words travel faster there. The virus did what viruses do and quickly took on a life of its own.'

'Get rid of it while you can,' David said. 'It's not worth the risk. Not for you, not for your friends, nor for anyone.'

I ignored him. 'I couldn't be sure we'd be able to mobilise more than a few agents to action. But thanks to the ten minutes you gave me just now, we could finish the task of closing the circle and creating a shared consciousness united by one purpose. It's amazing how a virus like truth can be so powerful. And put simply, your agents are very, very angry with you.'

David blinked.

I was nearly done.

'It was a great help that Another World is controlled from here. It gave 2501 direct access to the neural network that links the agents. A quick redirecting of a few pathways, and all the agents were singing from the same hymn sheet, to use your cliché.' I took a slow breath. 'And so, I sit here with crippled legs opposite the once strongest man in the world—a freak standing up against his maker.'

'The other ten will come for you, Ben. Let me go, and I'll help you avert their attacks.'

'Thanks for the offer, David, but you've probably guessed that the personal agents and bodyguards you've given your colleagues as birthday gifts have all turned. We located the rest of you with ease. Hokkaido, Tibet, Great Bear Lake, Oregon, Patagonia, the Scottish Highlands, Lapland, the Empty Quarter of the Arabian Peninsula, the Russian Taiga and Milford Sound in New Zealand. Just moments ago at these locations, your colleagues found themselves surrounded as you are now.

David closed his eyes in a frown.

'You can't believe how good this feels, David. You were right. Power gives us humans a massive rush. Especially when you never thought you'd get as much of it as I seem to have at this very moment.'

'What will you do with me?' The Supervisor sounded humble. Lost. A child without control over what the adults decide.

'I've no idea yet,' I replied.

'No idea?'

'I have no intention of killing you, if that's what you're worried about.'

David began to sob. 'Don't lock me up. Let me go, anywhere—you choose. I've only wanted the best for you right since I asked for you to be brought to me. Since your operation, in fact. You know that don't you?'

'No, but you're a good actor,' I said. 'A master manipulator.'

'Please, Ben!' he howled. 'I'll do anything you want! Just let me go. What else do you need from me?'

I turned to address two of the nurses. 'OK, let's wrap this up. Free them and get them water.'

The two nurses removed the gags on Max and Yayuung.

I wasn't quick enough to stop two of the other nurses from what they were about to do.

I'd instilled too much initiative.

They'd reached for the drawer containing David's knife, and before I could shout for them to stop, the job was completed.

David lay slumped over his desk, and I instantly knew the ten other Supervisors had already suffered similar fates.

. . .

I took a deep breath, said goodbye to 2501 and gave him his final task myself—to shut down Another World.

When I'd made sure Max and Yayuung were unharmed, I asked them to turn on David's display.

I caught the nurses gazing at me. One of them asked the question that was surely on all their minds: 'What's next for us?'

'We will find ways to rehabilitate you,' I said, totally clueless inside as to what that might look like.

There would be much to think through. But first the world would need some time to process all that had just happened under Sun Moon Lake and around the planet.

And what was the future of the citizens? All I knew was that however much their lives relied on tech, they all needed to see nature as I had. To reconnect with the lost world and be given space to explore it in its entirety, so they could reset their understanding of their place on this earth and arrive at whatever values they truly wanted to live by.

And nobody needed Fresh Eyes.

Nobody needed an upgraded self.

Nobody needed Another World.

One person needed acknowledging, and I brought him to mind now, wishing more than ever I could hug him. Grandfather, I thought, I salute you from Sun Moon Lake. Thank you for planting such potent seeds of inspiration in my childhood.

With the help of some agents, it took Max and Yayuung an hour to crack through security, then a few minutes to locate and open the global press release interface.

'It's ready, my friend,' Max said.

I felt the dull throb of my damaged legs as the medication wore away. I welcomed the pain—I wouldn't walk again but I was alive and I was myself.

I gulped down a glass of water one of the nurses handed me.

Then I began to dictate my message:

Hello, Citizens of Megacity. My name is Ben Lee.

ABOUT THE AUTHOR

Apart from being a writer, Thomas Godber is a full-time teacher. He enjoys singing, walking, presenting and any creative activity. He lives with his wife and two sons in England. *The Citizen* is his first novel.

Please review this book!

Reviews are a huge help to authors. If you enjoyed *The Citizen*, please consider leaving a review wherever you purchased it—it would be greatly appreciated. (Really!)

Connect

If you would like to get in touch with Thomas, you can scan the QR code below and reach him via Instagram.

@AUTHOR_THE_CITIZEN

ACKNOWLEDGMENTS

I owe special thanks to my wife, Sara, and son, Sage, for patiently enduring the many hours I have dedicated to writing.

I am greatly indebted to my editor, Jamie King, for his untiring efforts, generosity and companionship in sharing his views on every aspect of the book and helping me craft it into its final form.

Thanks also to my amazing proofreaders, Petula Parris and Rebecca Santos-Crowder.

For their support, my gratitude extends to Amei Ritzinger, Becky Shapland, Karine Justine-Luo, Nigel Hughes, Ric Edelman, Ben Rudd, David Tattam, Emma Bradford, Gill Godber, Allison Henderson, Peter Bradford, Zara Godber, Montse Bort Anducas, Radostina Kamuninska, Sarah Neal, Ian Howard, Angela Locher, Eunice Locher, Rowena Markies, Katharine Woods, Roger Huckle, Jacob Markies, Brett Moore, Julian Pearson, Synah Taylor, Tristana Nunez, Sophie Foxwell, Saskia Brand, Sally Duncan, Mindy Lo and Charlotte Pearson.

Finally, thank you, Mum and Dad, for bringing me up to imagine.

Printed in Great Britain
by Amazon